# MAIL ORDER BRIDE

# *Montana Adventure*

*Echo Canyon Brides*

*Book 3*

# LINDA BRIDEY

# Dedication

*This book is dedicated to all of my faithful readers, without whom I would be nothing. I thank you for the support, reviews, love, and friendship you have shown me as we have gone through this journey together. I am truly blessed to have such a wonderful readership.*

# Contents

# Chapter One

The temperature on the mid-January day in 1892 in Echo Canyon, Montana was a whopping nine degrees. That didn't stop Billy Two Moons from running across the street from his shop with no coat or shirt on. He rarely wore them, so the sight wasn't unusual around "Echo", as it was called. As he jogged towards the tiny post office, more than one pair of female eyes followed the progress of the powerfully built Indian man.

At the ripe old age of twenty, Billy had filled out very nicely thanks to a later growth spurt and his hard fight training. A combination of Nez Perce, Lakota, and Cheyenne Indians, with a splash of white in there somewhere, Billy's exotic dark eyes and light bronze skin were a very attractive combination. His medium brown hair with red highlights reached midway down his back.

Entering the post office, he encountered Vivian Nesbitt, an elderly woman who lived in an apartment next to his shop. His smiles caused women's hearts of all ages to beat a little harder in their chests.

Giving her one, he said, "Hi, Vivian. How are you today?"

"I'm just fine, Billy. Aren't you cold?" she asked.

Billy rarely got cold. "Nope. It's nice out. Well, for me anyway. If you wait for me, I'll get you back across the street; it's icy from the snow last week."

Vivian appreciated his concern. "All right. I won't refuse your offer. I don't want to fall and break a hip."

"Right," Billy said, going up to the counter. "Hi, Ian. Any mail for me?"

Ian Tompkins smiled at him, his blue eyes crinkling a little. "Yeah. A few letters came."

He found Billy's mail and thumped a thick stack down on the counter with a chuckle.

"Wow," Billy said. "I told the newspaper in Dickensville to stop the ad, but it must still be in circulation. I'm only interested in one woman's letter."

"You being an Indian artist is very exotic and romantic-sounding. You're attracting a lot of attention," Ian remarked.

Billy grinned. "Yeah. I'm not above using that to reel in a lovely lady."

Ian was about five years older than Billy. "I can't believe you're looking for a wife at your age. You haven't sown all your wild oats yet."

Billy grunted. "I've sown all the wild oats I need to, but I'm not gonna find a woman around here. No one wants their little girl to marry an Indian."

"I'd let you marry my daughter if I had one," Ian said.

"Thanks," Billy said. "I'm gonna get Vivian home and I gotta get back to work. See ya, Ian."

"See ya, Billy."

Walking over to Vivian, Billy offered his arm to her in gentlemanly fashion. She chuckled and tucked her hand into the crook of his arm. Vivian couldn't deny that she enjoyed the looks they got as Billy guided her across the slippery street. Once they were safely on the other side, Billy continued to walk with Vivian.

Not exactly conceited, Billy nevertheless was aware of his good looks and he wasn't afraid to use them to his advantage. He enjoyed flirting and he knew that Vivian was enjoying the attention. He escorted her to her apartment, kissed her cheek, and went next door to his shop.

As he walked away, Vivian murmured, "That boy is just too good-looking."

Billy unlocked the door to his shop and went inside. He flipped the sign to open, but he didn't expect to have a lot of customers that day since it was so cold. Most people would prefer to stay snug in their houses instead of traipsing around in the frigid air.

Going behind the counter, Billy flopped down on the comfortable blue wingback chair he'd put there. Sometimes when the shop was slow and he needed a break from painting, he napped there. If someone came in, the loud bell over the door woke him.

Sifting through the stack of letters, he found the one he wanted and ripped it open.

"What do you have to tell me today, sweet Callie?" he asked with a smile.

Last fall, he'd begun his search for a bride and had struck up a correspondence with Callie Carlisle from Mississippi. She'd told him that she was a buxom twenty-year-old with black hair and blue eyes. Her father and brothers were clockmakers.

Billy enjoyed her sense of humor and the stories she told about her family. She didn't mind a bit that he was Indian, which was a relief to him. As the only Indian living in Echo, he'd suffered discrimination even though he'd lived there all of his life and had been raised by white foster parents. Billy had found out the hard way that the parents in Echo weren't about to let their daughters marry an Indian.

In an effort to boost the town's population and save it from becoming a ghost town, Jerry Belker, who was now running for mayor, had suggested that the single men in town acquire brides by mail since single women were very scarce in the area. Although resistant to the idea at first, Sheriff Evan Taft had stepped up and started the experiment. His efforts had been greatly rewarded in the form of one Josie Bainbridge, and they'd fallen in love quickly and married. Now, they were the proud parents of little six-month-old Julia.

Next to give it a whirl was Dr. Winslow Wu, a veterinarian who'd advertised for a lady doctor to wed. Before Dr. Erin Avery had come to Echo to marry him, the town didn't have its own doctor. Dickensville, a bigger town about three hours from Echo, had been the only place they'd been able to find medical care.

Win, as his friends called him, and Erin had married only five days after meeting, as was stipulated in the bargain they'd made—that she would get her own practice in exchange for marrying him. Their arrangement had worked out well and they'd been married for almost a year. Seeing two of his closest friends successful in finding wives, Billy was ready to find his own true love.

Putting Callie's letter to his nose, Billy inhaled the light vanilla scent of the perfume she spritzed her letters with before unfolding the letter.

> *Dear Billy,*
>
> *I hope you're doing well. Things here are fine. The clock shop has been very busy. If they're not fixing clocks, they're making custom orders. I've been helping with the paperwork and so forth to free up more of Daddy and Cliff's time so they can be in the back working.*
>
> *How is business for you? Are you selling lots of paintings? I hope so. I've been giving your invitation to come to Echo serious consideration and I think that it would be a good idea. I've checked into travel arrangements and I could be there by the end of February, if that would be acceptable.*

Billy sat forward in his chair as he continued reading, becoming more excited when she said that she'd come into Cheyenne, which was a couple of days from Echo by wagon. Billy jumped up and let out a war whoop just as another one of his friends, Lucky Quinn, came into the shop.

"Well, I know ya like me, but ye don't hafta jump for joy when I come in," he joked.

Billy ran around the counter, grabbed Lucky's heavy denim coat, and shook the Irishman a little. "She's coming! Callie is gonna come here to meet me! She'll be here around the end of February. I'll go pick her up in Cheyenne. She's coming here!"

Billy shook him so hard that Lucky felt like he was in another earthquake. "All right, lad. Don't shake me up like I'm a butter churn. Sure and that's wonderful news."

Billy released him. "Sorry, but I can't help it. We'll meet and fall in love and get married and have babies and have such a wonderful future together!"

Lucky was usually the voice of reason to Billy's enthusiasm when the young man hadn't thought things through. "Slow down, Billy. Let the poor woman get here and see what's what. Don't propose to her on sight or somethin' like that."

"Why not? Win was going to marry Erin sight unseen. He's just lucky that she's such a pretty woman and, uh, very passionate from what he says," Billy replied.

Lucky frowned. "He ought not talk about such things. 'Tisn't proper." He had a strange sense of propriety about the relationships between men and women. He didn't like talking about the private lives between man and wife, but he didn't mind telling ribald stories and jokes when they went to Spike's or when it was just a bunch of men sitting around chewing the fat.

Billy smiled into Lucky's gray eyes. "That was all he said; she's passionate. No details or anything, so don't get your nose bent out of shape."

Lucky grunted. "Did ya forget what today is?"

Billy searched his mind, but couldn't come up with anything. "I don't think so. Why?"

Lucky rolled his eyes. "We're goin' to Dickensville to pick up those new goats. I've got the wagon all ready, lad."

Billy put a hand to his forehead. "I guess I did forget. Sorry about that. No problem. I'll go finish dressing and be right back."

Lucky chuckled and sat down in the blue chair. "I'll be right here. Go on with ya."

Billy ran through the doorway at the back of the shop that led to a small storeroom. Painting and framing supplies sat on the floor and lined shelves. His efficiency apartment laid further on. Stepping into the tiny kitchen, Billy took a swig of cold coffee from his mug; he'd forgotten about the coffee after making it. Whenever Lucky saw him drink cold coffee, he shivered in revulsion, which amused Billy.

Finishing it, he went through a small parlor and into his bedroom that was big enough to hold a full bed, a dresser, and a nightstand. From a small closet, he retrieved a blue western shirt that was slightly tight on him. This pleased Billy because it meant that he'd gained even more muscle.

Buttoning it up, he felt a twinge of pain in his left shoulder that reminded him of the unknown man who'd dislocated it last June. He frowned at the memory of the man getting the best of him; the mystery man had been a lethal opponent and Billy hadn't possessed enough fighting abilities to successfully combat him.

After the encounter, he'd begun honing his fighting skills and had become stronger so that he would be able to hold his own against any enemy. Between the Indian fighting that Lucky was teaching him and the karate and other combat skills Win was showing him, Billy was becoming a proficient fighter.

Billy put on his winter buckskin coat that Lucky had made for him. The Irishman had lived among the Cheyenne for three years and wedded a beautiful maiden named Avasa. During that time, Lucky had learned fighting, hunting, and tracking skills from the men and cooking, garment making, and beading from his wife.

The latter three skills weren't really something men were supposed to know, but he'd pleaded with Avasa so much that she'd taught him in secret. All of those lessons combined had served Lucky well over the last couple of years since coming to Echo.

Billy liked the way the coat looked on him and smiled at his reflection before heading back out to the shop. He stopped short when he saw Marvin Earnest standing in the middle of it, looking around at the various paintings. Billy's black eyes narrowed upon seeing the hated man.

With his golden blond hair and beautifully handsome looks, Marvin was hardly the type of man one would ever suspect of being evil and devious, but he was. He was one of the few people around Echo who had any real wealth. The Earnests had made their money from their gold and silver mines, as well as other various business ventures. The mines had drawn droves of people in search of riches and opportunity.

The mines had eventually died out and with them went the majority of families in the town, leaving behind too many single men and not enough women. The Earnests had survived the hard times, and now Marvin's careful management was paying off.

Stepping forward, Billy asked, "What do you want?"

Marvin smiled. "I'd like to engage your services as an artist in doing a portrait of Barkley." Barkley was Marvin's prized bulldog. For all of his other failings, Marvin adored children and animals, and treated Barkley as well as he would a child.

Lucky stood behind the counter, his gray eyes stormy with restrained anger and hate.

"Not interested," Billy said. "Find someone in Dickensville."

Marvin cocked his head at Billy. "Come now, Mr. Two Moons. I've seen some of their work and they don't have your talent. Besides, you know Barkley, and you'll be able to capture his essence. I'll make it worth your while," he said coaxingly.

Billy glanced at Lucky who rolled his eyes a little.

Marvin saw the look and asked, "Do you always ask Mr. Quinn's advice in these matters, or do you have a brain of your own?"

Billy resisted rising to the bait. "What do you call 'making it worth my while'?"

Marvin chuckled. "Three hundred. Half now and half upon completion of the piece."

Billy could use the money, especially since Callie would be coming to Echo soon. It would set him up nicely to be able to show her a good time and allow him to take care of some expenses for the shop. "Three fifty," he countered.

"Done," Marvin said, holding out his hand.

Billy looked at it as though it was a snake. He had no desire to touch Marvin, but it was business and shaking hands sealed the deal. He shook it as briefly as possible. Marvin pulled out his wallet and handed the appropriate amount of money to Billy. "When will you start?"

"Tomorrow."

"Very good. What time shall I bring him by? I'm assuming you'll want to do it in your studio," Marvin said.

"Nine. Yeah, the light up there is better than anywhere else."

"Splendid. I'll see you then. It's been a pleasure as always, boys," Marvin said, putting a hand on the doorknob. Turning back, he gave Billy a sly smile and added, "You should have haggled a little more, Mr. Two Moons. I would've paid five hundred." Then he opened the door and left.

Billy let out a string of swear words and as he took the money around the counter and put it in the lock box he kept there. He saw Lucky smiling and said, "Shut your trap, Irish." He took the lock box back into his apartment where he hid it under a floorboard and replaced the colorful woven rug that Evan had made for him over top of it.

Then he rejoined Lucky and the two men got underway.

When they returned that night, they went straight to the sheep farm that Lucky, Win, Billy, and two of their other friends, Ross Ryder and Travis Desmond, had started a couple of years ago. Ross, the local butcher, sold the majority of their mutton and lamb out of his shop. Travis provided them with a way to bring their sheep and goats to the farm without having to go the long way around.

His involvement was still a secret, since he worked for Marvin and wasn't yet able to quit and work the sheep farm full-time with the others. His job as the foreman at the Earnest ranch enabled him to keep food on the table and a roof over the heads of his wife, Jenny, and daughter, Pauline.

Marvin was fond of Pauline and once a week Travis brought her to see Marvin. The ranch owner paid Travis extra for allowing him to spend time with Pauline. Soon, Travis hoped be able to tell Marvin to go to hell and quit working for his difficult and sometimes cruel employer.

Pulling up to the barn, Lucky hopped down from the wagon and opened the barn doors so Billy could drive inside. The scents of warm animals, hay, and grain hit them and Lucky smiled at the pleasant aromas. As he lit a couple of lanterns, the sheep and goats bleated a greeting at the two sheep farmers. They put the six new arrivals over by the pen that had been set up for them.

Billy looked at them again. "I feel bad for them."

"Why?" Lucky asked as he opened the pen door.

"They have such tiny ears. It's not natural and it seems like they would get cold in this weather," he said.

Lucky laughed at him. "That's just the way they're bred. They don't know no better. We could always have Evan and Josie make 'em some earmuffs."

Evan was notorious around Echo for his crocheting abilities. He often went to Spike's, one of the two saloons in Echo, and sat crocheting at the bar. Of course, he didn't go there as often with a wife and daughter at home now, but he still hung out there at least once a week.

The image of six La Mancha goats running around with earmuffs on their heads made Billy laugh. "You know if you ask him to, he will."

Billy and Lucky finished moving the six does into the pen and shut the door.

"There now. You gals are gonna like it here. Ye have a bunch of handsome men, including yer very own vet, and a beautiful lady doctor watchin' over ya. Not to mention quality hay and feed. Tomorrow, I'll introduce ya to yer man and we'll see if any of ya are feelin' frisky."

Billy loved the way Lucky conversed with all of the animals. He knew practically each of them by sight and kept careful records of their lineages. He was an expert at the business since he'd grown up in a sheep-farming family back in Ireland.

As they stacked the crates off to the side, clip-clops sounded on the barn floor. Win's little burro, Sugar, came around the side of the wagon. She brayed at them and trotted over to be rubbed. It always cracked them up when they saw Sugar in her pretty sweater that Evan had crocheted for her at the beginning of fall. The deep red garment with white trim and a frilly collar was fastened down her back by fancy gold buttons.

The burro had been Win's payment for services rendered to a local rancher. At first, Win had been resistant to accept her in lieu of monetary compensation, but he'd ended up taking her home. She'd become strongly attached to him and went everywhere he did. He didn't have much of a choice, because she chewed through ropes, kicked out boards, and broke fences in order to be with Win. The Chinaman had finally given up and let her follow him.

The color of the sweater was a very nice contrast with her dark brown fur and she did look very pretty in it.

Billy said, "I see that Win wasn't successful in getting her sweater off her."

Lucky grinned. "He wasn't. She's so proud of it that she doesn't want to stop wearin' it."

Scratching behind her ears, Billy said, "You're such a pretty girl. You don't want to take off your pretty sweater, huh? I know you love it, but it's gonna have to be washed sometime."

Sugar closed her eyes and grunted in contentment as Billy's fingers found her itchy spots. He was the only person besides Win who Sugar would stay with and Win brought her to his place to be burro-sat. She loved coming upstairs to his studio and looking out of the large windows that lined the huge room.

On cold nights like this, Win and Erin let her sleep in the parlor in their cabin that sat on the farm. She knew how to open and close doors and usually let herself out to go potty or to her little shed next to the cabin. Most likely she'd heard them drive up and had wanted to come visit.

"Do you fellas need any help?" Win asked, coming into the barn. The well-muscled Chinaman stood only about five-foot-ten, but he was a lethal fighter.

"We don't," Lucky said with a smile. "I see herself there wanted her sweater left on." Lucky talked about people in those terms when they acted conceited.

Win smiled. "Nope. I tried, but she nipped me. I let her alone, but sent her to bed without her carrot."

Sugar's ears went back at his statement and she leaned against Billy's legs.

Win said, "Don't take her side like you always do. It's like parents— one's the disciplinarian while the other one can't say no. You reinforce her bad behavior."

"Sorry," Billy said. "She's just so darn cute." He took Sugar's head in his hands and turned her to face Win. "How can you look at that face and deny her anything?"

"Very easily," Win said, giving Billy an annoyed look and stepping over to the pen.

His wife, Erin, joined them. "Evening, gentlemen," she said. Her dark eyes shone with good humor as she looked at her friends. "How was your trip?"

"Cold," Lucky said. "Of course, lookin' at Billy ridin' along without his coat only made me feel colder."

"I can't help it that all you purebloods aren't as hardy as I am," Billy said. He called himself a mutt because of his mixed heritage.

Erin smiled at their bantering. With Lucky living on the farm as well, she heard it all the time and enjoyed it. She also enjoyed spending time in Lucky's tipi, playing knuckles or cards, and eating the Indian food he made for them. He'd built the tipi to save money so that he could one day go after his wife.

The military had rounded up their tribe, forcing them onto a reservation. Lucky hadn't been allowed to go with them since he was white. He'd begged, fought, and tried to bribe officers, but none of it had worked. He'd been heartbroken and his pain had been compounded because Avasa had been five months pregnant at the time of their capture and Lucky had never gotten to see their child.

Win stepped into the pen and examined the does. "They're some fine ladies, all right," he said, presently.

"I thought so," Lucky said. "I'm glad ya concur, Dr. Wu."

Erin had gone in the pen with Win. "Their poor little ears. Why don't they have any?"

Billy laughed. "That's what I said. We're gonna have Evan crochet them some earmuffs."

Win and Erin broke out into laughter.

"That's a slippery slope," Win said. "They'll get to expect you to put them on the same way Sugar does her sweater."

Sugar's ears swept forward at the word "sweater" and she stood a little straighter as if to say, "I have it on. Don't I look pretty?"

Erin laughed and kissed her nose. "Yes, you're a very pretty girl."

Win said, "You're as bad as Billy."

Billy and Erin exchanged a smile.

"Well, come have some coffee, guys," Win said. "I'm sure you could use some."

They murmured their assent and followed the Wu's from the barn after blowing out the lanterns. As they sat at the table drinking coffee and eating homemade bread with apple butter, Billy told Win and Erin about Callie's impending arrival in Echo. This was imparted to them in between huge bites of bread, which earned him dark looks from Lucky. Billy's lack of table manners irritated Lucky, who'd had them drilled into him by his mother and father.

"I'm also reluctantly doing a portrait of Barkley for Earnest, but only because of the money he's paying me. I'll need it for when Callie gets here and for the shop, too," Billy said. "Otherwise, I would have told him to go scr—"

Lucky kicked his leg under the table. He didn't like a lot of swearing around women.

Billy gave him an annoyed look and said, "Well, you get my meaning."

Win and Erin hid their smiles by either taking a drink or eating more bread. The older-younger brother rapport between their friends was always amusing. Before Lucky had come to Echo with Josie two years ago, Billy had had no clue what being an Indian was all about. Under Lucky's tutelage, he now was a very good shot with bow and arrows, fought well with a knife, knew how to track, and was talented at other skills Indians commonly possessed. Lucky had also taught him to speak Cheyenne and use Indian sign language.

"I don't envy you having to spend time with Marvin," Erin said. "I treat him, but I don't dawdle about it."

Marvin caused trouble wherever he could and had done so between Erin and Win in the early part of their marriage. The horrible scene on the night Marvin's former lover, Phoebe Stevens, had tried to murder Marvin came back to her. Bree Josephson, a family friend of Marvin's, had come to live with him and when she'd heard the struggle between Marvin and Phoebe, she'd come to Marvin's rescue and shot Phoebe.

Bree had come to get Erin because Phoebe had shot Marvin in the thigh, and he'd needed medical attention. Erin gave herself a mental shake, dispelling the vision of the woman lying dead on Marvin's kitchen floor. She'd seen dead people, of course, but knowing the woman had been with child filled her with sorrow at the thought of the innocent life that had been lost.

It was even more tragic because the baby wasn't Marvin's. It had belonged to Thad McIntyre, a long-time family friend of Evan's. The talented bounty hunter was known all over the Midwest for his uncanny ability to track down the wiliest criminals. He and Phoebe had been seeing each other, but he hadn't known she'd been two-timing him until that summer. Marvin had known about Thad, however, but he'd loved Phoebe so much that he'd been willing to share her. After Phoebe's funeral, Thad had left town. He'd needed some space and time away to heal. He hadn't been back yet, but he'd sent a few letters to let them all know that he was alive and well.

Win said, "You just watch yourself around him."

Billy smiled. "You act like I don't know him. I can handle myself. Well, I'm going home so I'm up on time. All I need to do is some sketching to get started, so the sitting shouldn't take very long. Thanks for the snack."

He kissed Erin goodnight and headed back out into the cold night.

# Chapter Two

Three weeks later, Billy finished Barkley's painting and was about to take it out to Marvin's when Lucky burst through his shop door, ringing the bell so loudly that Billy thought he'd go deaf.

"Damn it! What's the matter with you?" he demanded.

"Sorry," Lucky said.

Billy didn't like the look on Lucky's face. There was a wild look in his eyes and his jaw had an odd set to it. "What's wrong? Did something happen at the farm?"

"No," Lucky said.

That one syllable told Billy that something was very wrong. The only time the Irishman said "yes" or "no" was when he was being extremely emphatic about something.

"What is it?"

Lucky started pacing, running a hand through his light blond hair that had grown longer over the winter. "Wild Wind sent me a letter." Wild Wind was Lucky's closest friend from his Cheyenne tribe.

"Wild Wind did? I didn't know he could read and write," Billy said. "Besides, how did he get a letter to you? He's on the reservation, right?"

"Aye, he is. I taught him and a few of the others how to read and write. He must have bribed someone to send it," Lucky said.

"What did it say?" Billy asked.

"It says that part of their band is gonna be moved farther west in a couple of weeks, maybe three. Avasa is part of that group." Lucky's eyes flooded with tears. "Billy, I have a son. Avasa had a boy."

Billy gave a shout of joy and grabbed Lucky in a bear hug. Lucky returned the embrace as tears streamed down his face. "I'm so happy for you! That's incredible!" Billy said. "What's his name?" he asked, releasing Lucky.

"*Otoahnacto*. Bull Bear," Lucky said.

Billy laughed. "How about that. Well, your Cheyenne name is Yelling Bear and you have a bull tattoo on your back. Maybe that's Avasa's way of honoring you."

Wiping more tears from his face, Lucky said, "I think yer right. I'm leavin' for Oklahoma tomorrow, Billy."

"Tomorrow? That's sort of short notice," Billy said.

"There's no time to waste. I'm goin' after her and Otoahnacto. I can't miss the opportunity." Lucky gave Billy an uncertain look and added, "I need your help."

"Sure. Whatever you need," Billy said. "What can I do?"

"I need ya to go with me. Ya said ya would."

Billy's eyes widened. Callie was due in Echo within a week's time. "Oh, Lucky, you're putting me in a hell of a position here."

Lucky nodded. "I know, lad, but if it wasn't so serious, so dire, I wouldn't ask, ya know that. I know yer lady is comin' soon, but I'm sure when Win tells her what's happened, she'll understand. We'll come back just as soon as possible and then ya can be with her."

"Win? Win knows about this?" Billy said.

"Not yet. I know that he'd go get her if we ask him to," Lucky said. "Billy, I'm askin' as one brother to another, will ye please do this for me?" He put a hand on Billy's shoulder.

Billy knew what it cost a man to plead for something. Lucky was practically begging and that fact broke through his initial resistance. Besides, getting Lucky's wife and child back was more important and he was right; there would be time with Callie when he got back.

With a smile, he said, "Well, I guess we'd better get packing. I got Earnest's painting done just in time, too. I'll go out and get my money from him today so we have it for traveling."

Lucky hugged him so hard that Billy thought his ribs would crack.

"I'll owe ya the rest of my life," Lucky said. "Let's go."

That evening, they had supper with Evan and Josie. Evan's Aunt Edna lived with them. She was what Lucky called a "lusty one", which meant that she liked to flirt outrageously with their male friends. They played a game in which they weren't allowed in the house unless they were shirtless so she could get an eyeful of them. It was all harmless, but it wasn't something they spread around. Evan usually scolded Edna and rolled his eyes, but it was all part of the game.

As they sat down to the meal, Edna said, "So Lucky has a son. I can't tell you how happy I am for you."

Lucky took the hand she held out to him and grinned. "Aye. I woulda been happy either way, though."

"I know," Edna said, watching Billy load his plate.

Evan's green eyes followed the motion of Billy's arm as he piled stuffing onto it. "Hey, Two Moons, you wanna leave some of that for the rest of us?"

Billy smiled and passed the dish to Josie, who sat to his right. "I'm loading up now because I'm not gonna have any home cooked meals for a while and no one makes stuffing like Josie."

"Thank you," she said. The blue-eyed blonde smiled and said, "I can't wait to meet Avasa and … I can't pronounce your son's name, Lucky. I'm sorry."

"That's ok. Ya won't be the only one. I think it'll be good to call him Otto. I'll have to talk to Avasa about it, of course, but I think it'll solve that problem," Lucky said.

Erin said, "Otto Quinn. I like it."

Evan got up from the table and got some glasses down from the cupboard along with a bottle of bourbon. He passed the glasses out and gave each of them a finger of liquor. Holding his glass aloft, he said, "To Lucky's son, Otto Quinn. Congratulations, Lucky."

They drank to his toast and Lucky had to blink back tears. Josie's heart went out to him. He'd waited so long to know what sex his child was and she knew that if there was any chance that he could get Avasa and their child, he had to take it. She and Lucky had met on the train from her hometown of Pullman, Washington.

The big Irishman had befriended her and had saved her life when the trail had derailed. He'd also been coming to Echo Canyon, having bought a large tract of land from an old man who'd gone out west after the collapse of the mining trade. The man had sold the land for a song and Lucky had snapped it up. They'd developed a close friendship and Josie regarded Lucky as an older brother.

As Billy shoveled food into his mouth, he chewed thoughtfully. He hated to leave Callie in the lurch, but Win would take good care of her and she would be befriended once she got back to Echo. She seemed like a kind woman and he was sure that once Win informed her of the seriousness of the situation, she would be understanding. At least he hoped she would be.

He was excited about her coming and he didn't want her to go back home before he even had a chance to meet her. Looking over at Lucky's happy face, he knew that no matter what happened with Callie, he would never regret helping Lucky get his family back.

# Chapter Three

"Wild Wind said that we needed to be at the south side of the reservation at two a.m. on March 12th," Lucky said as they started out the next morning.

"We have some hard riding ahead of us then."

"Aye. I have it all mapped out, though. Just pray that we don't run into any bad weather," Lucky said.

"I will. We don't need to be slowed down any," Billy said.

"We don't," Lucky agreed.

Billy said, "This is exciting. I've never been farther away than Dickensville. I just realized that."

Lucky quirked an eyebrow at him. "Yer jokin'."

"No. I've spent my whole life right around here."

Grinning, Lucky said, "No wonder ya were such a scoundrel with the girls. Ye had nothin' better to do."

Billy laughed. "That's partly true. It used to get pretty boring, but it was also fun to fool around with them."

"I'm glad to see that yer maturin' and ready to settle down."

A frown settled on Billy's face as he thought about Shelby, an older woman he'd had a relationship with a couple years ago. She'd been a young widow with two children. The twenty-three-year-old woman had been lonely and when she and Billy had met, she'd been attracted to him despite his age.

They'd seen each other for about a year until she'd ended things. He'd been in love with her and would have married her and helped her raise the kids, but Shelby had known that that would have been impossible. She'd have been shunned if she'd married an Indian and her children would have been the objects of ridicule. The age difference and the fact that he hadn't had regular employment had also factored into her decision to break up with him.

For a long time, Billy had been bitter and depressed over the situation. He'd grown to hate his Indian heritage because it caused him such heartache. However, he'd eventually come to embrace it thanks to Lucky and the support from his parents and friends. Although he would always have a tender heart, he'd hardened it to ridicule, learning how to turn it back on others instead of letting it make him bitter.

As their sheep farm started making more money and his shop was making a little profit now, his self-confidence had grown and he was proud of his accomplishments. He felt certain that he could take care of a wife and family now, which was why he'd begun searching for a bride.

So lost in thought was he that he didn't hear Lucky's question.

"Billy!"

"Huh? What?"

Lucky asked, "Are ye sure you want to go with me?"

"I'm here with you, aren't I? Of course I want to go. I'm honored you asked me," Billy said. "Besides, I'll get to meet Avasa and Otto first."

Lucky smiled. "I better not catch ya flirtin' with her. She's a gorgeous creature, so I couldn't blame ya, but just the same."

"Don't worry; I'm not in the habit of stealing someone's wife," Billy said, smiling.

Lucky's expression darkened. "Unlike someone else we know."

Billy's countenance matched Lucky's as he thought about the way Marvin had duped Thad for so long. He couldn't imagine being so depraved that he would keep seeing a woman once he knew that she'd been sleeping with someone else at the same time. It turned Billy's stomach. "Yeah. There are times when I can barely keep from smashing him in the face."

Lucky said, "Me, too, but we won't have to. Evan will figure things out there and make Marvin sorry he was ever born."

"I know. I just feel so bad for Thad. I can't imagine losing a child like that."

"'Tisn't an easy thing," Lucky said. "But it's different in his case. At least my son is alive. Thad never even got the chance to see his child and when I think of that poor little life lost like that, well, it tears me up, it does."

"Me, too," Billy said. "Thad needs to find a wife, too, but I'm not sure he's the marrying kind. Not with the way he's always out on the road."

Lucky chuckled. "Well, maybe if he had the right incentive, he might not stay away so much."

"Maybe not," Billy said. "I know that once I'm married, I won't want to be away from her."

"And once I have Avasa and our lad back in Echo, I'll never feel the need to roam, either."

Billy smiled and fell silent as he daydreamed about what it would be like when he was married.

Riding up the lane to Marvin's ranch, Evan prepared his mind for the visit ahead of him. His uncle, Rebel Taft, had been one of the toughest sheriffs in Montana and he'd learned at his side. Reb, as he had been called, and Thad had been friends since childhood. While Reb had decided to become a part of official law enforcement, Thad preferred to be a bounty hunter because he didn't have to obey rules and regulations.

He could be creative in the pursuit of criminals and didn't have to answer to anyone about it.

Reb and Thad had taught Evan to be creative and determined in his approach to his job. After the traumatic events of the past fall, Evan had regrouped and he was taking Lucky's advice in coming at Marvin from the side instead of straight on.

When he knocked on Marvin's front door, he worked hard on keeping the disgust from his face. A beautiful brunette with brown eyes named Bree Josephson answered the door. She'd come to live with Marvin last summer, but the two of them were only friends. There had never been anything romantic between them.

"Hello, Sheriff," she said in a cool tone. She was not enamored of Evan or Thad after Thad had essentially called her a whore and accused her of sleeping with Marvin. "What can I do for you?"

He smiled and said, "I was wondering if Earnest was around. I'd like to talk to him."

Bree said, "Is this official business?"

"No. It's purely personal."

"Wait here. I'll see if he's free," she said.

"Sure."

She shut the door again and went to Marvin's office. He sat behind his desk, looking through a ledger.

"Hello, m'dear," he said pleasantly.

"Hi. Sheriff Taft is here. He says it's a personal matter. Do you want to see him?"

"Personal?" Marvin thought that odd, but he was intrigued. "Yes, I'll see him."

"I'll let him in, and I'll be upstairs in my room if you need me," she said.

Marvin smiled at her. "Thank you. You're too good to me."

"No more than you are to me. I'll be back."

Leaning back in his chair, Marvin ruminated on the sisterly way he felt about Bree. He'd have never thought it possible for him to feel that way about a woman, but he did. She'd also saved his life, for which he was grateful to her.

Bree brought Evan to his office and then went upstairs.

Marvin motioned to a chair. "To what do I owe the pleasure, Sheriff? What evil thing do you suspect me of now?"

Evan gave him a sheepish smile. "Nothing. It's taken me a long time to come to you like this, but I felt that an apology was long overdue. I'm sorry I didn't believe you about Louise's baby. Back then you never told me that you'd had an injury and that you couldn't have children."

Marvin said, "Well, it's not something you just go around telling people, is it? It's not an easy thing for a man to admit, you know."

Evan nodded. "But we were friends until you slept with Louise. Why would you do that? Didn't our friendship mean anything?"

Marvin was very good at reading body language. He saw nothing in Evan's posture except regret. "Of course it did, but I admit to not being able to resist a beautiful woman and she tempted me several times before I gave in. I've always regretted it," Marvin said with honesty. "It should have never happened."

"No, it shouldn't have," Evan said. "Just like you shouldn't have slept with Phoebe all that time."

Marvin's face turned stony as he said, "I've explained that. I was so in love with her that I couldn't give her up. I don't expect you to understand. I really did think she'd choose me. I certainly have more to offer a woman: financial security and a stable home. I would've done anything for her. But eventually, I just couldn't stomach the rejection anymore, so I ended it."

Evan nodded. "So you've said. I believe you. It's not something I'd be able to do, but I know we're different on a lot of levels."

Marvin said, "Perhaps. I want the same thing as most people: love and a family. It's what I've wanted for a long time. You understand that. How are Josie and little Julia?"

Evan's smile was genuine as he thought about his little girl. Julia had his black hair and Josie's blue eyes and she was a happy baby. "They're fantastic. I'm a lucky man. If it hadn't been for that earthquake, Josie and I might not have made up and gotten married."

Marvin smiled inside. "Oh? You don't think so?"

"I'm not sure. We were so mad at each other. Whoever kidnapped me really knew what they were doing. I just can't figure out what their game was. I mean, I realize that keeping me from my wedding and making it look like I had cold feet was their goal. But why would they want to do such a thing?"

Marvin shook his head a little. "I can't think of a reason. You've always been such a good, upstanding man. You're right; why would someone want to do that? I know you suspected me, but as you know, I was right here. Besides, I don't have the strength to haul you around. Not with my hernia. It's repaired, but if I lifted anything too heavy, I could undo it all. Dr. Avery thinks I'm going to have to have another surgery as it is."

Evan said, "I know. You were here when Thad and the guys came searching for me. They said it took some time to search the place. It's huge."

Marvin smiled. "Yes it is." *You don't know the half of it.*

"Why would you want to stay in such a big place all by yourself?" Evan asked. "I don't think I could."

"I suppose it's because this is where I grew up and it's been in the family for a long time. I really don't mind living alone, although I would prefer to have someone to share my life with," Marvin said. "Perhaps someday I will."

Evan said, "How many bedrooms does this place have, anyway? You never did give me a tour like you promised."

Marvin grinned. "Didn't I? There are seven." He rested his head back on his chair and asked, "Why the sudden bonhomie, Evan? You've done nothing but hate me for the past four years and now all of a sudden you want to buddy up to me."

*Tread lightly, Evan.* "Aunt Edna and Uncle Reb taught me to own up to my mistakes, and after everything that came to light in October, I know that I've been wrong about a lot of stuff. My conscience won't let me not at least try to make it right."

Marvin thought this fit with what he knew about Evan. "I see. Well, I appreciate the sentiment."

Evan said, "You know, I feel bad for both you and Thad. You both lost Phoebe and he lost a child."

Marvin closed his eyes against the tears that rose in them. "You don't know how much I hate what happened that night. I just wanted to get the gun from her. I was afraid she'd get hurt, but I didn't have the strength to get to the gun first. I know you won't believe me, but I also feel badly for Thad. Not being able to father children, I can only imagine the loss he must feel, knowing that his child perished."

Evan was shocked to see tears leak out from under Marvin's closed eyelids. If this was an act, it was a damn good one. "As a father, I can't imagine losing Julia. I know it was a shock to him at first, with him being fifty-eight, but he was starting to get a little excited about the prospect of becoming a father."

Marvin took out a handkerchief and blotted away his tears. Clearing his throat, he said, "I'm sure he was. I certainly would be no matter what age I was."

Evan nodded. "Well, I just wanted to stop by and tell you how sorry I am about not believing you about it all. I'll get out of your hair. I'm sure you're busy."

"Oh, come see the portrait Billy did of Barkley on your way out," Marvin said, rising.

Evan did want to see it—he hadn't had a chance to. Following Marvin into the ornate parlor, he looked at the beautifully rendered portrait. "Dang, that kid does great work, huh? He looks like he could just walk right out of the painting, doesn't he?"

Marvin said, "Yes. Billy is very talented. I do hope people come to appreciate his talent, Indian or not. It's a shame the way others judge people based on assumptions. So what if Billy is part Indian? He's a very nice young man, and popular with the ladies from what I understand."

Evan nodded. "I agree. Well, I better be getting back to make sure everything is calm in town. Again, I'm sorry."

Marvin shook the hand that Evan held out to him. "Apology accepted." Then he walked Evan to the door and closed it after him. "What are you up to, Evan?" he asked. "Whatever it is, I'll enjoy the game."

# Chapter Four

Irish and the Indian, as many people in Echo had dubbed them, rode hard for Oklahoma. Normally Lucky wouldn't have pushed their horses so hard, but time wasn't on their side. Wild Wind would bring Avasa and Otto to the meeting place and then he and Billy could get them safely home.

He was looking forward to seeing his good friend again, too. They'd had many good times together and he had missed his Indian brother. Looking over at Billy riding next to him. Lucky smiled as he thought about how he'd gained another Indian brother. He certainly hadn't expected to when he'd come to Echo, but he was grateful to the Great Spirit for bringing Billy and the rest of his friends into his life.

Billy saw Lucky smiling at him. "What? Are you planning some prank on me?" They were always doing that to each other.

"No. I was just thinkin' about how I never thought I'd become friends with another Indian when I came to town," Lucky said.

Billy grinned. "Yeah, and then you insulted me by saying that I wasn't a real Indian."

"Well, ya weren't. Ya didn't know how to do anything that Indians do. I had to show ya it all, but ya caught on fast. Yer on the way to being an Indian," Lucky said.

That fact made Billy feel proud instead of bitter like it used to. "I guess I am. I just can't field dress the game I kill. I wish I could stand blood. I've tried and tried. It makes me feel like a sissy. I'm glad you always warn me when you're gonna make blood soup." Just the thought of that turned Billy's stomach.

Lucky chuckled. "Ya can't help it. But other than that, you're doing just fine. You've become a good marksman and ya don't mind runnin' around in a breechcloth. Ya look good in it, too. Edna sure likes it when ya go over there in it."

"Oh, yeah. It irritates Evan like heck, but she loves it. She tells him to let an old lady have her fun," Billy said.

"I know. She always wants me to show her my tattoos." On Lucky's left shoulder was a tattoo of a griffin and on his right was a charging bull. They faced each other, both poised to attack. Billy was envious of the artist who'd done the intricate works of art.

"Julia's getting big," Billy remarked.

Lucky nodded. "It's hard to believe she's seven months old now. The time went fast. Otto will be three by now. I've missed so much time with him that I'll never get back."

"I know, but we'll get them and then you can have the future together that you've been dreaming about," Billy said.

"Aye, that we will," Lucky said.

They put their horses back into a canter, intent on making the meeting time and reuniting Lucky with his family.

Both men thanked the Great Spirit for helping them reach their destination without mishap. During their travels, their friendship deepened even more. Lucky had thanked Billy repeatedly for going with him and finally Billy told him to shut up about it.

"I've been wonderin' somethin', but I've been a little worried about askin' ya about it," Lucky said a couple of days before they reached the outskirts of the reservation.

"Go ahead. You can ask me anything. You know that," Billy said.

"Well, with Callie comin' and all, I wondered if you ever think about Shelby," Lucky said.

Billy smiled. "I do, but it doesn't hurt anymore. She did what was right for her and the kids and I can't fault her for that. It taught me a lesson, though. Don't have unrealistic expectations. That's what I did with Shelby, but I won't repeat that. That's why I think Callie and I will make a good fit. She's down to earth and we both want the same things."

"I'm glad to hear it. I'm glad that you can look back on it that way. Yer right to look to the future. I guess we're both doin' a lot of that," Lucky said.

*Ain't that the truth* Billy thought. He wondered how Callie had taken the news about him leaving town with Lucky right when she would have arrived.

⁓

Callie Carlisle paced back and forth in her room at the Hanovers' boarding house, the closest thing Echo had to a hotel. She'd been hiding her anger and anxiety fairly well since Win had picked her up in Cheyenne. It had been a big shock to discover that her intended had gone off to rescue his friend's wife. She could understand, given the situation, but she'd been looking forward to meeting Billy and it was a disappointment to her to have to wait longer.

There was no telling when Billy would return and she wondered what she would do in the meantime. She'd been in Echo for two days now and Billy's friends had kept her occupied and shown her around. Evan's wife, Josie, had taken her out to see the sheep farm and she'd been charmed by the fluffy animals. She'd enjoyed feeding them and playing with the frisky lambs.

Josie had also showed her Billy's shop and studio, and she'd marveled at his talent as she'd looked at the wide variety of things he'd

29

painted. There were landscapes, still lifes, portraits, and a couple of bizarre ones that Josie said he'd painted when he was still on laudanum from when his attacker had dislocated his shoulder.

As she paced, Callie had an idea. Billy was losing money with the shop closed. She could keep it open and sell his work for him. She grinned at the idea and wanted to run it by Josie to see what she thought.

Going downstairs, she encountered Gwen Hanover, who owned the boarding house along with her husband, Arthur. Gwen tended to be a little flighty, but she had a good heart. She was tall with red hair and brown eyes, while Arthur was a little shorter and round like a barrel.

"Hello, Callie. How are you?" Gwen asked.

Callie smiled at her. "I'm fine, thank you. And you?"

"Oh, just fine. Is your room still to your liking? Are the meals all right? Did you sleep well last night?" Gwen asked.

"Yes to all three questions," Callie said with a chuckle.

Gwen laughed. "Sorry about that. I do get a little excited from time to time. Arthur calls me 'high strung'."

"That's ok. Well, I'm off to see a friend, but I should be back for supper," Callie said.

"Good. It'll be nice to have the company," Gwen said. "We haven't had many boarders lately and Arthur and I only have so much to talk about."

Callie smiled. "Well, I'll keep you entertained with stories about my family."

"Wonderful!" Gwen said. "I look forward to it."

Callie went on her way then, enjoying the fresh air as she walked to the Tafts' house. She didn't mind the walk, it gave her time to think, and a chance to really see the town. Arriving at the Tafts', she heard Julia crying and smiled, thinking that hopefully things would work out with Billy and they'd have a baby someday not too far in the future.

She knocked on the door and heard Edna call out, "Come on in!" She liked the feisty woman who was in her mid-sixties.

Stepping inside the house, she saw Josie walking back and forth with

Julia, humming to the baby. Josie had a beautiful soprano voice and played guitar. She played a couple times a month at Spike's. Billy usually accompanied her since she'd taught him to play guitar; his melodic baritone voice blended perfectly with Josie's.

"Hello, ladies," Callie said.

"Hi, Callie," Edna said. "Julia is fighting sleep. I think she's afraid of missing something around here if she takes a nap."

Josie cut a glance at Edna. "Who does that remind you of?"

"Ha ha. Very funny, young lady," Edna said.

Callie liked the way the two women bantered. It was easy to see how close they were.

Josie asked Callie, "What are you up to today?"

"Well, I was wondering something. With Billy away and his shop closed, he's losing money. Maybe I could run it for him while he's gone. At least that way he'd be making some money. I'm experienced in running a shop, so I'd do a good job. What do you think?"

Josie looked at the dark-haired woman who stood about five-six and had curves in all the right places. "I think that's a very considerate offer. What do you think, Aunt Edna?"

Edna said, "Well, she's got the know-how and the time. Why not? I think Billy will be grateful."

Josie smiled, bouncing Julia a little. The baby burped and then smiled. Josie said, "Maybe that's what was wrong. She had gas in her tummy."

Julia babbled a little as if confirming that statement. Then she put her thumb in her mouth and leaned against Josie, sucking contentedly on it.

Callie said, "I guess that was the problem."

"I guess so," Josie replied, walking towards the kitchen. "Here's the key to the shop. All of Billy's friends have a key. Let us know if you need help with anything. Do you want to come to supper?"

Callie smiled. "No, thank you. I would, but I promised Gwen and Arthur that I would keep them company."

Edna said, "They're lonely without Phoebe there."

"It's so awful what happened," Callie said. "Billy told me about it in his letters. He warned me about Marvin and I'll keep my distance. I don't need any trouble like that."

"You're right about that," Josie said. "That's all he causes."

Callie nodded. "Ok. I'm off to open up. I hope we get some sales today."

"Good luck," Edna said.

"'Bye," Callie said and went on her way again.

After she left, Josie said, "She's a lovely girl. Billy's a lucky man."

Edna nodded. "She's a looker, too. That won't hurt a bit." She chuckled. "Someday, there'll be little Two Moons running around Echo."

Josie laughed. "I can't wait to see that and I can't wait to meet Lucky's family."

"Me, neither. I just hope they have safe travels."

"Me, too," Josie said and went to put the now-sleeping Julia in her crib.

Callie hummed to herself as she dusted the paintings and shelves in Billy's shop. It made her feel good to know that she was helping him and she enjoyed the work. She was at the back of the shop when she heard the bell over the door clang. Putting down her duster, she went out front to see who had come in.

The man who stood in the shop was a large, muscle-bound specimen with brown hair and brown eyes.

He smiled upon seeing her and said, "Hello, miss. I happened to see you in here. I'm a friend of Billy's, Ross Ryder."

"Hello, Ross. I'm Callie Carlisle. You're the butcher here in town and you're in business with Billy, right?" she asked.

"Yes, ma'am," Ross said. "Are you running the shop?"

"Yes. I thought with Billy being gone I could help out until he gets back," she said.

Ross took in her beautiful blue eyes, pink lips, and sweetly curved figure and thought that Billy was a fortunate man. "That's very kind of you. I'm sure he'll appreciate it."

"I hope so," she said. "Was there anything I could help you with?"

"No, ma'am. I just stopped by to introduce myself and welcome you to Echo. If I can be of help to you in any way, just let me know," Ross said.

"Thank you very much, Mr. Ryder," she said.

"You can call me Ross. I'm not really the formal type." Ross fidgeted a little, not wanting to leave quite yet. "Billy says your pa is a clockmaker."

Callie nodded. She liked the way his eyes crinkled at the corners and his dimples showed when he smiled. He had a strong jaw and a nice, straight nose. "That's right. He makes all kinds of clocks."

"He doesn't happen to have a catalogue, does he?" Ross asked. "I've been looking for a clock to replace the one we had in the parlor. Roxie's dog gnawed on it and it looks terrible. Plus it's not keeping the right time. I've looked in Dickensville, but I didn't find any that I liked."

Callie found herself a trifle disappointed to know that he was married. "Oh, well, I don't have a catalogue with me, but I can have Daddy send me one."

Ross was mesmerized by her southern accent and her eyes. "That would be great. I'd be much obliged to you."

She smiled. "I'm sure that Daddy has something that would appeal to you and your wife."

"Wife? Oh, I'm not married. Roxie is my sister," Ross said.

Callie tried to squelch the happiness that statement brought her, but didn't quite succeed. She was here to marry Billy, yet she felt a tug of attraction towards Ross. Firmly, she put that out of her mind. "I see. Well, I'll let you know as soon as the catalogue comes."

Ross smiled and she felt a little fluttering in her stomach. "Thanks. I look forward to it. I hope you don't think me too forward, but, um, Billy's lucky to be getting such a pretty lady."

Callie blushed, pleasure filling her breast. "Why thank you. That's very nice of you to say."

"I mean it. Well, I'd better get back over to the store. Take care, Callie," he said.

"You, too." Callie looked out the window, following his progress down the street until he disappeared out of sight. She sighed as she thought how nice-looking he was with all those muscles and that spectacular smile. He seemed so nice, too. "Stop that, Callie! You're not here to meet any other man but Billy. Now get back to work and stop this foolishness!"

With resolve, she returned to her dusting, but every so often, an image of Ross flashed across her mind.

# Chapter Five

Lucky and Billy arrived at the meeting place a half hour before time and Lucky couldn't sit still. His excitement ran high and he felt a little giddy knowing that very shortly he would be reunited with the woman he loved and meet his son. He willed the minutes to hurry by, hoping that nothing prevented Wild Wind from bringing them safely to him and Billy.

As he passed Billy another time, he heard a soft dove call. His face broke out into a huge grin. "He's here." He sent back a bobcat screech.

Billy searched the dark and saw shadows moving in their direction. They'd lit a lantern around the time they were to arrive and an Indian brave stepped into the dim light. Billy had only seen one other Indian in his lifetime and that was when he'd been little. It had also been from a distance. Seeing one up close was a whole other story.

He was about his height, his long black hair done in braids with eagle feathers woven into them. His black eyes moved back and forth between Lucky and Billy, settling on the latter. Even though he wore heavy buckskin clothing to ward off the cold, Billy could see that he was strong. He moved with grace and confidence and Billy couldn't help feeling a little intimidated. He also felt that he was lacking somehow in the brave's eyes, as though he knew that he wasn't a "real" Indian.

Then the brave dismissed Billy and concentrated on Lucky. Billy saw warmth enter his eyes even before he smiled.

In Cheyenne, Wild Wind said, "It has been much too long, Yelling Bear. You look well."

Lucky laughed. "It has been too long. You look well, too."

The two men embraced and laughed, slapping each other's backs, and Billy felt a pang of jealously. Immediately he brushed away the petty feeling. Of course they were happy to see each other.

"Wild Wind, I would like you to meet my very good friend, Billy Two Moons," Lucky said.

Billy stepped forward, holding out his hand. "It is good to meet the man Yelling Bear calls brother."

Wild Wind took his measure again and grasped arms with him. "It is good to meet a friend of Yelling Bear's. It seems like he meets Indians wherever he goes," he said with a smile.

Lucky watched the two of them, happy to introduce Billy to his good friend. Then he asked, "Is she here?"

Wild Wind nodded and let out another dove call. Lucky's heart began thudding in his chest as he saw Avasa come towards him. She smiled the radiant smile he remembered and tears stung his eyes. He couldn't believe he was finally seeing her again. Everything in him wanted to embrace her and kiss her.

However, he knew it would be incredibly inappropriate to do that. He would have to wait for a more private time. Going to her, he held out his hands to her, and she placed hers in his.

"Is this a dream?" he asked. "I am finally with the woman I love again."

Her smiled slipped a little and a prickling of warning broke out over Lucky's shoulders.

"It is good to see you, Yelling Bear. I have thought about you much since we were separated."

"I have thought of you all this time and I have kept my vow to come for you and our child," Lucky said.

Avasa regretted that she could no longer return Lucky's feelings, but she had to be honest. "Yelling Bear, I divorced you."

"I know, but I could not accept that," Lucky said. "We were meant to be together and had the military not separated us, we still would still be."

She shook her head a little bit. "But that is not the case. I have remarried. This is Red Boar, my husband."

Lucky had been so focused on Avasa that he hadn't noticed the other brave. Looking up, he saw Red Boar and hated him on sight. Avasa saw Lucky's gray eyes light with anger.

"Yelling Bear, I love him. He is a good man and has been good to your son," Avasa said.

Lowering his gaze, Lucky saw the little boy who stood in front of Red Boar and he fell in love with him right then. He resembled Lucky quite a bit, being much fairer than Avasa. His dark blonde hair fell to his shoulders and had a little curl to it. His dark eyes watched the adults with interest. He was a stout little fellow and showed no fear.

Avasa called him to her. "Come, Bull Bear."

He walked to his mother and stood by her when she crouched down. "This is your father, Yelling Bear. We have told you about him. Do you remember?"

"Yes," he said with a nod as he looked Lucky over.

"And do you remember that you are going with him?" Avasa asked.

"What?" Lucky asked. "What do you mean?"

Avasa picked up Otoahnacto and said, "I want you to take him with you. There is no future for him here. Starvation and suicide are rampant. I know this will hurt you, but his white blood has already caused him to be picked on by some of the older children who are angry with the soldiers and Indian agents. He will be better with his father. You will be able to teach him how to survive in your world and he will have more opportunity for happiness with you than he will here."

"But you are his mother." Lucky responded. "As much as I want him, should he not stay with you?"

Avasa held Otoahnacto tighter and said, "With all my heart I want him to. He is pure joy, but I love him too much to keep him here where he will end up killed or become a drunk. Please, Lucky," she said, using his English name for the first time. "Please take him with you so that he will grow into a fine young man and have a future."

"Avasa, come with me," Lucky said. "We can all have a future together. I have a sheep farm now and we are starting to make money. We can all be happy." He didn't care that her husband stood right there.

Avasa put a hand to his jaw. "I am sorry, but I would never survive away from my tribe. I do not think I could learn the ways of the white people. I loved you very much, and I still do, but my heart belongs to Red Boar now. Please take your son."

Lucky fought against the crushing pain her pronouncement brought. To hear her proclaim her love for another man was excruciating. He'd dreamt and planned for this reunion, and now all of his dreams had been dashed by her one statement. Lucky knew there was no use arguing with Avasa. He saw the truth in her eyes and he knew that her heart was no longer his.

His sense of honor warred with the urge to smash the face of Avasa's new husband. With his indomitable will, Lucky managed to shove the hate and fury down enough to step over to Red Boar and hold out his arm.

"Even though I would like nothing more than to fight you and cause you great pain, I will not do that. If you bring Avasa happiness, so be it. My love for her is stronger than my anger. Take good care of her and never take her for granted."

Red Boar smiled a little and grasped arms with him. "I have heard the stories about you and I see now why you are called Yelling Bear. I have no doubt that you can be very angry and deadly. If I were in your place, I would feel the same way, so I cannot be angry with you. I promise to do as you have asked."

Lucky nodded once and let Red Boar's arm go. He returned to Avasa and said, "I will take him. At least I will always have a part of you. My heart is broken, but I will honor your request and raise our son well."

Avasa's eyes grew moist as she nodded. Hugging Otoahnacto tightly she said to him, "You must listen to me, my son. I love you more than you will ever know and I only do this because I love you so much. One day you will know that I have done the right thing. Never forget how much I love you. You must go with your father now. Do you understand? Be a brave boy and do not cry."

She gave the boy to Lucky along with a sack of his clothing with some toys in it. Otoahnacto looked at his mother, his eyes swimming with tears, but he didn't make a sound as he tried to be strong. However, he did hold out his arms to her in a silent plea to not give him to this strange white man.

Avasa kissed one of his little hands and gave him a watery smile. "I love you. Remember that. I love you." Then she turned quickly and left before she changed her mind. Red Boar faded into the night after her.

Lucky stared into the night, willing his love to come back and tell him that she'd changed her mind. The shaking of Otoahnacto's little body in his arms drew Lucky's attention away from the place where Avasa had disappeared. Although his crying was silent, he sobbed, his little heart aching for his mother.

Stroking his son's soft hair, Lucky said, "I feel the same way, my son."

Otoahnacto looked at Lucky and said, "Yelling Bear is sad, too?"

"Yes. I am very sad, but we must do what your mother wants and be brave. We will be brave together," Lucky said, mustering a smile. "It will be hard for a while, but it will get a little better each day."

Wild Wind stepped close to Lucky and said, "We must go quickly before they notice I am missing."

Lucky gave him a sharp look. "What do you mean 'we'?"

His friend smiled. "I am going with you. You heard Avasa. There is nothing here but despair and death. Cruelty and heartbreak. We are not allowed to be ourselves here. They have taken our weapons, we are not allowed to hunt, and we are expected to act grateful for the scraps they throw to us. I do not wish to live in such conditions. You have one Indian friend and he looks healthy and happy. What is one more Indian friend?"

Billy waited to see what Lucky would say to that, but after what he'd just heard, he couldn't stand the thought of Wild Wind going back to the reservation. "Of course you can come," he said in English, forgetting himself. "You can't go back there to that sort of life. Let's get moving before someone comes after us."

Wild Wind was taken aback and turned to Lucky, who was smiling. "You heard him. Let's go. While we're traveling, we're going to call Otoahnacto 'Otto'. It'll be his English name. Most people won't be able to pronounce his Cheyenne name."

Wild Wind nodded. "Ok."

Billy doused the lantern and they made their way back to the three horses they'd brought. As Lucky mounted, he tried not to think about how the third horse had been for Avasa, but he failed. As they trotted away into the night, he and Otto cried silent tears together.

Later that night, they camped out a safe distance from the reservation, but they didn't make a fire. If anyone had been following them, they would be harder to spot if there was no telltale fire. Lucky had offered to take the first watch because he knew there was no way he would sleep. He sat with his back up against a tree trunk, his son sleeping by his side.

The poor tyke had finally cried himself to sleep, but Lucky knew no matter how much he cried, it wouldn't tire him out enough to slumber. He looked skyward, railing a little at the Great Spirit, asking Him why he'd let Avasa fall in love with another man. He doubted he'd ever get an answer, but he asked anyway.

For the past two years he'd envisioned their family living in happiness on the sheep farm, watching his child run around with the sheep and dogs. He'd seen himself carrying their child down the street while Avasa walked beside them, laughing and smiling. Part of those dreams was coming true, but there would forever be an enormous hole in his heart left there by Avasa's absence.

Billy wasn't sleeping either. He was too worried about Lucky, knowing that his best friend must be in misery. He'd been hoping and praying that Lucky would have the happiness he wanted and deserved. It was disheartening to watch Lucky's heart be broken and he planned to do whatever he could to ease Lucky's pain. He knew how painful it was to be rejected by the woman you loved.

There was no sound, but Billy saw a shadow move in the trees. He saw that Wild Wind still slept. Rising, Billy crept out around Lucky, who looked at him questioningly.

Billy whispered in his ear and told him to stay with Otto. Lucky nodded and watched Billy leave their camp.

Billy moved cautiously, following the unknown intruder. It reminded him of what had happened last year and he wasn't about to let history repeat itself. He tensed his shoulder muscles as he closed the distance between them.

Leaping on the person, Billy heard their breath leave them in a rush, a high-pitched cry of fright escaping them. They landed and Billy pinned them down. The person felt weak and soft and very feminine judging by what was under his hand.

"Please do not hurt me," a woman's voice said, confirming Billy's suspicions.

She spoke Cheyenne. Billy moved his hand from where it was to her shoulder. "Who are you?"

"Nina. I followed you. I overheard Wild Wind talking to Avasa tonight and I knew that it was my chance to escape. Please take me with you. Please!" she whispered.

This was serious. If she had overheard that conversation, it was possible that someone else had, too. "Did anyone else follow you?" he demanded.

"No. No one. I swear," she insisted.

"Why should I believe you?"

Wild Wind had come up behind him. "It is true. I knew no one else was there. Avasa and I purposely made sure she would hear us. I knew she would follow me."

"Why would you do that?" Billy asked, getting off the woman. He rose and pulled her up with him, keeping a firm grip on her arm.

"For the same reason Avasa wanted Bull Bear to go with Lucky. Nina is white. A Kiowa captive who was traded to our tribe when she was perhaps eight winters old. She has not had a good life, especially since coming to the reservation. She will be better off with us."

Nina said, "Please do not send me back. I will do anything. I will cook, clean, become your wife. I will be no trouble." She grasped Billy's coat as she tried to find his eyes in the dark.

"I do not know," Billy said.

Nina became even more desperate. "I will beg. I have already had one drunken husband, I do not wish to have another. They will give me to the highest bidder and not care about what I want. Please!"

The thought of a woman going through something like that filled him with disgust. He'd been taught to respect women and part of that meant protecting them. He couldn't leave her behind. Billy sighed and said, "Fine, but no one else better be following us. If you have led someone to us, it will not go well for you."

Wild Wind smiled a little at his firm tone. It was the appropriate thing for him to say in light of the situation. He himself would have made the same decision. "Come. We should go back to Yelling Bear."

# Chapter Six

"Please, Father! Don't! I'll be good, I swear," the eight-year-old Shadow begged.

Wesley Earnest approached the boy, a belt wrapped around his hand. "It's too late! Look at that mess!"

Shadow didn't want to look over in the far corner of the cage at the chamber pot there. It was so hard to see what he was doing in the dark when relieving himself. He tried to spare the single candle he had because it had to last him so long. One candle a week was all he was allowed, so he hadn't lit it last night.

"I'll clean it up! I'm sorry!" His words weren't always clear because he had so few opportunities to speak. His father was the only one he ever saw.

"You're damn right, you will! I should have killed you at birth, but your mother wouldn't hear of it."

"Why can't I see Mother?" Shadow asked.

"What did I tell you would happen if you kept asking me that?" Wesley asked, fury in his cold blue eyes.

Shadow cowered even more. "I'm sorry."

*"You certainly are. Sorry and stupid and filthy! Time for your punishment and then you'll clean up that mess!"*

*"Please don't! Father, no!" Shadow screamed as Wesley unwound the belt.*

"Shadow!"

Someone shook his shoulder and Shadow recognized Bree's touch and voice. He lay still, willing his breathing to return to normal and the fright to recede. He hadn't had such a vivid nightmare in a while and he felt shaky from its intensity.

Bree stretched out against him, lending comfort through her closeness and body heat. Marvin's twin rolled in the bed and gathered her to him as he expelled an unsteady breath. They lay in their bedroom in the underground house beneath the one Marvin lived in. Bree put her arms around his muscular body and laid her head on his shoulder.

"It's just a dream. You're safe," she said.

He thought it ironic that a woman he outweighed by sixty-odd pounds should make him feel safe, but she did. Burying his nose in her thick, wavy hair, he inhaled the exotic scent of the expensive soap he had Marvin buy for her. It was some sort of wildflower from the tropics and it always had a powerful effect on him.

"Thank you, my little counterfeiter," he said.

She smiled at his reference to her former occupation, if it could be called that. Being captives was something that she and Shadow shared, something they had recognized in each other soon after meeting. "You're welcome, my holy terror."

Shadow laughed. He was always amazed that she accepted his very dark nature and could joke about it. "Yes, I am. Both yours and a holy terror," he agreed.

Pressing a kiss to his bare skin, she said, "It's almost evening."

"Is it?"

"Yes. You'll want to go out soon," she said.

"Mmm hmm." He nuzzled her neck and scored it lightly with his teeth, laughing softly against her skin when she shivered against him.

Bree sighed and held him closer. Since meeting him the prior winter, they'd slept in the same bed every night and she'd fallen in love with him, but she hadn't let him make love to her yet. She was too frightened—not of Shadow, however. She didn't fear him in the least. She'd been held prisoner for at least six years by men who only wanted her for two things: her talent at creating inks and dyes to make counterfeit money with and the pleasures her body could offer them. She now had an aversion to physical intimacy because there had never been any pleasure involved for her.

But Shadow's touch, kisses, and softly whispered words gave her tremendous pleasure. They'd graduated from simple things like holding hands and embracing to passionate kissing and caressing, but as of yet, Bree hadn't been able to go farther. Shadow never became angry when she halted things. Frustrated, but not angry. He'd promised her from the beginning that he would never force himself on her and he never had.

With infinite patience and skill, he'd begun introducing her to the way the physical aspects of a relationship were supposed to feel. She'd grown to crave his touch and the feel of him under her hands. Shadow gently encouraged her but never demanded anything from her.

As Shadow kissed his way to her lips, the last vestiges of his nightmare left him. As much as he needed Marvin, as much as he loved his brother and was devoted to him, he was just as devoted to Bree, the woman who'd stolen his heart without even trying. Marvin was his protector and always had been, but Bree was the one who chased away the bad dreams and gave him emotional refuge.

Holding her and not making love to her drove him almost insane with desire, but he would never go back on his promise to her and he'd been faithful to her. Not once had he gone to see any of the women he used to before meeting her.

As their kissing turned more passionate, Shadow knew that it wouldn't be too long before Bree began pulling back, but he was determined to get every second he could before that happened. When she did, he felt a flash of anger—not at her, but at the men who had harmed her so much. If he'd been able to, he would have killed more than one of them the night when he'd stumbled upon Bree and the man who was beating her. He'd wasted no time in snapping his neck like a twig and he'd do it a million times if necessary to keep her safe.

Shadow was surprised to feel tears prick the back of his eyes at the thought of her being so mistreated. When their lips parted, he said, "Bree, you have to know by now that I love you. Don't you? Can't you feel it when I kiss you? Hear it when I say your name? Just in case, I'll say it plainly. I love you, Bree."

Joy quickly spread through her and Bree said, "I thought you did, but you've never said it before now."

"I'm finding that love is a scary thing," he said with a laugh. "Me, scared. Ironic, isn't it?"

"All of us have fears, Shadow," she drew back and looked into his eyes. "I love you, too. So much."

His sensual mouth curved. "I know. I feel it, see it, hear it, and sense it. Sometimes it feels as though it fills whatever room we're in."

She kissed him and said, "For a murderer, you're very poetic."

"Maybe I have hidden talents," he said, running his hand down her arm. "Or maybe I'm just hidden."

She giggled at that. No one outside of her and Marvin knew of his existence. He and Marvin hadn't known about each other until they were sixteen. While Marvin had been showered with the finest things in life, Shadow had been held in a cage until Marvin had accidentally discovered him in the vast basement under the house.

Shadow loved making Bree laugh. He knew that she'd had little to laugh about until meeting him. He kissed her and caressed her back before whispering, "Bree, let me make love to you. You know I won't hurt you. I want to show you how much I love you."

Bree trembled in his arms, but she didn't move away. "What if I don't please you?"

His deep voice grew slightly husky with emotion. "Everything about

46

you pleases me. Why would that be any different? What if *I* don't please *you*?"

Bree hated hearing Shadow say anything negative about himself. "Of course you will. How could you not? You're so handsome it hurts me to look at you sometimes, you're gentle and kind, and it feels so good when you kiss me and hold me—"

"Easy, little one. I didn't mean to upset—"

This time Bree was the one to interrupt. She brought her mouth down on his in a demanding kiss and Shadow was thrilled in the change in her demeanor. Bree had never been forceful before and it was maddeningly exciting to him. She'd been eager and playful, but never forceful. He responded in kind until things reached a fever pitch.

Shadow groaned and broke the kiss.

Bree asked, "Where are you going? I thought you were going to make love to me?"

"Am I?" he asked.

"Yes, you are," she said. "So get back here and don't stop again."

Shadow grinned. "Yes, ma'am."

Although he slowed things down, he didn't stop, and for the first time in his life, Shadow made love with a woman. It was far more exquisite than anything he'd ever experienced before. He cared more for Bree's feelings than his own—something that had never happened to him before—and he savored every second of it.

Bree had never known such joy and she felt foolish for waiting so long to share it with Shadow. He was tender and generous, making her feel cherished and so very loved. The sweetness was too much to bear at one point and she was helpless to stop several tears from falling. Shadow kissed them all away and held her close, telling her of his love again and again.

When Marvin heard someone knock on his door that night, he'd thought it was Evan coming by to accuse him of something. However, when he opened the door, he was surprised to see a redheaded woman standing on the veranda.

"May I help you?" he asked.

"Perhaps," she said. "I understand you're looking for a cook and housekeeper."

Marvin's previous cook, Fiona, had quit after the whole Phoebe debacle, leaving him to fend for himself. He didn't mind in some ways; he was fairly skilled in the kitchen and he did a lot of the cleaning himself so that no one was snooping about. It was another precaution he took to keep Shadow a secret.

"Yes, actually, I am, but I normally interview people during the day," he said.

"I understand and I'm sorry about the late hour, but it was the only time I could get away since I needed someone to watch my daughter. My name is Veronica Hendricks."

Marvin said, "Pardon my bad manners. Marvin Earnest. Come in out of the cold. After all, you did come all this way."

Veronica looked around at the beautiful foyer that boasted a crystal chandelier.

"May I take your cloak?" Marvin asked politely.

"Yes, thank you."

Marvin hung the garment on the coatrack next to the door and motioned towards the parlor. "Come sit by the fire and warm yourself. Did someone bring you? They're welcome to come in."

"No. It's just me," she said.

The parlor was a large room filled with expensive furniture. A sofa and love seat lined one corner while a grouping of three red upholstered wingback chairs created a cozy half circle around the fire that blazed in the hearth.

She took the one on the right and Marvin sat in the one on the other end. He crossed his legs and laid his hands on his lap in an elegant, relaxed pose.

"Now then, did you bring a resume with you?" he asked.

"No."

Marvin nodded slightly. "What sort of experience do you have?"

"I took care of my uncle until he passed and I did all of the cooking and cleaning for him. I'm a very good cook and I keep a house spotless," she said.

"How long did you take care of him?"

"Five years."

"What kinds of things do you cook?" Marvin asked.

"Anything, sir. All types of breakfast food, roasts, chicken, and desserts. I'm a very good cook."

"So you said," Marvin responded.

"Did I? I'm sorry. I didn't mean to repeat myself."

Marvin smiled. "That's all right. Here's what I'm looking for. I only need someone for breakfast and lunch. Keeping the kitchen tidy is the main concern, and perhaps dusting downstairs. I don't need anything done upstairs, however. I take care of my room and Miss Josephson takes care of hers. She's a family friend who lives here."

"I understand," Veronica said.

Marvin asked, "When can you start?"

"Immediately," she said. She tried not to stare at him, but it was hard not to because he was so handsome.

The devil that usually sat on Marvin's shoulder made him say, "Well, then come with me. I'd love to have an omelet and then I can assess your cooking skills. I'm rather partial to them."

Veronica watched him rise and thought he was joking. She didn't move from her chair. Realizing that she wasn't following him, Marvin turned around and asked, "Well?"

"I meant that I would start tomorrow," she said.

"Well, if I like your omelet, I'll hire you and you can start tomorrow. Think of this as your audition," Marvin said. "Come. I'm hungry."

He left the room and Veronica had no choice but to follow him. She could tell that he was used to others following his orders, but she wasn't the type of person to be ordered about. As they entered the kitchen, he lit two lamps.

Veronica said, "You could say please."

He arched an eyebrow at her snippy tone. "Forgive me. *Please* make me an omelet so I can see if you're good enough for me to spend good money in hiring you."

She shot him an indignant look and Marvin smiled. He liked getting a rise out of people and he liked it even more when they gave it back to him. Seating himself at the table, he didn't offer her any assistance in finding things and it turned out that he didn't need to.

The cook stove was already hot to provide heat in the kitchen, so she didn't have to start a fire. She found a skillet and put it on the stove. Going into what she assumed was the pantry, she found eggs, milk, and some cheese. As she worked, she ignored Marvin for the most part, concentrating on her task.

Marvin's kitchen certainly was the nicest one she'd ever worked in and it was well equipped. She not only made an omelet for Marvin, she made one for herself. She sat the two plates and two cups of coffee she'd made on the table and sat down with him.

Marvin admired her pluck in making food for herself and sitting down to eat, too. That was certainly something he hadn't expected. Taking a bite of the cheese omelet, he chewed thoughtfully, exploring its taste. It was fluffy with just the right amount of cheese.

"You're hired. It pays seventeen a week and you may also take your meals here, if you prefer," he said.

Veronica smiled. It was good money. "Well, there's one thing that may influence that decision."

"Which is?"

"I need to bring my baby with me to work. She's a very good baby and doesn't cry very much. I've no one else to watch her," Veronica said.

"I'm assuming your husband works days. Don't you have any family who could take care of her?"

"You're assuming I have a husband," Veronica retorted. "I'm a widow. He was a soldier and he was killed shortly before Eva was born."

"That's horrible. I'm so sorry. Please accept my condolences," Marvin said.

"Thank you. My mother and father didn't like me marrying a military man and it put a strain on our relationship. David and I moved out this way a year and a half ago. Eva is ten months old so there's the matter of needing to feed her," Veronica said, not mincing words.

Marvin nodded. "Well, I suppose there's nothing for it then but to bring her. I'll play with her while you cook my breakfast."

"What?" she asked loudly. "That won't be necessary. I don't let strange men play with my daughter."

"But I'm no longer a strange man. I'm your employer, you know my name, and you have now broken bread with me. Besides, I love children. My foreman brings his daughter Pauline to see me once or twice a week. We struck up a friendship—sort of like an uncle, I suppose. She's a delightful child. You'll see."

Veronica said, "That's all well and good, but I'll take care of Eva while she's here, thank you very much."

Marvin raised his hands in surrender. "Very well. I meant no harm." He liked her protectiveness as well as her fiery red hair and snapping dark eyes. "Very good coffee, by the way."

"Thank you," she said. "If you're finished, I'll wash the dishes."

"That's not necessary. I'm sure you'd like to get home to Eva."

"Of course I'll wash them. I don't want them to get dried overnight and have to scrub them harder tomorrow," she said.

Although irritated, Marvin found himself enjoying her bossiness. "Fine. Have it your way. In fact, while you wash them, we'll go over a couple of other rules."

Veronica put water for doing the dishes on to heat. "Ok."

"The basement is completely off limits. And I mean *completely*. There are spiders down there and a few years ago, one of my cooks was bitten very badly. I've tried to get rid of them, but they keep coming back. So no going down there. I won't have another cook harmed."

"Spiders? Do they come up here?" she asked.

Marvin smiled. "No. They seem to like it where it's dark and dank. They're not fond of the light." *Oh, Shadow will love it that I compared him to a poisonous spider.*

"Oh. All right. I hate basements anyway, so that's fine with me," she said.

"There's a washroom on the first floor here for you to use," Marvin said. "Also, my office doesn't need any attention. I'm very particular about where things go and I don't like them moved around."

Veronica nodded. "All right."

"Good."

"What time do you prefer to eat in the morning?"

"Eight is fine unless I inform you differently the day beforehand."

Marvin watched her move around, noting her slim curves. She was graceful and confident. He smiled. *This could be fun.*

# Chapter Seven

In Billy's dream, he was snug and comfortable. There was something warm and soft lying against him, too. He skimmed a hand over it, discovering slim, womanly curves. Suddenly he knew he wasn't dreaming and his eyes popped open.

The sun was just peaking over the horizon, the light illuminating their cold camp. Billy stared into a pair of vivid green eyes set in a very beautiful female face. Their irises held gold flecks and these fabulous eyes were framed by long, black lashes. His artist's eye noted that a very pretty nose started between her eyes and ended in a slightly pert tip.

Below this nose was a full, pouty mouth and a delicate jawline. Dark, golden-blonde hair done up in braids and well-defined cheekbones all combined to create the most beautiful face Billy had ever had the pleasure to see.

She smiled and Billy's heartbeat went a little haywire. "Good morning," she said in Cheyenne.

"Good morning," he returned in kind. Waking up in such close proximity to a gorgeous woman had caused in his brain to fog up, but then it lifted and he remembered where they were. "Nina?" He hadn't had a chance examine her closely the night before since they hadn't had a fire.

"Yes."

Billy thought she was a couple of years younger than he was. "Uh, why are you here? Under the blankets with me?"

She gave him a sly little look and said, "Because it is warmer when two share their body heat."

He couldn't fault her logic, but ... "This is not proper," he said, moving away and throwing off the blankets.

She made a noise of protest when the cold air hit her and pulled them back over her as he rose. Looking around, he saw that they were the first ones up. Under extra blankets, Lucky was sleeping with his body curled around Otto to keep the boy warm since they hadn't built a fire to sleep next to. Wild Wind was still under his blankets, only the top of his head visible.

Billy stretched and then picked up his bow and arrow quiver. Bending down to Nina he said, "I am going hunting. Let the others know."

She looked at him and nodded. Once again her eyes cast a little spell and he sent her a smile, which she returned. Then he shook himself a little and left their camp. Once he was gone, Nina rose and went to take care of her business. She didn't go far, not wanting to leave the protection of Yelling Bear and Wild Wind.

Going back, she gathered a little wood along the way and started to build a small fire so that when Billy came back with some game, she could cook it. Wild Wind stirred and looked over at her.

"Good morning," he said, sitting up and yawning. "Where is Billy?"

Nina smiled at the mention of the handsome man's name and said, "He has gone to hunt breakfast."

Wild Wind grunted his understanding, seeing her slightly pink complexion. He smiled. It would seem that she was smitten with Billy. He rose and began rolling up his blankets. He tied them up and walked over to the horses, tying them to the back of the saddle of the horse he'd been given.

Coming back to the camp, it came to his attention that sometime during the night, Nina and Billy had shared sleeping robes. He drew this conclusion from the fact that there was only one pile of blankets instead of the two there had been when they'd gone to bed. He frowned. Had they been intimate? No. Not with him and Lucky so close.

"Nina, did you spend the night with Billy?" he asked. Normally, he wouldn't have been so forward, but he didn't want anyone to take advantage of her. She was a sweet girl who'd been through a lot of heartache and he didn't want her to be hurt.

Nina smiled. "Just for warmth. He did not even know I was there. It is so cold and I could not get warm by myself," she said.

Wild Wind said, "It is not right and you know it."

Her eyes shot sudden fire at him. "Who are you to tell me what is right? You are not my father or my brother. Not even a cousin. Besides, I am a widow and it is my prerogative if I take a lover or not. I am done with men telling me what I can and cannot do. Stay out of my business."

"She is right," Lucky said, even though his eyes were still closed. "Besides, Billy will not harm her, nor take advantage of her."

Wild Wind snorted and left the camp. Lucky sighed. His friend could have a little bit of a temper. He hadn't gotten up yet because he was letting Otto sleep a little longer and didn't want to disturb him. Also, he was waiting for the sun to warm things up a little so it wasn't so cold when they got out from under the covers.

Opening his eyes, Lucky looked down at the little boy. *My son.* Those words and the sight of Otto's cute little face filled Lucky with pride. He smiled and tickled Otto's cheek. He moaned a little and brushed Lucky's hand away. Lucky chuckled and did it again. This time Otto opened his eyes and gave Lucky a displeased look, his dark blond brows drawn together.

"Good morning, my son," Lucky said with a smile.

Lucky's smile was infectious and Otto smiled back a little. "I have to pee. Where is Mother?"

Sorrow and pain speared Lucky's heart. "She is back on the

reservation. You are coming with me now, remember?"

Otto nodded as the memory of Avasa leaving him came back to him. Tears welled up in his eyes. "I want Mother," he said.

Lucky gathered him to him and said, "Me, too. Otto. Me, too."

He had been made to understand that this was his English name, so he didn't protest Lucky's use of it. "She does not love me? Was I bad?"

Lucky kissed his forehead and said, "No, you were not bad. Your mother loves you so much that she gave you to me so I can take care of you. You will understand some day. We are going to my home. It is now your home, too. You will like it there. I live in a tipi."

Otto rolled over to face Lucky. "You live in a tipi? You are white."

"Yes. It is a nice tipi," Lucky said. "I raise sheep."

"Sheep?"

"They are fluffy, white animals. Smaller than cows. They are good to eat and we make things from their wool—their fur," Lucky explained.

Otto examined the face of the man his mother had told him was his blood father. His eyes traveled over his blond hair and noted his gray eyes and strong jaw. In a broken piece of mirror they had in his tipi, Otto had seen his reflection. His hair wasn't as light as Lucky's, but it was blond. He could also see that he had Lucky's smile. Otto put a hand to Lucky's face and felt the stubble there.

"You have hair," he said.

"That is right. White men have hair on their faces and some of us shave it to get rid of it every day. It grows fast." He took Otto's hand and kissed it.

Otto smiled and Lucky smiled with him. *He's beautiful. He has Avasa's eyes and her forehead.*

Billy returned with four rabbits and held them up. "How's that for a breakfast? You get to clean them, Irish."

Lucky laughed. "Aye. I will."

Otto said, "Aye?"

Lucky said, "That means 'yes' in English."

"Aye," Otto said.

"Good."

Lucky got up, but tucked the blankets around Otto to keep him warm.

"Father? I have to pee," Otto reminded him.

Billy said, "I'll take him. That'll get me out of here while you do that."

Nina came over and took the rabbits from Lucky. "It is my job," she said.

Lucky relinquished the rabbits to her. "We'll have to remember that this type of thing is her domain, Billy. Cheyenne women get angry when you interfere in their work."

Billy smiled at Nina and said in Cheyenne. "I will not fight you about doing the cooking. Do not worry."

She chuckled and said, "I told you I would make a good wife."

Billy's smile faded. "You are not my wife."

"I know." She turned to her task then. *But I could be. You are very handsome and very nice. You are also a good hunter and would be a good provider.*

Billy looked at Lucky, but his friend wasn't any help. Billy could see that he was fighting laughter. In English, Billy said, "This isn't funny. I don't know where she got such an idea. Callie is waiting for me back in Echo."

Lucky cleared his throat and said, "You'll have to explain that to her."

"Why is she focusing on *me*? Why not you or Wild Wind?" he asked.

"Because you're the one who gave her permission to come with us. She thinks you're in charge of her, so to speak," Lucky said.

"In charge of her? I'm not in charge of anyone," Billy said. "I have a woman in Echo. Once we get there, she'll find someone, but it won't be me."

Billy went over to Otto and held out his hand. "Come with me," he said with a smile.

Otto gave him a shy one in return and took Billy's hand. "You are Father's friend?"

"Yes."

Otto gave Billy his hand and they began walking from camp. Billy thought that Otto was very cute with his wavy blond hair and dark eyes. His skin tone was much the same color as Billy's—a shade darker than Lucky's pale skin and not as dark bronze as Wild Wind's. Once he helped Otto go, they came back to camp.

Wild Wind had returned by this time. With his back to Nina, he signed, "What are your intentions towards Nina?"

Billy blinked and signed, "None. I have a woman waiting for me at home."

"But you shared her robes last night."

Continuing to sign, Billy sent back, "I had nothing to do with that. I woke up and there she was."

Wild Wind saw that Billy told the truth and suddenly he found the situation funny. A small smile turned up the corners of his mouth. "So the intentions are all on her part?"

"Yes!" Billy signed. "This is not funny! I will explain it to her so that she will not have any more intentions towards me. She is beautiful. Why do you not want her?"

Wild Wind almost laughed. "I am simply not attracted to her, but it sounds like you might be."

Lucky let out a snort of laughter since he had a clear view of their conversation. Billy's dark eyes lit with anger. "I am not! I am an artist and I notice how things and people look, that is all."

Lucky came over to sign, "You could do worse for a wife. She is young and beautiful and skilled at homemaking."

Wild Wind grinned. "She is also a widow, so there is nothing really wrong with sharing her robes."

Billy's fists clenched before he signed, "I have a woman in Echo! You know that." He looked at Lucky as he said this.

Lucky sobered and nodded. "Yes, I know. I was just teasing you," he signed.

Wild Wind signed, "You are an easy target

Billy fumed inside, but didn't say anything more about the situation. Instead, he went to his blankets and began rolling them up. Then he took them to his horse and lashed them to the saddle. *Why are they trying to push this woman on me? She's a widow? What happened to her husband? Last night she said that she'd had one drunken husband and didn't want another. Do they really sell captives? That's slavery. White people used to, but I didn't know Indians did it. Do all tribes or just some? I feel bad for her, but I'm not responsible for her.*

"Billy, don't be sore," Lucky said from behind him.

Billy smiled. "I'm not. I just don't want her to have the wrong idea about me. I'll explain it to her after breakfast."

Lucky smiled. "Good idea. It's ready. Come eat."

Billy asked, "Was she really sold like a slave?"

"Some tribes do that, aye. The Cheyenne don't as a rule, but it's possible she was won by men who were gambling. I don't know her story," Lucky said. "She wasn't with our tribe when I was."

Billy's brow furrowed and Lucky could tell that he didn't like that idea.

"Come have breakfast so we can go. The sooner we're on the road, the sooner we get you home to Callie," Lucky said.

Billy smiled. "That's right. I can't wait to meet her."

They went back to the fire and Billy sat down, accepting a large piece of rabbit meat from Nina. He was ravenous and broke off large chunks, shoving them in his mouth rapidly. He complimented Nina on the meat.

"I am glad you like it," she said with a coy look at him.

Billy found himself responding to her flirtatious smile in spite of himself. Then he remembered Callie and frowned, returning his attention to his meal. It didn't take him long to eat. A chuckle to his right made him look in that direction.

Wild Wind grinned. "You eat like the camp dogs. Do you even chew?"

Lucky let out a loud shout of laughter at his statement. Billy smiled and shoved more meat in his mouth, eliciting a frown of disapproval from Lucky. He heard Nina giggle and Otto laughed at him. Lucky sat cross-legged and Otto sat on Lucky's legs. Billy would have liked to have painted them and then remembered that he had his sketchbook with him.

"Stay right there, Lucky. Keep him with you." He got up and jogged over to his horse, withdrawing a large pad of sketch paper from a saddlebag.

Coming back, he sat down directly across from Lucky and Otto. "It won't take me long to do the preliminary sketch, but I have to get it while I have the right light."

Nina was curious about what he was doing, but she didn't interfere. Instead, she watched his eyes go back and forth from the paper to father and son. She liked the way Billy's dark brows drew down as he concentrated and the graceful movements of his well-made hands.

Creeping up behind him, she looked over his shoulder and stared in wonder at the way he made the drawing come to life. He perfectly captured Lucky's strong jaw, tussled hair, and wide shoulders. Lucky didn't mind being a subject for Billy and he held still. Nina saw Billy create Otto's likeness as well, including the clothing he wore and the way his little hands lay in his lap.

When Billy was done with the drawing, he got up quickly, bumping into Nina. He grabbed her to prevent her from falling. "Are you ok?"

Nina frowned at the unfamiliar words. She hadn't learned English since she preferred to stay as far away from any white people as she could. In fact there were few people she trusted, Wild Wind being one of them. He never spoke English around her because there was no need to.

"Ok?" she asked.

In Cheyenne, Billy said, "That means 'yes' or 'all right'. I asked if you were all right."

"Ok," she said with a smile.

Billy nodded and released her. Then he stowed his sketchpad again. Camp was broken and they readied the horses. Otto rode with Lucky and, much to his dismay, Nina rode with Billy. As soon as he mounted, she came to his horse's side and held up her hand. Billy looked at Wild Wind, but the brave was talking to Lucky about something. He knew that even if he hadn't been, Wild Wind had no intention of riding double with Nina.

He helped her mount and gathered the reins while she settled herself behind him. The sensation of her moving against him sent a wave of desire through his body. She put her arms around him and leaned her cheek against his back, which didn't help his situation any.

*This is bad. Very bad. Why did she have to come with us? Lucky and Wild Wind aren't helping me any, either.*

As their little group started out, Billy tried to put the fact that a very desirable woman was pressed up against his backside out of his mind, but he wasn't very successful. He couldn't wait until they stopped for lunch so he could put some space between them.

# Chapter Eight

Evan sat at Spike's, crocheting and nursing a beer in between contemplating his next move with Marvin. He'd seen Marvin a couple of times in town and he'd been civil but not overly friendly. Since that day in Marvin's office he'd backed off, knowing if he'd suddenly seemed to do an about-face, it would tip Marvin off that something was afoot.

During one of his contemplative moments, he had an idea that brought a smile to his face. He should have thought of it sooner, he realized, but that's the way it went sometimes; something that seemed so simple couldn't be seen until another time. He'd had his eyes closed, so he wasn't expecting the nudge he felt to his arm.

Opening his eyes, he saw Thad smiling at him, his dark eyes shining.

"Hello, Sheriff," he said.

With a grin, Evan said, "It's about damn time you got back home. Spike, a whiskey for Thad on me."

Thad sat down and Evan clapped him on the back. "Everyone has been missing you. You better come home so you can see my women."

Thad nodded. "I will. How's things?"

Evan said, "Good. Julia's getting so big. Wait until you see her."

Spike, an older man in his mid-sixties with white hair and blue eyes, sat a full shot glass down in front of Thad. "Well, if it isn't our long-lost bounty hunter. Good to see you."

"Thanks," Thad said. "It's good to be back." He tossed the shot back and indicated that he wanted another.

Spike filled the glass again. "That one's on me. So how many crooks did you chase down this time?"

"Three," Thad said. "I'm set up for money pretty well, so I guess I'll stick around for a while."

"Glad to hear it," Evan replied.

"What are you working on right now?" Thad asked.

Evan shrugged. "Not much."

This was the code phrase the two men used to let each other know that something of importance was occurring. Spike was notorious for spreading gossip, so they didn't talk about cases in front of him.

"Good. I'm hankerin' to beat you at poker. Let's go," Thad said.

Once they'd started their game, Thad asked, "What's goin' on?"

"You got back to town just in time," Evan said. "How'd you like in on a long-term surveillance mission out at Earnest's?"

Hatred so strong it almost took his breath away flooded Thad, but he stayed calm. "Tell me what you're thinkin'."

Evan said, "Well, whoever he's got working with him is gonna have to show up at his house sooner or later. I've done some on my own the past week, but it seems that Marvin's a homebody most of the time. The couple of times he did go out at night it was just for a drive. He didn't meet up with anyone and he didn't stop at the Burgundy House.

"The only person I saw come to visit him was a woman. From what I gather, he hired her as his new housekeeper. I asked Travis about Bree and he said it's funny because she doesn't seem to be around a lot during the day, but he never sees her go anywhere and her horse is in the barn most of the time.

"Where is she going? Does she sit in her room all day? That's another funny thing. I've been there at various times after dark, but there's only light in one of the bedrooms, which are all upstairs. I'm assuming it's Earnest's. Where is she sleeping? I don't know how, but something tells me that all of it is somehow connected."

Thad knew that Evan didn't approach law enforcement quite like other people. He liked to examine farfetched theories, and sometimes they turned out to be right. He'd caught criminals that way in the past. Maybe getting more creative might work in going after Earnest. He had to admit that it did sound a little funny. "Maybe she really is sleeping with him and that's where she stays."

Evan shook his head. "I thought about that, too, but I never see anyone in the parlor at night with him. You know he reads a lot. I've peeked in the window once or twice, but she's never in there. Even if she was in a part of the room I couldn't see, he would have talked to her at some point. No, he's alone at night."

"I still don't see what you're gettin' at."

Evan said, "I think she's his go-between with this guy. I think she's how they communicate."

"But you said no one comes and no one goes," Thad said.

"You're gonna think I'm crazy, but what if there's another way in and out of that house? It would explain how this person can disappear like he does. It would also explain how she might get in and out without being detected."

Thad rubbed his jaw as he thought about it. "It's possible. That might be why I never saw any activity the three nights I watched the place. And there are different tunnel systems all over Montana that people don't realize exist. What if old man Earnest had something like that built? If he did, where's the entrance?"

"Exactly," Evan said. "I also think that Earnest was taking care of the guy that Lucky shot that night. I haven't seen him go to any woman's house, so I know he's not seeing anyone. I know deep inside that the murdered guy Lucky and Billy found has something to do with Bree. I think she's the woman whose tracks Billy found."

Thad said, "But she didn't come to town until a month or so after they found that guy."

"What if Earnest was hiding her? If there's a tunnel system, maybe she stayed down there."

"But this stuff with Earnest has been going on for years. How do you think she's linked to this guy if he's been around for so long?" Thad asked.

"I don't know, but we're gonna find out. Win's gonna help and Jerry and Travis, too. We're gonna look for the tunnel entrance tomorrow and we're gonna start around the place where the guy was killed," Evan responded. "You wanna help?"

"Hell, yeah," Thad said. "What time are we starting?"

"About eight. Meet me at my place in the morning," Evan said.

"That won't be hard since I'm gonna sleep on your sofa. I gotta find a place to stay. I can't go back there," Thad said.

In the past whenever he'd come home to Echo, Thad had stayed at the Hanovers', but since Phoebe's death, he hadn't been able to lodge with them. There were too many memories of them there. Thad had suffered a triple loss; he'd lost his relationship with Phoebe upon learning of her cheating. He'd lost the woman he loved and the unborn child he'd never known. It had taken him a long time to get his head on straight and do his normal job. The funny thing was that his heart wasn't in it quite like it used to be.

Evan saw the grief in Thad's face and a surge of sympathy flowed through him. However, he knew mentioning it would make it worse for Thad who didn't talk about things that hurt. "I'm sure you'll find a place. I'll help you."

"I don't need a big place."

Evan nodded. "Well, let's get home and get some shuteye."

"Sounds good," Thad said.

"Do you know who you need to talk to?" Edna asked the other people in the Tafts' parlor.

Thad smiled. "Who?" He held Julia and made faces at her, making her laugh.

"Brock Kincaid. He's older than dirt and knows practically everything about Echo. He's probably pushing ninety," she said. "He might be able to shed some light on the Earnests. It never really occurred to me before."

Evan said, "I've heard of him, but I don't think I've actually met him. Doesn't he live out past the Burgundy House a little ways?"

"That's right," Edna said. "If anyone knows anything about the Earnests, it's him."

Josie said, "I could go talk to him while you men look for a secret entrance." The prospect of helping to possibly solve some of the mystery surrounding the Earnests was very exciting. "You know how Marvin finds out everything, so if you went, that might be of interest to him, but if I went under the guise of putting together a history of Echo, it really wouldn't rouse his suspicions."

Evan had to admit that the idea was a good one, but the thought of Josie in that part of town made him uneasy. "I don't like you going alone out there. I know, we'll see if Remus can go with you. Just tell him the same story. I don't want to tip off anyone about this."

Remus and Arlene Decker were Billy's parents who lived next door to the Tafts.

Josie nodded. "I'll ask him right away in the morning. With him retiring last year, I'm sure that he'd have some time."

"You just be careful," Evan said. It made him feel better that a man would be going with her.

Josie smiled at him. "I will. I promise. I'm just going to talk to him."

Evan nodded. "Let's get some sleep. We all have a big day ahead of us tomorrow."

―――――

"Thank you so much for seeing us, Mr. Kincaid," Josie said as he let her and Remus in.

Brock smiled, showing several empty spaces where teeth had once been. "No trouble at all. It ain't like I got much to do these days."

The slight statured man shuffled his way into a small parlor that looked like it hadn't been cleaned in some time. He pointed to a sofa and sat in an old threadbare chair with tufts of stuffing coming out here and there.

"How can I help you?" he asked.

Josie took out a notepad and pencil. "Well, as a newcomer to Echo, I don't really know much about the history of the town and I was told that since you've been here for so long, you most likely have a lot of information on the town."

Brock's laugh sounded rusty, as though he didn't use it much. "My goodness. Someone actually cares what I think about Echo. How 'bout that? I can do a lot better than just talkin' about it. I've got a lot of journals you're welcome to take with you. There're newspaper clippin's and the like, too."

Josie's eyebrows rose. "Really? That would be wonderful. I would make sure to return them to you, of course."

"Oh, you can keep them. I know what's in them word for word and I ain't got no grandkids or kin that wants 'em. I'm the last of the Kincaids to live in Echo," Brock said. "Is there something specific you wanted to know?"

"Well, with the earthquake and mine subsidence, it got me thinking. I know there are tunnels around Montana, ones where people hid the Chinese from some townspeople to help them. Well, supposedly. I was wondering if there were any such tunnels around Echo since it was a mining town," she said.

"Hmm. Let me think."

Josie and Remus waited while he ruminated on the subject. Josie felt a hum of anticipation run through her body. She hoped to uncover something that would be of use to Evan's investigation.

"You know, it does seem to run in my mind that a few of the bigger mining families had some tunnels. I guess sometimes they did house the

Chinese down there, but more times than not, it was a place to hide their loot," Brock said.

Josie wrote this down. "And which families were they?"

"Well, the Mosbys, Lancasters, Earnests, and the Wintersteens. Those were the largest operations as I understand it."

Josie made sure not to react to Brock's inclusion of the Earnests in the possible families who had tunnels. She jotted down all the names. "I'd love to see them. It would be fascinating to walk through them. Such a part of history."

"I reckon the entrances would be hid good since they didn't want anyone to find the gold. I've never heard where any of them are, though."

Josie requested that Brock give her a rundown of the histories of the main mining families. She paid particularly close attention when he talked about the Earnests.

"Outside of their money, they didn't have very much luck with things," he said.

Remus asked, "What do you mean?"

"Well, as I recall, they had several babies that died in childbirth or soon after. Marvin was the only one that survived and I guess they quit tryin'. It's a shame really. He had a twin, but the boy died when he was just a baby," Brock said.

Josie did think that was a shame. "Edna says that Marvin wasn't quite the same after his father died. How did his father die?"

"That's a little bit of a mystery. I guess Marvin had come home from boarding school one summer. He was maybe fifteen or sixteen; I don't really recall exactly. There was some sort of urgent business abroad and both of his parents left for England. His mother got sick not long after they arrived over there and passed away.

"Now, you'd have thought that Wesley would have come home to be with Marvin after Marilyn had died, but he stayed in England for a couple of years. Marvin had an overseer, Richard Drewmore, but once word came that Wesley had been killed in a boating accident, Marvin inherited everything, so he let Drewmore go and started running things himself. Some people think the Earnests are cursed, but I don't buy that," Brock told them.

"Why do they think they're cursed?" Josie asked.

"Drewmore was robbed and stabbed to death in his home a few months after Marvin fired him. If it wasn't for Marvin's money and the fact that jobs are so scarce, no one would work for him. This latest incident out there has only strengthened that feeling. It's why his cook quit. She didn't want to work in a kitchen where a woman had been killed. She thought it would be bad luck and that she might run into a ghost or something.

"Anyway, after Wesley died, Marvin started acting nasty with people, especially the people working for him. I think he was bitter over his parents deserting him like they did. He had no one else, no friends around here since he went to boarding school every year. Once he was sixteen, he didn't go anymore though. He finished his schooling here in Echo," Brock said.

Brock didn't have much more information to tell her about any of the families, but Josie and Remus took the journals and photo albums that he had since they'd brought her buggy. On the way home, she and the big, gray-haired man chitchatted about everything Brock had told them, but the whole time, Josie's mind worked on the information about the Earnest family, hoping that it might somehow help fill in some of the holes they were missing.

# Chapter Nine

By the time Lucky and company reached a little town in Colorado named Hayden, Billy was almost beside himself with exasperation. Nina was almost his constant companion. It didn't help that he found himself intensely attracted to her. He'd told her about Callie, but it didn't seem to faze her.

When they made camp for the night in Hayden, Billy went to get some firewood and she was right there. He let out a groan and put the armload of wood he carried down.

"Nina, we need to talk," he said, glad that he could communicate with her in Cheyenne since she was still learning English.

"Yes?" she asked.

"Did you not understand when I told you that I have a woman at home waiting for me?"

Nina looked at the ground. "Yes. I understood. But you are not married to her. She is not here. I am. I will be a second wife, if you like."

Billy passed a hand over his face. "No, I do not like. I will marry only one woman and she is first in line, whether she is here or not. When we get to Echo, I will help you find a husband."

Nina became frightened. "No! I do not want anyone else. You are nice to me and you do not yell at me. I do not know those men and I do not want to. Is this other woman pretty?"

Billy said, "I do not know. I have never met her. I have explained to you that we were supposed to meet, but that I came with Lucky right before she arrived in Echo."

Nina arched a brow at him. "You are to marry a woman you have never met? What if she is ugly?"

"I doubt she is, but I will find out once we meet," Billy said.

Nina nodded and lowered her gaze. "I do not know where I will stay when we get there. How will I survive?"

Billy's kind heart couldn't help feeling sorry for her. "We will help you. You will see."

Nina didn't answer him. She bent and picked up some of the firewood. "We should get this to camp and make the evening meal."

Billy caught the sheen of tears in her eyes. "Nina, wait." He put a hand on her shoulder to halt her.

Even though tears trailed down her cheeks, she met his gaze with a proud expression on her face. "What?"

"I am not trying to hurt you. I am trying to honor a commitment to someone."

"I understand," she said, looking into his black eyes.

After her husband had drank himself to death, she'd vowed never to get involved with that kind of man again. However, it seemed as though the matter was out of her hands, and she'd known that it would only be a matter of time before she was given to some other man. When Billy had first attacked her, she'd only sought for them to take her with them.

Then she'd seen how nice and handsome he was and had thought to secure her future by enticing him into marrying her. Over the past week, she'd come to sincerely like Billy. He was funny, talented, strong, and kind. He was good with Otto and had told her that he'd taken care of a few children while he was growing up. He was a good hunter and had a successful business.

He was everything she could ever want in a husband, but this other woman complicated things. While she respected his sense of honor in upholding his commitment to this Callie, it hurt her to think about it. On more than one occasion, she'd snuck under the covers with him while he was asleep. There had been a couple of nights when he'd put his arms around her and they'd slept that way. He made her feel safe.

"I will not bother you anymore," she said. "I am sorry for doing so."

"It is not that you are bothering me, it is just that I do not want you to expect something that is not going to happen," he replied.

She brushed away her tears and said, "You are right. I have been foolish. Of course you would want this other woman. She is of your world and I am of no world. I am a white woman who has lived as an Indian. I do not know your language or your customs. Why would you want someone who does not belong anywhere?"

With angry movements, she gathered the firewood again and turned to go back to camp. Billy couldn't let her leave after that statement. He knew exactly how she felt. He stopped her and cupped her face in his hands.

"I don't belong, either. I'm an Indian raised in white society and very few people are truly my friends."

She didn't understand what he was saying because he'd slipped back into English. "What?"

Instead of repeating it in Cheyenne, Billy said, "The hell with it." Lowering his head, he kissed her soft lips, savoring the taste of them.

Nina wasn't sure what to do at first. Should she pull away? Hit him? Kiss him back? She did the latter because his kiss was intoxicating and she let him pull her closer and wrap his arms around her. Burying her hands in his thick hair that was the color of chestnuts, she offered herself to him, letting him know that she enjoyed what he was doing.

Never before had Billy felt such a powerful attraction to a woman. Not even Shelby had roused his desire the way Nina did and he was helpless to fight it anymore. It was like trying to fight the ocean— impossible. He'd spent too much time with her body pressed against him, her arms around him, and it had been a couple of years since he'd been with anyone. He hadn't even kissed a girl in all that time.

A sound intruded on them and Billy recognized it as Lucky's tuneless whistling. He abruptly ended the kiss, and was left feeling dazed. Looking at Nina, he saw that she felt the same way. Quickly, Billy began picking up firewood even while his body still thrummed with desire.

Nina did the same thing, also gathering small twigs to use as kindling. Lucky came into view just then.

"There ya are," he said. "We were beginnin' to wonder about ya."

Billy said, "Just getting some wood so we have a good fire tonight."

Lucky said, "Good. It's gonna be another cold one. At least ya have someone to help keep ya warm." He winked at Billy.

Billy just shook his head. "I don't encourage her and you know it." *But I just did and, heaven help me, I enjoyed every second of it.*

Lucky wasn't sure what to tell Billy about the situation. He could see that Billy was attracted to Nina. The way Billy looked at her when he thought no one was watching gave him away. It was the way a man watched a woman he thought was beautiful. Wild Wind had also seen it and remarked to him about it. He respected Billy for trying to stick to his guns about keeping his commitment to Callie, though.

"I know ya don't, lad. Ya can't blame her for likin' ya, though. Yer a good-lookin' man and nice besides. It's not like ya don't know the ladies like you."

Billy smiled at that. "I can't refute that statement."

Lucky chuckled as they went back to camp. Once supper had been eaten, they sat around the fire and Wild Wind told them some stories. Billy couldn't concentrate on them, however. His mind worked on the problem of Nina and Callie. He had no solution to it, but he did know that he liked Nina. She was sweet and feisty. He'd found out that her name meant "strong" and he thought that it fit her. She'd had to be strong to survive being captured when she was little and taken away from her family like that. She'd survived being a captive and being married at a young age to a man she hadn't loved and who hadn't treated her well.

Suddenly, Wild Wind stopped talking and stood up. The sound of several guns being cocked stilled all activity around the fire. A man brandishing a revolver walked into the firelight.

"Well, now. Looks like we got some trespassers, boys," he said. "Keep your hands where we can see them."

They all raised their hands. Lucky said, "We're sorry, sir. We didn't know that we were on yer property. We don't want any trouble so we'll just pack up and go on our way."

"You always travel with Indians?" the man asked.

Lucky said, "They're good friends of mine and peaceable, the same as me."

Billy said, "Yeah, we're just passing through. We just needed a place to sleep for the night."

Otto didn't understand what was going on and buried his face against Lucky's chest. He put one arm protectively around his son. "I'd appreciate it if ye'd not scare my boy."

The man lowered his gun. "Well, I don't want to frighten the little fella. He's a cute boy. How old?"

"He's three. Sir, please just let us go. We'll be gone before ya know it," Lucky said.

Nina had been sitting close to Billy like usual and she grabbed his hand, scared that these men were going to shoot them or try to take her away from them.

The man saw the movement and asked Billy, "Is that your woman?"

Billy saw one of the other four men looking appreciatively at Nina. "Yeah. She's mine," he said, staring the other man down.

The man in charge nodded. "You married?"

Billy's stomach clenched. "Well, no."

"Oh, I see. You're engaged then. It's not proper you traveling together like this when you're not married. Well, all of you can come with us. We got a barn you can bed down in. All except the lady. She can bunk in with my girls. Then in the morning, we'll get Preacher Simms to marry you proper-like."

"What?" Billy shouted. "You can't do that!"

"You just said she was your woman, or were you lying about that?"

Nina's heart raced as her fear increased and she hid behind Billy a little more, squeezing his hand harder.

Billy looked at Lucky for help, but Lucky had no idea what to tell him. He didn't normally approve of lying, but in this case it was the prudent thing to do. Turning back to the man, Billy said, "No, I'm not lying. She's mine. It's just that I wanted my folks to be at the wedding. We're heading home to be married. My ma will be really upset if she misses our wedding."

"I can understand, but I'm a God-fearin' man and I just can't abide any sort of improper conduct. Nope. You'll get married in the morning and then we'll let you go on your way," he said.

Lucky said, "So yer kidnappin' us and forcin' him to get married without his own preacher and his loved ones bein' there? That doesn't seem very Christian of ya."

"Well, neither is lettin' them run around unmarried. Seems like I have more morals than you. Now, get your things and let's go," he said with a menacing wave of his gun.

They rose and began packing up.

Lucky said, "The least ya could do is tell us yer name. I'm Lucky, this is Billy, Nina, Otto, and Wild Wind."

"I guess you're right about that. I'm Walter Peterson and these are my boys, Paul, Jacob, Harlan, and Brice."

Although each man raised a hand to their group, they kept the shotguns trained on their captives. Once they were finished packing, Wild Wind and Billy each took some of Lucky's gear so he could carry Otto and comfort him. Lucky walked close to Billy.

"Maybe we can get away before morning," he whispered in Cheyenne.

Billy had thought of that, but he said, "Not if Nina is in the house.

They will probably watch us overnight to make sure we do not escape."

"I know."

"Looks like I will be a married man come morning. How do I explain that to Callie?" Billy asked.

"You could get it annulled once we get home as long as the marriage is not consummated," Lucky whispered.

Billy was prevented from answering when Brice said, "Quiet and talk English."

Billy said, "How can we be quiet and talk at the same time?"

Brice gave Billy a shove and said, "Shut up."

Billy turned around and said, "You touch me again and I'll wrap that gun around your thick skull."

Brice's blue eyes narrowed and he pointed his gun right at Billy's head. "Go ahead and try it, Injun."

Lucky saw Billy's nostrils flare and knew that something bad was going to happen. He grabbed Billy and turned him around. "Don't mind him, lad. He's just nervous about tomorrow, that's all."

Billy saw Nina's fearful expression and forced himself to smile at her. "They are making us get married tomorrow in front of a white man's shaman. You will have to spend the night with this man's daughters. We will be married in the morning and they will let us go."

Nina clutched Billy's hand hard. "No! I want to stay with you. I do not know these men and they are holding us prisoner. What if they keep me?"

"I said talk English," Brice said.

Billy ground his teeth together. "She doesn't speak English, so I have to explain it to her this way. She's scared to death. Put yourself in her position. You're strange to her, holding us at gunpoint, and you're taking her away from us overnight. I'm warning you, if something happens to her, you'll regret it."

"Aye," Lucky said. "I echo that sentiment. If we don't show up at home by a certain date, our friends will come lookin' for us and one of them is a sheriff who doesn't give up. Our friends aren't the sort you want to be on bad terms with."

Walter got a little nervous at his statement. "Don't worry. We'll take good care of her and you'll be let go just as soon as you're married. Keep moving."

They fell silent, Billy trying to give Nina comfort by keeping an arm around her shoulders. Looking skyward, he prayed silently for a reprieve from the night and what the next morning would bring.

# Chapter Ten

Nina sat on a bed in the bedroom of Walter's two daughters, Ella and Bernice. She huddled in the corner, watching everything suspiciously. The two girls smiled at her and chatted, but she had no idea what they were saying. She drew her legs up and just stared at them. They'd made her change into what they'd called a "nightgown". The material was soft, but flimsy against the weather. Of course, the house was toasty so there was really no need to wear anything heavy.

She'd planned to stay awake and sneak out of the house as soon as everyone was asleep. Then she'd remembered that Billy had told her they would be guarded, so even if she could get out, there would be no way to get around the four men with guns. The next best thing was to remain vigilant and wait for dawn to come.

Eventually, the girls gave up trying to talk to her and blew out their lamp. One of them lay down on the bed where she sat and Nina pulled further away from that side of the bed. As she thought about the impending nuptials, there was a part of her that regretted not being able to marry Billy at a proper wedding, but the other part was happy that he would become her husband.

She knew that he didn't love her and that he was angry about being forced to marry her, but she was going to do everything she could to make him happy so that one day, he wouldn't regret marrying her. Her cheeks heated as she remembered the way his kisses had made her lose all sense of control. His lips were soft and warm, his hands gentle. Closing her eyes, she saw his smiling face and the hungry look in his eyes she'd caught now and again when he'd looked at her.

She'd heard his beautiful singing voice the one night when Lucky had made him sing them a few songs. She didn't understand the words, but she'd sensed the emotions behind them and she'd been disappointed when he'd stopped singing. She was grateful to the Great Spirit for letting her overhear Wild Wind so that she could come with them and meet Billy.

Laying her cheek on her knees, she filled her mind with images of him to combat her fear. He often went without a shirt even though the temperatures were so cold and she'd admired his muscular upper body. She also knew how good it felt to be in his arms and she knew that she wouldn't mind sharing his sleeping robes in all ways.

When she fell asleep, Nina didn't know, but it seemed as though the sun came up very fast. Her legs had pins and needles running through them from sleeping in such an uncomfortable position. Hope filled her as she realized that she would soon marry Billy and then they would be free.

While Nina had been able to slumber, Billy hadn't been that fortunate. Guilt and anger kept him wide-awake in the empty stall where he, Lucky, Otto, and Wild Wind slept. They, too, had thought of escape, but they knew they'd never be able to get Nina out of the house undetected even if they'd been able to get past their guards.

Like it or not, by noon, he would be married to a woman he didn't love. Billy thought about Callie and he felt a huge sense of regret because the first thing he had to tell her was that he was married and that her trip to Echo had been made in vain. That was not a meeting he was looking forward to by any means.

The other two men didn't really sleep, either—just dozed fitfully. When the sun came up, Lucky looked at Billy's profile and saw that he was wide-awake. A groom was always nervous on his wedding day, but not angry, as he could tell Billy was. Usually he was able to put things into perspective for Billy, but he had no words of comfort for him today.

However, Wild Wind tried to help him. "Billy."

"Yes?"

They spoke in Cheyenne so they at least had that much privacy.

"I know this is not how you wanted to get married and it is not to the woman you were expecting, but it will not be terrible. She will be a good wife to you. She is a good woman."

Billy said, "Says the man who did not want Nina, either."

Wild Wind smiled. "Yes, but *you* want her. I have seen the way you look at her. Can you honestly say that you are not attracted to her?"

"Attracted to is a far cry from marrying. I am supposed to meet another woman. Why does this keep happening to me?"

"What do you mean?" the brave asked.

"The Great Spirit or whoever has it in for me. I am cursed when it comes to love," Billy said. He fought against the despair he hadn't felt for so long. "Never mind. I do not want to talk about it anymore. I just want to get this over with and go home."

Wild Wind looked at Lucky who just shook his head a little. He knew by Billy's tone of voice that he was done with the conversation. The brave sighed and fell silent again.

Ella and Bernice were eager to help Nina dress for the wedding, but Nina was resistant to wear the dress they wanted her to put on. It was foreign and constricting. They were insistent, however, and Nina figured it was easier to go along with them. It wasn't a wedding dress per se, but it was a pretty lilac shade with silver embossed flowers down the front.

Ella had picked it out and Bernice styled Nina's hair. After brushing out the thick, straight mane, she pulled it up on the sides, fastening it in the back with a pretty comb. Looking at herself in a mirror, Nina thought she looked pretty enough. She hoped that Billy would think so. Maybe he would be more accepting of her since she looked like the women he was used to.

Walter appeared at the doorway of the girls' room and informed them that it was time to go. They conveyed this to Nina by gestures. She gathered up her things and shoved them in her buckskin bag, carrying it protectively because she didn't trust them not to take it. Nina glared at Walter for several moments before following the girls down the hallway.

The wedding was the most somber one Lucky had ever attended. Billy seethed with anger, Wild Wind was hyper-vigilant against more trouble, and Lucky attempted to be cheerful. However, he couldn't muster very many smiles. Billy's expression was downright malevolent as he stared at Walter and the man knew that given the chance, Billy would have hurt him.

Preacher Simms turned out to be a short, thin, balding man with a scraggly beard. He smiled benignly as if it were normal for people to get married at gunpoint. Billy knew that it happened, but normally it was the fathers of the brides holding the shotguns, not some man deciding the fate of two complete strangers.

Billy glowered at the preacher. "I just want you to know that I'm doing this under duress. We weren't hurting anyone and we wanted to get married at home with our families present. I can't believe you're going along with this. You're supposed to be a man of God, but you're allowing them to force us to get married now. That's not what I call a man of God. You're nothing more than an accessory to a crime—a common criminal."

Preacher Simms just smiled. "Son, one day you'll thank me for helping to save your soul so that you will be permitted to pass through the Pearly Gates."

"You're as crazy as they are," Billy said, motioning at the group of gun-bearing men.

"Simmer down, son," Simms said. "Here comes your bride."

Billy looked at the doorway to the Peterson's parlor where they'd been herded. Nina stood there shyly. Walter's wife, Mabel, looked highly pleased to be hosting a wedding and Billy wondered just how many weddings like this had taken place in their home.

If Billy hadn't known Nina's background, he'd have thought she was any other white woman. The pretty dress she wore emphasized her lithe figure and golden skin tone. Her hair was done very nicely and her dazzling green eyes were the only adornment she needed. Despite the circumstances, she made a lovely bride.

Billy sent her an encouraging smile, trying to convey to her that things would be all right now. She smiled back at him and then looked away. Mabel prompted her to walk over to where Billy stood. Instinct made Billy hold out his hands to her and she placed hers in his.

Lucky said, "I'll translate for everyone."

Preacher Simms said, "That's fine. Let's get started."

Lucky told Nina to repeat the words he said to her and she told him she understood.

As the preacher conducted the ceremony, it all felt surreal to Billy. This wasn't the woman he was supposed to be marrying. He'd wanted to be in love when he married. His vows were supposed to have been said as part of a voluntary commitment, filled with meaning and promise, not said fearfully because if he didn't he might wind up dead.

Staring into Nina's eyes, Billy said those words to her, trying to mean them in case they couldn't get the marriage annulled when they got back to Echo. He smiled at her as the words passed over his lips, but it was to convince their kidnappers that they were a happy couple.

While it was a happy occasion for Nina, Billy's tense stance and clipped words told her that he was anything but happy. She recited her vows and promised once again to be a great wife and make Billy happy. When she'd followed Wild Wind, she'd only been seeking freedom, not expecting to find a wonderful man. In her mind, she thanked the Great Spirit repeatedly for giving her Billy.

Preacher Simms said, "I now pronounce you man and wife. You may kiss your bride."

If they'd been standing in front of Pastor Sam at home in Echo, Billy wouldn't have been nervous to kiss his bride, but standing in a parlor surrounded by men with shotgun took the joy out of the moment for him. Still, he had to continue to play his role so they could safely be on their way.

When Lucky translated to her what was about to transpire, she smiled brightly and Billy was caught up in that little spell of hers again. Of its own accord, his mouth curved in response to her smile and he suddenly wanted to kiss her very much. Their lips met and Nina felt the world shift a little as elation filled her. This kiss meant that they were now married and her happiness was almost overwhelming.

Billy kept the kiss respectable, but it had a powerful effect on him. He'd just kissed his wife for the very first time and a tiny thread of gladness wound its way through him. As the kiss ended, there was applause from the women present and a few of the men, including Lucky and Wild Wind, who looked a little uncomfortable with the unfamiliar custom.

Although the men still held guns on them, Walter said, "Congratulations, you two. We'll get your things and off you go."

They were marched outside and given back their horses and belongings. They mounted up and the Petersons waved farewell to the group as though they were old friends instead of former captives. They rode away silently, ignoring the Petersons.

Lucky looked over at the young couple. Nina rode behind Billy, a smile on her face as she held on to him. Billy, however, stared ahead, his jaw thrust forward and his eyes stormy with anger. The Irishman sighed and didn't speak to Billy. Instead, he entertained Otto, trying to dispel any lingering fear over seeing all the men with guns. He also prayed that no more misfortune would befall them before reaching Echo.

They decided to stay at a hotel for the night instead of camping out again. Lucky didn't know what to do about the sleeping arrangements. By all rights, Billy and Nina were now free to sleep in the same bed, but he didn't know what Billy preferred. He suspected that Nina would have no qualms about it.

As they were dismounting outside the hotel that had seen better days, Lucky pulled Billy aside out of earshot of the others.

"Uh, I don't know how to ask this except to just ask. Will ya be stayin' with Nina or with us men tonight?"

Billy's eyes got bigger. He'd been so caught up in anger and disappointment that he hadn't given that any thought. It was their wedding night, so there was no moral issue to the rest of society, but Billy didn't know what to think.

Lucky saw his indecision and said, "Billy, she's gonna be expectin' ya to stay with her. In her eyes, you're truly married now."

Fury burned throughout Billy's body. "If I stay with her she's going to expect … marital relations. That can't happen for there to be any chance of getting an annulment."

"I know, but maybe this was meant to be, ya know? She's a comely lass and good wife material. I saw the way ya looked at her when ya kissed her today. There's attraction there. Would it really be so bad being married to her?"

Billy's jaw clenched for a moment. "If you had someone waiting for you back in Echo and this had happened to you, what would you do? This isn't fair to Callie. She's expecting me to court her and very possibly marry me."

"I understand, but the Good Lord works in mysterious ways, as they say. Maybe this is one of them. Look, ye've sometimes been sharing sleepin' robes. I know that's been without your knowledge most of the time because she waits until you're asleep to climb in, but nothing's happened between youse yet. Ya could sort of do the same thing and see how ya feel about it," Lucky said.

Billy let out a sound of frustration. "This is a hell of a wedding day and wedding night. The Lord definitely has a sense of humor, but I don't find this one bit funny. I guess I'll try your suggestion. Go ahead and rent the rooms. I need to walk a little bit and clear my head."

Lucky said, "Try not to be angry with Nina. It's not her fault this happened. You're a great catch and she knows it. After what she's been through, ya can't blame her for wantin' someone like you."

"I know," Billy said. "I'll be back."

Lucky nodded as Billy walked away.

# Chapter Eleven

When Billy had returned, they'd all gotten something to eat in the hotel restaurant. Although it wasn't the best place, the food was decent. Wild Wind and Nina weren't used to eating with utensils, but they copied what Billy and Lucky did so they didn't look out of place. Billy had given Wild Wind a set of his clothes to wear so he looked a little tamer.

Wild Wind didn't like the strange clothing, but he wore it since he didn't want any more trouble for them. Thanks to Lucky, he knew English and could speak it quite well, so at least he'd be able to communicate in the white man's world. He knew he was going to have to do that once they reached Echo, but he was willing to do it in order to be free.

Otto was a source of amusement for them as he sat on Lucky's lap and tried to learn how to use a fork and spoon. He tried bites from everyone's plates. He seemed to like it all and the adults were indulgent in sharing their food with him. Billy could see a lot of Lucky in him and he enjoyed watching the two interact. He was amazed again at Lucky's fortitude in dealing with the terrible blow he'd suffered in losing Avasa for good. Even though Lucky's heart was broken, he was rising to the challenge of suddenly being a single father.

As they talked and laughed, Billy thought he should follow Lucky's example and make the best of things. Looking at Nina, he knew that he could do a lot worse for a wife, but how would she adjust to life in a completely different culture? She was strong, but would making the transition be too much for her? He guessed they'd find out.

Having been married before, Nina knew what to expect on their wedding night. She made Billy wait outside their room so she could get ready. Without the garments she would have normally worn that night, she made do with the chemise under her dress, liking the way it looked on her. She hummed a little as she made herself presentable for her new husband.

Billy stood uncomfortably out in the hallway. Wild Wind had grinned at him and told him to have a good time. Lucky, while finding it funny, had shoved him inside their room. When he turned to Billy, however, he didn't know what to say. The normally vocal Irishman had found that happening a lot lately and it was disconcerting.

"Billy?"

"Yeah?"

Lucky became as uncomfortable as Billy. Finally he said, "I'll see ya in the morning," and went into his room.

Billy smiled a little at how sensitive Lucky was about these things. The door to their room opened and Nina smiled at him. He followed her inside and shut the door. His pulse rate accelerated upon seeing what she wore. The thin garment did little to hide her body in the lamplight.

Her beautiful eyes locked on his and he couldn't move as she came to him. She took his hand and raised it to her lips, kissing his palm. Billy was touched by the gesture.

"Nina, I do not know …" He didn't know how to tell her about annulments because there was no such thing in her culture.

She smiled at him. "Do not worry. I will show you."

His brow furrowed. "What?"

"Do not be shy," she said. "You are so handsome. Does the way I look please my husband?"

Billy grinned. She thought he was a virgin. "I have been with a woman before." His eyes moved over her. Everything about her was pleasing, from the shape of her body to her inviting lips, glossy hair, and vibrant green eyes. What man wouldn't want to be with her? "Yes, you please me."

She gave him the sweetest, most beautiful smile and he was helpless to resist her. Billy watched her small, pretty hands undo the buttons of his shirt. Parting the shirt, Nina pressed her lips to Billy's muscular chest and pushed it off his shoulders. Flinging his shirt aside, Billy groaned a little and cupped her face before bringing his lips down on hers firmly.

His fiery kiss thrilled Nina and she ran her hands up his sides, enjoying the smoothness of his skin and the hard muscles under her palms. He responded to her touch, his hands roaming over her possessively. She'd never felt such desire before and she welcomed the intense feelings.

Billy couldn't get her undressed fast enough. She was sensual and exciting and he'd wanted her since the morning he'd woken up to find her cuddling against him. The chemise fought them and Nina giggled as he tugged her this way and that to get rid of it. Finally it was off and Billy threw it away from them.

His breath left him as he stared at the most beautiful sight he'd ever had the privilege to see. She fueled his passion even more and he rid himself of the rest of his clothes before wrapping his arms around her. Picking her up, he kissed her and laid her on the bed.

She gave him a wicked little smile and asked, "Does this mean that my husband is pleased with me?"

His return smile was roguish. "Yes. Let me show you how much."

She laughed and raised her arms to him. Billy accepted her invitation and embraced her again. This wasn't how he'd imagined his wedding night, but, suddenly, all regret fled his mind. As they held each other that night, giving and taking pleasure, he briefly wondered if Lucky had been right and that Nina really was the woman he was meant to be with after all.

⌒〜〜〜⌒

Evan put his hands on his hips and critically surveyed the ground around the area where the stranger had been murdered. There was nothing remarkable about it. It was in a wooded area and covered by leaves, twigs, and other debris. While there were two deer trails leading away from it, they hadn't found any human prints. Of course, none of them were the tracking experts that Lucky and Billy were.

"We could really use Irish and the Indian," he remarked to Win and Thad.

Win said, "I agree. Who knows how long it'll be until they get back, though. We can't wait around for them."

Thad wasn't paying them much attention. Instead, he was looking at the formation of the mountainside near where they were searching. Moss and vines covered some of it and trees had grown near it. Pushing his way through the trees, Thad began exploring along the rock wall, looking closely for anything that looked out of place.

"What do you got, Thad?" Evan asked.

"Nothin' yet. It just seems to me that there's gotta be a door around here somewhere, if this is the right area. There's no kind of a trap door out where you are. We stomped around enough that we'd have found it by now. Besides, he's able to disappear so quickly that a trap door doesn't make sense."

Win said, "You're right. It's got to be big enough that he can just slip through and lock it behind him." He went to the wall a distance away from Thad and began working towards him. As he moved slowly along, Thad saw a large branch leaning up against the wall, much like the way someone leans a broom against a porch wall.

His right ear buzzed a little the way it always did when he was onto something. He didn't pick up the branch, but he looked it over. The end

89

of it was smooth, like the handle on a cane that was used often—something that wouldn't happen unless it was handled often. Leaving the branch where it was, he continued examining the wall. The buzzing in his ear grew louder.

Passing his fingers over a spot near the branch, he found what felt like a seam. "Win. Come here." Win joined him and Thad asked, "What does that feel like to you?"

Win examined it closely and a smile spread across his handsome features. "I think you just found our door. This seam is roughly the shape of one and big enough for someone to get through quickly."

Evan had come to see what they'd found and had heard Win. "Way to go, guys. I'm gonna kiss my wife as soon as I get home and thank her again for all of her research."

Thad chuckled. "She's a good detective all right."

Win said, "We need something to pry it open with."

Evan shook his head. "No, we're not going in there without knowing where it leads. If there's a whole tunnel system, we could get lost and end up trapped. Since most of the activity seems to happen at night, we'll get here by dusk and lie in wait for them."

"Good thinkin'," Thad said. "I can't wait to nail this son of a bitch."

Win smiled. "Me, neither, but if this is the same guy who hurt Billy, we're gonna have to be careful. He's skilled in close combat, so stay out of his range with your guns. I could disarm you in a heartbeat if I wanted to and I'm betting so could he. Make no mistake; this man is very dangerous."

Evan said, "Yeah. He's not afraid to hurt people, which makes him twice as dangerous."

"Right," Thad said. "Well, we have our plan. I can't wait for tonight."

Evan said, "Me, neither."

"More of your crazy theories are working out. That's what I love about you. You have a knack for turning the impossible into the possible," Thad said.

"Thanks. I learned that from you and Uncle Reb," Evan said as they walked along the trail leading to the sheep farm where they'd left their horses.

"You learned a lot from us, but you've got a creative streak all your own, son," Thad said.

Evan smiled modestly, but didn't comment. Thad's praise made him feel good, but he just considered it all a part of doing his job.

# Chapter Twelve

Shadow was a little later than normal in going out that night because he hadn't been able to leave Bree without making love to her first. He craved her the way an addict craved opium and he could rarely curb his desire for her. He smiled as he thought about his lady love and how incredible it was that they'd been brought together—two broken people who somehow formed a whole.

Slipping from the tunnel, he shut the door, making sure it latched behind him. He took about five steps from the door and stopped. Years spent in almost pitch-black darkness had honed his ability to see in low lighting. While not as powerful as a cat's or other nocturnal animals, his night vision was stonger than most humans'. This allowed him to see his surroundings quite clearly after dark while other people fumbled around.

However, it wasn't anything he saw that made him stop, it was the scent of cologne. He knew it wasn't his because he never wore any. It would tip someone off that he was around. The soap he used also had very little scent for the same reason. A man had been through this area and very recently, too.

Remaining motionless, Shadow carefully surveyed the area while continuing to sniff the air. The scent of cigarette smoke reached his nostrils and he knew that it had to be very recent for the odor to linger so strongly in the air. He continued to search for any movement or noise, but there was none. Still he waited, but there was nothing.

One step at a time, he moved forward towards one of the trails he used. The smell of smoke grew stronger and seemed to be coming from his right. Looking there, Shadow saw something move. He moved swiftly and silently. As soon as he made out the shape of a person, he attacked, his intent to kill the intruder.

The man let out a startled grunt and then swore, which Shadow found amusing. It was also amusing because he recognized the voice as Thad's.

Pinning him down, Shadow said, "Mr. McIntyre, you should have stayed off my land. Now you'll find out what happens to trespassers."

Thad was thoroughly confused. "Earnest?"

"Who else?" Shadow was having fun. It was rare that he had a chance to impersonate Marvin. "Was there someone else you were expecting?"

Thad wondered when Win and Evan were going to move in. "Well, yeah. Where the hell did you learn to fight like that? I'd never take you for a fighter."

"I have many talents that people don't know about. One of which is punishing trespassers," Shadow said. "Even the good sheriff would have to agree that people who trespass should face consequences. What do you think *your* consequence will be?"

Something wasn't adding up to Thad. The voice sounded similar to Marvin's but it wasn't an exact match. Also, the man straddling his chest felt heavier than Marvin looked. Given that Marvin had a botched hernia repair that was going to have to be redone at some point, he didn't think the man was capable of taking someone down the way that this man had.

Shadow heard a gun cock behind him.

"The only one who's gonna suffer any consequences here is you, Earnest. Let him up now," Evan said.

Shadow growled low in his chest and the animalistic sound sent fear coursing through Thad. He'd never heard a human make such a noise before.

"That ain't Earnest, Evan," he said.

"Get off him!" Evan fired a shot into the ground near the two men. "The next one goes in your brain. Get up."

"Go ahead and shoot me," Shadow said. He'd rather be dead than locked up again.

Evan said, "That might be a good for you, but think of Bree. She'd miss you and I'd have to ask her a lot of questions. Maybe even send her off to jail."

Shadow didn't want to go to jail, but he would do anything to protect Bree. He rose swiftly, pulling Thad with him into a standing position. Evan knew what kind of strength that took because Thad was no lightweight.

"You leave Bree out of this. She's done nothing wrong," Shadow said, shoving Thad away from him.

Thad windmilled backwards into a tree, his breath knocked out of him from the hard impact.

Another voice said, "Well, well. Aren't you chivalrous?"

Shadow said, "Hello, Dr. Wu. How's your lovely wife?"

Win grew angry, but remained calm. "Just fine. Now how about you step out onto that trail?"

Evan asked, "You all right, Thad?"

"Yeah. Great. Never better. I think he just fixed what was wrong with my back," Thad quipped.

Evan put another round in the ground close to Shadow's feet. "I got plenty of ammo so I can do this all the way back to the office, Earnest, or whoever you are."

Shadow calculated his options as he began walking slowly towards the trail. He could run, but they'd only go to the house and hound

Marvin ceaselessly or put him in jail because they thought it was him. Shadow would try to keep any inconvenience to Marvin and Bree to a minimum. No, there was no way out of this and Shadow quickly came to accept that the time had come for the world to know about him.

He kept his hands up as he stepped onto the trail. While Evan and Win kept their guns on Shadow, Thad lit the lantern they'd brought with them and held it close to Shadow. Shadow recoiled from the sudden light, closing his eyes and putting up a hand to block it.

"Sweet mother of God," Thad said, his voice full of wonder. "There's two of them. Two Earnests."

Evan and Win came around so they could see what he meant. Aside from the dark hair color and a more powerful build, he could have been Marvin. Evan recalled Josie telling him that Marvin had had a twin who died in childbirth. That story had apparently been fabricated for whatever reason; here stood living proof that Marvin's twin had lived and thrived.

"Good gravy, look at the size of him," Thad said. "I said Bree was sleeping with Earnest. I just had the wrong one."

This appealed to Shadow's odd sense of humor. He often laughed at things that others didn't find funny.

He laughed and said, "Surprise!" the way people did when throwing a surprise birthday party.

To his delight, Thad actually laughed with him. Evan and Win gave the bounty hunter disapproving looks. Thad shrugged and said, "What? That was funny."

Shadow laughed even harder and started walking along the trail.

"Whoa," Evan said. "Where do you think you're going?"

"You said you wanted to go to the office, didn't you? We won't get there any sooner by standing around here all night. I'm sure you'll want to get home to your family at some point, Sheriff," Shadow said and kept on walking.

Afraid that Shadow would get too far ahead of them and run off, Win decided to prevent that from happening. He handed Thad his gun and ran at Shadow, delivering a kick to his left knee. Shadow felt his kneecap pop out of place, but he never let out a sound of pain as he went down. As he lay on the ground, Shadow felt his kneecap go back into alignment, but he knew that damage had been done to the joint and that it would take a while to heal. There were a lot of other joints Win could have picked, but Shadow knew that knees were integral to keeping one's balance and hitting accurately. Win had made it harder for him to attack anyone and impossible for him to escape.

"Well done, Dr. Wu, but that was counterproductive to getting to our destination," Shadow said.

He didn't ask for assistance in getting up, figuring that none would be granted. His captors knew that he was too dangerous to get close to. Getting up, he waited a few moments to assess whether he was going to be able to bear weight on the injured leg. Gingerly he put his toe to the trail and hitched a little. It wasn't great, but he could hobble along.

"Move," Evan said.

"I was trying to when Dr. Wu—"

A bullet hit the ground right beside him and Shadow shielded his eyes from the dirt that flew up.

"Shut your mouth," Evan said. "Not another word."

"As ye like it," Shadow said with a chuckle. "Any word from Irish and the Indian? They've been gone a while now. I do hope that they're all right."

Something hit his back with tremendous force and Shadow went down again. His injured knee hit the ground and he grunted at the pain that radiated up into his thigh. He dragged himself onto his feet again and kept going down the trail. Once they made it out to the sheep farm, they made Shadow stop and Evan put cuffs on him while Win and Thad pointed their guns at his head.

Shadow submitted, not for his sake, but for Bree and Marvin's. He would sacrifice himself to make things easier for them. The other three men affixed ropes to him and made him walk to town, because Evan suspected that Shadow would try to use a horse to make an escape. Echo was quiet at that time of night, for which Evan was glad; he didn't want anyone to know about his prisoner before he'd gotten some answers from Marvin's twin. And he had a lot of questions.

Shadow didn't panic until they reached the office. Evan lit a couple of lanterns and carried one into the cell area. Shadow could see the cells and he began to tremble. He was already half insane, but he knew he'd go completely around the bend if he was put in a cage again.

Evan opened the first door and Thad and Win began pushing Shadow towards the other room. Shadow shook his head and refused to budge. "No."

Evan saw terror in Shadow's expression. "Yes," he said. "Now move it."

"No. I can't go in there. You don't understand. I can't be locked up again. You can hurt me more, you can kill me, but I won't go into that cage."

Shadow's trembling increased until his long bangs moved with the motion.

"You've been in jail before?" Evan asked.

"No. Not jail. Jail would have been kinder. Of course, death would have been kinder, but he was not a kind man," Shadow said.

Thad gave Shadow a rough shove. "Just get in there and stop talking in riddles."

"No!" Shadow shouted. "I will not!"

Win, looked at Evan, who rolled his eyes and motioned towards Shadow. Raising his shotgun, Win rammed the butt of it against the back of Shadow's head, knocking him out. Shadow dropped to the floor and remained inert. Thad rolled him over and the three of them got a better look at him.

Win said, "If his hair was dyed blond, I'd never know the difference between them."

"Me, either," Evan said. "Let's get him in there before he wakes up. I think he was on the verge of some sort of episode."

Win and Evan dragged Shadow into the cell and hoisted him up onto the cot inside it. Evan decided to leave the cuffs on him since they didn't know what he'd be like when he woke up. Locking the cell door, Evan and Win rejoined Thad in the other room. Thad had sat down and lit a cigarette.

Evan sat down at his desk and Win took the other chair and the three men looked at each other.

Exhaling a puff of smoke, Thad said, "Just when I thought it couldn't get any more bizarre, it does."

Evan nodded. "Brock told Josie that Marvin had a twin that died either in childbirth or soon after, but that's obviously not the case."

Win said, "I'm around Marvin's age and I've lived here all my life. I've never heard of Marvin having a brother. I never saw any other kid who looked like Marvin. I'd remember."

"Like I said, where's he been all this time? Did they hide him away for some reason? If so, what reason could there possibly be?"

Evan said, "He's intelligent, strong, and has a sense of humor of sorts. He sounds a lot like Marvin when he talks."

"Yeah, but that growl was what tipped me off that it wasn't Marvin. I've never heard anyone make that kind of noise before. It scared the bejesus out of me."

Win laughed. "That *was* a little scary. He knows who all of us are and he knew our voices."

Thad nodded. "Yep. And how did he see me? You know how dark it was. There wasn't even a moon tonight. Yet he made me out. I'm just lucky that you fellas were with me or else I wouldn't be sitting here right now. That boy's deadly. You were right about that, Win. He had me pinned in seconds."

Win nodded. "Why was he so afraid of the cell? He said he'd been locked up before, but not in jail. And who was he talking about when he said 'he was not a kind man'? 'Was' implies the past, not the present, so he couldn't have been talking about Marvin."

Evan said, "I can't wait to see the look on Marvin's face when I tell him that we have his brother. I'm gonna savor every second of it."

"I'd love to go with you, but I'll stay here and guard Earnest number two in there," Thad said. "Besides, I'm sure Marvin will want to come see him."

"I'm not gonna give him a choice. He's got a lot to answer for," Evan said. "Well, you both go get some sleep. Thad, you can spell me in the morning and I'll go get Earnest. Marvin, I mean. This is gonna be confusing for a while. We don't even know what this one's name is."

Thad laughed. "I think we were all too shocked to ask."

Win smiled. "You're right. I'd better get home to Erin. She'll be wondering what happened. Let me know if you need more help, Evan."

"I will. Thanks for everything," Evan said.

Win nodded and bid them goodnight and Thad wasn't far behind him. Evan took out a tablet and pencil and propped his feet up on the desk. He began writing down every question that came to mind about his prisoner, Marvin, and Bree. It was a productive way to pass the time until dawn came.

# Chapter Thirteen

Shadow woke to bright sunlight in his face. He threw his arm over his eyes and moaned from the pain in his head. It took him a few moments to remember where he was, but when he did, he bolted up on the cot. Dizziness engulfed him and he almost passed out again. His knee also protested the movement and prevented him from rising as quickly as he wanted.

Once he was on his feet, he hopped over to the opposite side of the cell, out of the direct rays of the sun. He opened his eyes in slow increments and, while it was still too bright for him, he could tolerate it for short amounts of time. He saw Thad sitting at a table out in the other room, playing solitaire.

He looked at the bars of his cell and panic set in again. He tried to fight it, but soon it held him in a powerful grip.

"Thad," he said.

"Good morning, sunshine," Thad said. "Have a nice rest?"

Shadow chuckled. "I like you. I always have."

"So you know me, huh?"

"Yes. I know almost everyone. Please let me out of here. I won't go anywhere, I swear. I can't leave the building."

Thad got up and came into the cell room. "You're damn right you won't leave. You're not getting out of that cell, either."

He saw the way Shadow shook and held his stomach. It reminded him of men he'd seen going through withdraw. "Are you on something? Opium?"

"No. I don't partake of drugs nor do I smoke. I drink a little whiskey now and again, but that's it."

"What's wrong with you then? Do you always shake like that?" Thad asked.

"It's the cage. The cell. Please let me out. You can handcuff me to a chair or something. I can't leave the building," Shadow said.

"Ok, I'll bite. Why can't you leave the building?"

"The light. I can't see during the day and bright light is excruciating to my eyes. So, even if I were to roam free, I'd still be trapped," Shadow said. "Please. He kept me in a cage all those years and I just can't be in one again. Please?"

Thad watched sweat trickle down Shadow's cheeks and drip from his chin. The look in his eyes was akin to the kind that Thad had seen in the eyes of trapped animals.

"Get over there on that cot," Thad said.

"No. It's too bright over there," Shadow said. "Please let me out. I'll be good, I swear." In his mind, Shadow went back in time. "I won't cause any trouble. I do whatever you tell me to, Father. Just let me out."

Thad's eyebrow arched. "Father? What the hell are you talking about?"

Shadow shook even harder and sweat soaked his shirt. "Please let me out. I didn't do anything. I ate all my food and did everything you told me to."

Thad was stunned when Shadow sank slowly to the floor and curled up into a ball. He had no idea what to do, but he wouldn't have been human if he didn't feel badly for Shadow. There wasn't an actor on the planet who could pull off such an act. He decided to go get Erin. Maybe she could shed some light on what was wrong with Shadow.

By the time six-thirty a.m. came, Marvin and Bree knew that something terrible had befallen Shadow. He was always home by daybreak, but he hadn't shown up.

"You stay here in case he comes back and needs help and I'll go look for him. There are some places he goes and I'll start there," Marvin told Bree.

"Ok," she said. "Be careful."

"I will." He kissed her temple and opened the front door to see Evan riding up the lane. He let out an angry sound. "I don't have time for him today!"

Marvin stepped out onto the veranda and quickly went down the steps.

"Not now, Evan. I'm busy," Marvin said, walking towards the barn.

Evan smiled. "Looking for your brother?"

Marvin paled and stopped in his tracks. There was no use denying that Shadow was his brother. "Where do you have him?"

"At the office. Where else?" Evan asked.

Alarm made Marvin's heart lurch. "In a cell?"

Evan nodded. "Yeah."

Terror and anger contorted Marvin's face into an expression that scared Evan a little. Marvin ran for the barn, leaving Evan to stare after him. Marvin didn't waste time saddling a horse. He put a bridle on one, led it from the barn, and threw the reins to a shocked Evan. Marvin hurried to the house and told Bree where Shadow was.

"I need blankets," he said, running upstairs. Coming back down, he used a belt to bind them together so he could carry them.

Bree said, "I'll have Travis saddle a horse for me and I'll be right along."

Marvin nodded and flew back out the door. Running to his horse, he pulled himself onto its back. Once mounted, he pulled the reins from Evan's hands and tore down the lane with Evan in hot pursuit.

The sheriff wasn't going to let Marvin go. Getting ahead of Marvin's horse, he brought them to a stop.

"Mind telling me what's got you all in a snit here besides the fact that we caught your brother?"

"We have to get him out of that cell now or something very bad will happen. He can't stand being in a cage. He lived in one until he was sixteen and I'll not have him in one again. We need to get to him *now*!" Marvin maneuvered his horse out around Evan and put his heels to its sides.

Evan spurred his horse to catch up to Marvin. His mind digested what Marvin had just told him. Above the sound of the horses' hooves, Evan yelled, "He lived in a cage?"

Marvin nodded. "Yes. Our father was pure evil. You think I am? I've never kept anyone in a cage or degraded them the way he did."

"He kept his own son in a cage? Why?"

Marvin said, "I'll tell you more when we get to your office."

Evan fell silent as they galloped towards town.

When they reached the office, Marvin slid off his horse and let the reins drop. He raced inside the office, his eyes wild. He saw Shadow lying on the floor in a cell.

"Let me in that cell!" he demanded of Thad.

Thad's eyes were wide as he looked at Evan who'd just come through the door. Evan took one look at the man who lay shaking on the floor and hurried to it. He unlocked the door and Marvin shoved him aside to get to his brother.

Kneeling on the floor, he took Shadow's face in his hands and said, "Shadow, it's Marvin. I'm here. You're safe. It's all right. I promise. You're safe. He's not here. He's dead. Remember? He's gone. It's ok."

Marvin continued talking to Shadow until he began coming out of the fugue state in which he'd been trapped. Looking into Marvin's eyes, he asked, "Marvy? Are you really here? Am I dreaming?"

Marvin smiled at him. "No. You're not dreaming. I'm here and you're safe. I promise."

Shadow grabbed Marvin, holding on to him as though he were drowning. "Don't leave me. Don't let them keep me in here. I can't. I'll die. You know that. He was here and he was so angry. He—"

"Shh. It's all right now. He's not here. He'll never hurt you again. It wasn't real. Just a flashback. But it wasn't real. I promise that you're safe. Come and get off the floor now. Sit on the cot. I'll stay with you. Bree will be here soon," Marvin told him.

"Bree's coming? I don't want her to see me like this," Shadow said.

Marvin said, "She's not going to care. We're just glad you're safe. When you didn't come home this morning, we knew that something had happened to you. I'm just glad Sheriff Taft had you instead of someone else."

Marvin rose and saw that Shadow's left pant leg had been cut up to his thigh. Pulling his pant leg up, he saw that his knee was twice its normal size and it was dark purple in color.

"What happened to him?" Marvin asked as he helped Shadow get up.

Shadow leaned on Marvin and hopped over to the bunk. The sun had moved by this time and it wasn't as bright there as it had been. Marvin eased him down onto the cot.

"Stay right there," Marvin said.

Evan said, "He almost ran away from us last night. Win made sure that didn't happen."

Marvin shot him a look full of fury. "I'm sure Dr. Wu enjoyed that."

Erin had been out in the main room reading a sedative for Shadow. "I'm glad you were able to get him up. I haven't been able to assess his knee properly yet."

"Oh, good. Dr. Avery. It's good to see you as always, despite the circumstances," Marvin said.

He went out to the main room and dragged a chair into the cell room. Unrolling the blankets he'd brought with him, he stood on the chair and began tying a blanket to the bars as best he could.

"Do you always redecorate sheriff offices or is it just this one?" Thad asked.

Shadow laughed at his remark and Thad couldn't help but smile at him. Marvin was glad to hear Shadow laugh. It was a good sign. He finished with that window and repeated the process with the other window, darkening the room considerably.

"Open your eyes, Shadow," Marvin said.

Shadow did and sighed in relief. "Thank you."

Evan felt as though he was watching a strange play. "Ok, why did you do that?"

Shadow and Marvin exchanged a look, hearing each other in their minds. "It's time," Marvin said.

Shadow nodded. "Yes. Time for the monster to be revealed." Now that he could look around with a fair amount of comfort, Shadow looked at Evan. "Our father, and I use that term loosely, was a member of a fanatical group of the Klu Klux Clan and believed in racial purity. Blond hair and blue eyes, which both he and my mother possessed.

"When I was born and he saw that I had dark hair, he deemed me unworthy and was going to kill me. Mother wouldn't let him and they argued about it. They compromised by deciding to keep me locked away. I would have been an embarrassment to his fellow clansmen and he couldn't have that.

"So for the first sixteen years of my life, I was locked in a cage, never allowed out of it. It's in the cellar at the ranch. I lived in almost total darkness except for the one candle I was allowed each week and the lantern light when Father came to feed me and berate me, beat me, or perform whatever other forms of torture struck his fancy. I never saw my mother. He wouldn't let her come to see me and after a while, she stopped asking about me. I begged to see her, thinking that maybe she would help me, but it only made him angry with me."

"You never saw your mother?" Evan asked.

"Not once. Marvin showed me a picture of her. We look like her a great deal," Shadow said.

Evan looked at Marvin. "Where were *you* all this time?"

"Since I was away at school so much, I didn't know about Shadow until we were sixteen. There were a few summers when I went home with a friend because they were doing some traveling and I was going to go along. When I was home that particular summer, I became curious about why Father was down in the basement so much. He'd always been warning me not to go down there, but I finally had to know why. I followed him one day, but I hid from him.

"Once he went back upstairs, I went to the very back of the basement and found Shadow. I'd brought a candle with me. Imagine my shock and horror at seeing my own face staring back at me through bars. Neither of us could speak for a few moments. I heard Father coming and told Shadow that I'd be back for him."

Erin hesitantly entered the cell, Evan right by her side.

"I think you should take this sedative. I'd like to give you some cocaine injections in your knee to help with the pain. Will you let me look at your leg?" she asked.

Shadow smiled. "If you're asking if I'll hurt you, the answer is no. You have nothing to fear from me."

Evan began to close the cell door behind them and Shadow growled. Evan wanted to keep him calm, so he opened it again. Thad was right outside the cell, his gun drawn, so he felt comfortable about doing so.

Erin got to work. As gently as possible, she examined Shadow's knee. "My husband certainly knows what he's doing when it comes to injuring people," she said.

Shadow blocked the pain her probing fingers caused. "I guess that's why you make such a good pair. He hurts people and you patch them up."

The brothers laughed briefly and the corners of Erin's mouth twitched a little. To Evan and Thad, it was eerie how much they sounded alike.

"I have a delicate question, Shadow," Erin said. "Do you want me to ask now or in private?"

Shadow smiled. "As you can see, there's nothing very delicate about me. Go ahead."

"Have you ever had syphilis or some other venereal disease?"

The Earnests burst into laughter and Thad was hard pressed not to join them. He had no idea why he seemed to share Shadow's sense of humor, but he did.

Sobering, Shadow said, "No, I've never had anything like that. Why?"

Erin's face was a little pink as she said, "I was wondering if it could be contributing to your sensitivity to light, that's all."

"Oh, I see. It's just because I lived in the dark for so long. Marvin tried to get me used to the daylight, but my eyes just can't take bright light. Cloudy days aren't so bad or right at dawn or dusk," Shadow said.

"I have something that might help. Tinted glasses. They're normally made for syphilis patients, but people with other eye ailments use them, too," Erin said.

"Tinted glasses? They make such things?" Shadow asked.

Erin didn't get to answer because Bree hurried into the office and caught sight of him.

"Shadow!"

Marvin moved out of the cell so Bree could sit by his brother.

"Are you all right?" she asked, embracing him.

Shadow put his arms around her and said, "Yes, I'm fine."

Bree saw his leg. "What happened? What did they do to you?"

"It was my own fault. It'll heal," he assured her.

Evan thought it odd that Shadow wouldn't try to shift blame to him and his men.

Erin said, "I'm going to give you two injections. Hold still."

Shadow nodded. Bree couldn't tolerate needles and pressed her face to Shadow's chest. "It's all right, little one. It'll be over quickly."

She nodded, but didn't comment. When Erin was done, she put her instruments away and stood up. "I'd like you to take this cannabis, Shadow. Is that a nickname?"

"No. I'm the youngest, born in Marvin's shadow, he used to tell me. He'd told Marvin that I died soon after being born," Shadow said. "It's my real name."

"Ok, well, I want you to take this to help you stay calm when they close the cell door," Erin said, holding out the pills.

Marvin spoke up. "He can take a whole bottle of pills, but they won't help if that door gets closed. So, unless you want him to have a complete psychotic break, don't close it."

Evan watched the fearful way Shadow looked at the cell door. He put his hand on it and saw Shadow's face tense. When he took his hand from it, Shadow relaxed again. Shadow took the pills Erin handed him and dry swallowed them, not bothering to ask for water.

"Here's what I'm willing to do for you, Shadow," Evan said. "In exchange for information, I'll leave the cell door open and cuff you to the bars."

"Done," Shadow said. "What would you like to know?"

"I think we'll chat in private," Evan said. "Come out of here, everyone. Earnest, er, Marvin, I'd like you to take Bree home now."

Bree said, "No! I don't want to leave him."

Evan said, "You can come back this evening to visit for a little while. This is official business and I'm not gonna put up with any interference. Please go with Marvin, Bree." His voice let them know that he wasn't to be trifled with.

Shadow caressed Bree's cheek. "Go with Marvy. I'll be fine. Go on. I love you."

She nodded as tears of fear welled in her eyes. She didn't want him to see her cry, so she smiled as best she could, kissed him, and left the office.

Evan stepped over to Shadow and said, "Are you gonna sit up or lie down?"

Shadow was starting to feel fuzzy. "Lie down." When he was in position, Evan cuffed him to an iron bar. "All right, Marvin. You go, too."

"I'll see you this evening, Shadow," Marvin said.

Shadow raised a hand to Marvin and quickly fell asleep.

Marvin gave Evan a cold look. "Might I have a word outside with you, Sheriff?"

Evan nodded and followed him outside. "What is it?"

"I'll warn you now, if there're any other injuries to Shadow when I come back, there'll be hell to pay," Marvin said. "And you and I both know that I have the connections to make your life very uncomfortable."

Evan moved closer. "The only Earnest I'm interested in hurting right now is you. Get going."

Marvin grinned. "I knew your sudden friendliness was false."

"Oh, I meant the apology in a way, but I found out exactly what I wanted to know," Evan said. "You should know by now, Marvin, I don't stop until I get what I'm after any more than you do, no matter how long it takes me. Now, if you don't mind, I'm going to go get your brother some food for later. Oh, and I have a lot of questions for you, too, but they can wait. Have a good day, Earnest."

As Evan walked away, Marvin admired the sheriff for his cunning. Then he collected his horse and he and Bree went on their way.

# Chapter Fourteen

The day after she and Billy were married, Nina set out to show him that she was a good wife. When they got up, she took out a comb and made him sit on the bed so she could comb his hair.

Billy asked, "Why are you doing that? I can do it."

"Wives groom their husbands to show them how much they respect them. Husbands will do the same for wives that they also hold in high regard," Nina told him.

"I see. Did your first husband do this for you?" he asked.

Nina said, "No. The only thing he held in high regard was whiskey. I was only there to serve him. Wives are supposed to, but husbands usually show their appreciation in some way."

Billy didn't like that. "I will never make you feel that way. I do not drink much and I was raised to show women respect, whether or not they do anything for me."

Nina smiled. "You are a good man, Billy. He was not. I do not want to talk about him. That was my old life, but you are my future, and I am very lucky."

Reaching behind him, Billy grasped her wrist and brought her hand around so that he could kiss her palm. "So am I."

She said, "I know that I was not your first choice for a wife and had those men not made us get married, you would have married that other woman. I will be a good wife to you, though. You will see."

Billy nodded and released her hand. He didn't know what to say because she was very possibly right. His sense of propriety wouldn't have let him stop resisting Nina, even though they'd kissed. Nina's attentions made him feel languid and he could have gone back to sleep. She was gentle as she worked out the rats in his long hair and smoothed it. The color of it reminded her of an otter's fur—brown with a little red mixed in.

Taking a leather thong from her bag, she braided his hair into a single braid and tied it off. She scooted off the bed and came around to look at him. She smiled and kissed him. "My husband is very handsome."

Billy put his hands on her hips and said, "My wife is very beautiful."

"You told me that many times last night," she said, smiling.

He laughed. "I meant it, too."

She caught the gleam in his eyes and said, "No. I do not want to be responsible for making us start out late. There will be time for that at lunch."

"Lunch? That is so far away," he said, giving her a coaxing smile.

Nina almost gave in to his charms, but held firm. She wanted him as badly as he did her. Her first husband had never made her feel beautiful or told her how good she made him feel. There had been no appreciation with him, but Billy was completely different. She may have been married before, but he'd shown her that there was a whole other side to marital relations.

Billy hugged her around the waist and then stood up, hoisting her over his shoulder. She squealed.

"Put me down!" she said with a giggle.

"I thought maybe you were tired from last night and would like me to carry you downstairs for breakfast," he said, walking towards the door.

"No! Wait! We need our things," she said.

Billy went back to the bed where their bags sat. "Pick them up, please."

She grabbed them and he headed for the door again. When he opened it, Lucky was on the other side, hand poised to knock.

"Good morning, Yelling Bear. My wife and I are going down to breakfast. Will you join us?" Billy asked.

Lucky tried not to look at Nina's buckskin-clad rear end, but it was hard since it was pointed right at him. "Yes, we will join you," he said and then mouthed, "Annulment?"

Billy grinned and shook his head. "Come, wife. We do not want to keep the others waiting."

Nina giggled and pulled the door shut as Billy walked forward. She waved back at Lucky, who laughed and went to his room to get Otto and Wild Wind.

Billy had grown up seeing how non-Indian marriages worked, but he was surprised by a lot of things Nina did. At lunch that day, she served Otto first and then Billy, making the other two men wait. She also gave him the nicest portion of meat. Startled, Billy looked at Lucky and Wild Wind, but they didn't look perturbed in the least. Then she served them and then herself. When Billy looked about to protest, Wild Wind caught his attention and shook his head, his eyes wide. He looked at Lucky, who wore much the same expression.

He refrained from saying anything. However, once the meal was over, he was going to help her clean up and discovered that Nina had a very fierce side to her.

"Put that down!" she commanded when he picked up the pot to take it to the stream they were camped by. "Do not interfere in women's work, husband. I do not tell you how to hunt, do I?"

"No, but—"

"Then do not make me feel less of a woman by trying to do my work," she said.

"I was not—"

She stopped him with an angry look that made him move away from her. Once she'd gathered things up and left to go down to the water's edge, Billy looked at Lucky.

"What the hell just happened?"

Lucky and Wild Wind laughed. "You had much the same look on your face, Yelling Bear."

"It took me a while to get used to it, too, Billy. Never, ever try to do what a woman deems as her work. Think of your ma and the way she doesn't let ya in the kitchen. Don't get in Nina's way when she's cookin', cleanin', makin' clothes, or anything like that. That includes haulin' water or cleanin' up from meals," Lucky told him.

"So what am I supposed to do around the house?" Billy asked. "We're gonna live in a house and I don't hunt every day."

Lucky chuckled. "Work on your art or come out to the farm to help. Pretty much what ya do now. Ye'll never have to worry about yer place bein' clean."

"But what if she's not home and I'm hungry? Am I allowed to cook? Can I make a sandwich?" Billy asked.

"Sure, but when she's around, best to stay out of the kitchen. Of course, ye'll have to show her how things work first."

Wild Wind laughed at the anxious look on Billy's face. "He has just found out that wives can be scary."

Lucky laughed at Billy, too.

Nina finished with her chores and then flashed Billy a smile. "I would like to take a walk with my husband."

"Ok," he said, smiling back at her.

"Ok," she repeated. "You must teach me English."

"All right. Let us start while we are walking," Billy said.

As the couple disappeared into the trees, Wild Wind chuckled. "I think we will be waiting a while."

Lucky smiled and nodded even though he cried inside. He remembered taking those kinds of walks with Avasa, barely able to restrain their desire until they were somewhere private. Laughing and loving through the night hours. He even missed their fights. Looking at Otto, he was very grateful to finally be with his son, but it hurt so badly that they would never be a complete family without Avasa.

There were still times when Otto greatly missed his mother, but whenever he began to cry, Lucky held him for a little and then began distracting him with something. Lucky distracted himself from his own grief by entertaining his son. Wild Wind was also helpful, telling Lucky funny stories of how they'd embarrassed soldiers or outwitted some of the officials on occasion. He stayed away from the subject of Avasa completely, for which Lucky was grateful. One day he'd be able to talk about her, but that day was a long ways off.

Traveling with three Cheyenne people and one who acted Cheyenne, gave Billy a sense of what living with a tribe would be like. The men hunted while Nina took care of Otto, repaired clothing, and got things ready so she could begin cooking as soon as they returned. There were other days when they pressed onward, eating cold meat from the day before.

Guided by Lucky and Wild Wind, Billy came to feel genuine pride in his heritage. There was much to learn and he was amazed at the intelligence, ingenuity, and strength it took to live the way Indians did. Although they stayed at a hotel here and there, they mainly camped out in the woods where they could to take advantage of the cover and protection from the wind.

They ran into a couple of storms as they hit the northern part of Wyoming, but they weathered them well thanks to a couple of lean-to's they'd built. Huddling together with Nina in theirs was a very pleasant experience for Billy. He enjoyed holding her and listening to the snow fall outside their little shelter.

Outside of keeping fed, making sure their weapons were in working order, and that they were protected, things were idyllic as they worked their way back into Montana. It was as though he'd been given a glimpse back in time to how the Cheyenne had lived for thousands of years and he was grateful and better for the experience.

Having Nina as a wife gave Billy tremendous pleasure and matured him somewhat because someone now depended on him for survival. It would be the same back in Echo. Although his role would change back into an artist and part-time sheep farmer, he would still have to provide for Nina, and he took that very seriously.

As Nina rode behind him every day, she was the happiest she'd ever been. Having a husband like Billy was a dream she'd thought would never come true. He was passionate, sweet, funny, firm about things at times, and considerate. She discovered that he was a patient teacher and that he had a creative perspective on many things.

Sometimes, he took out his sketchpad while they traveled and drew something quickly before it was lost again. He was also good at telling stories and after watching him play with Otto, she saw that he would be a wonderful father.

She became nervous the one day when they'd stopped for lunch and Billy had asked her what was wrong.

"We will arrive at your home tomorrow," she said. "I do not know anyone there. What if they do not like me?"

He gave her an encouraging smile. "They're gonna like you very much."

"Are you sure?"

Looking in her eyes, he said, "I'm sure."

They had spent the past few days speaking only English and she was mastering it quickly.

"Do you want me to dress like a white woman so I fit in?" she asked.

"I want you to wear whatever you're comfortable in," he said. "You're beautiful no matter what you're wearing."

She smiled. "You're a very lenient husband."

Billy nodded. "Do you know why that is?" She shook her head as he put his arms around her waist and said, "*Né-méhotátse*, Nina. I love you."

Nina's eyes grew bigger. "You do?"

"Yeah, I do. I don't know how it happened or when exactly, but I fell in love with you," he said.

She gave him a big smile and said, "*Né-méhotâtse*, Billy. I love you, too."

Billy's heart filled with happiness and it was as though his life became complete in that moment. Nina felt it, too. The kiss they shared was sweet and joyful as they stood by their horse while Lucky and Wild Wind finished packing their horses. As they mounted and began the last leg of their journey, both of them were confident that the future held only good things from then on.

Shadow was the strangest prisoner Evan had ever kept in the jail. Although he was capable of great violence, the only aggression he ever showed was whenever the door to his cell was closed. He tried not to panic, but it was just too much for him. While Evan was sweeping the floor one day, he'd accidently closed it. With his back turned to Shadow, Evan had continued on down the line of cells.

The next thing he knew, it had banged open again. Shadow had stretched himself out until he could kick the door back open. "That's better," he said.

"Oh, sorry about that," Evan said.

"It's all right."

One afternoon Evan came into the cell and gave Shadow an odd look.

"What's on your mind, Sheriff?" he asked.

Evan leaned against the wall. "I'm not sure what to do with you. I know you're guilty as sin of some stuff, but I don't have any proof, and I can't beat it out of you. My morals won't let me. I'm worried that if I let you go, you'll go back to doing whatever it is that you do."

Shadow had been wondering about that himself. He couldn't confess anything Evan without implicating Marvin and he would never do that. However, he certainly couldn't spend the rest of his life in the town jail. "I'm not sure what to tell you, Evan. I've been a good boy and what good would it do me to commit crime now that you know about me? You'll just come arrest me and we both know that I'll kill myself before letting myself be thrown into prison."

"That's true. I will come after you and if you tried to run, I'd just send Thad after you and he can track down anyone," Evan said. "I'll figure it out."

"Soon, I hope. I miss my home and my little family. I'm sure you can relate," Shadow said.

"I can't believe you live in a basement," Evan said.

Shadow smiled. "It's not just any basement. It's essentially an underground house. If you let me out, I'll show you."

Evan was very curious about Shadow's lair, but he wasn't ready to let Shadow loose. "Tempting, but not just yet." He had an idea about how to neutralize both Shadow and Marvin in one fell swoop, but he wanted Thad's opinion first.

That night, he asked the bounty hunter over for dinner and told him and his family his concept. They were silent after he'd spoken.

Josie and Edna looked at each other and then waited to see what Thad's reaction. Thad stared at the ceiling as he thought about it. He saw that it could work, but everything hinged on Shadow.

After a little bit, Thad smiled at Evan. "You're crazy as a fox. That's why I think you're so creative. No one else would have come up with such an insane but potentially successful plan."

"Do you think it'll work?" Evan asked.

"I think it could definitely work," Thad said.

Evan had let out a shout of laughter without thinking and Julia began to cry in the nursery upstairs because he'd startled her.

Josie smiled sweetly at Evan and said, "Guess who gets to put her back to sleep, Pa?"

Evan laughed. "Don't worry, I'll get her back down quick."

Seeing Evan in his role of father made Thad think about his own baby. It was hard not to. How could you grieve for something you hadn't even known you wanted, he wondered. To ward off his dark thoughts, he started telling Edna and Josie about one of his more humorous escapades.

# Chapter Fifteen

Evan startled Shadow the next day when he came into his cell and unlocked his handcuffs. "Come on out here with me. You try anything funny and I'll shoot you down. Got it?"

"Yes." Shadow got up and followed him.

Although his knee was still painful, it felt good to walk a little more than he'd been previously allowed. As he came out into the bright office, he turned his head away from the sunlight. It stabbed at his eyes and made his head hurt.

Evan said, "Oh, sorry. I forgot. Sit here."

He guided Shadow to a chair, took a blanket from the supply shelves, and hung it across one of the windows, dimming the light.

Coming back to the table and sitting opposite from Shadow, he asked, "How's that?"

Shadow opened his eyes in increments, letting his eyes adjust. "Tolerable."

"Good. Now, I have a proposition for you and your freedom depends on whether you accept it or not. If you don't, I'll keep digging and find proof of some of your misdeeds and have you locked up in prison. You can kill yourself if you want or go stark raving mad. Or, you can take my offer and be free to live your life."

Shadow gave Evan a measuring look. "Go on."

"I'm offering you a job," Evan said. "I know you guys have money, but what're you gonna do with your time now that you won't be out causing trouble?"

"A job?" Shadow asked. "I'm not interested in manual labor. I also don't type or write shorthand."

Evan smiled. "You have the exact skills I'm looking for. Strong, almost fearless, intelligent, lethal fighter, good with weapons, so you say, and you have no problem hurting people."

Shadow was perplexed. "I fail to see what position you're talking about."

Evan pulled something from his pocket that he laid on the table and pushed over to Shadow. Shadow picked it up and looked at it in disbelief. The laugh he let out filled the office and Evan couldn't stop himself from laughing along. It took Shadow a little while to get himself under control again.

"You can't be serious," he said.

"Dead serious," Evan said. "What's your answer?"

"Forgive me, but you truly want me to become your deputy? Is this a trick?" Shadow asked.

"Nope. No trick. I figure it this way: I need a deputy, you really don't need to be paid much, you get to go free, and once you put on that badge and take the oath, you're honor-bound to report crime of any kind—no matter who it involves. If I find out you're not doing that—and I will check up on you—I'll haul you off to prison," Evan said.

Shadow mulled that over. "I have a counter offer. If I do this, once I put on the badge and take the oath, I am absolved of any and all hypothetical past crimes that I may have been involved in. And Marvin, too."

"You're asking for immunity for the two of you in exchange for becoming my deputy," Evan said.

"That's right. *If* we strike this deal, we both have a clean slate, and *if* we do make this deal, I will haul in whomever I find doing wrong. You'll have to define wrong for me, though, since I have a rather warped sense of that," Shadow said.

Evan smiled. "That means no senseless murder, unnecessary violence, robbing, looting, larceny, bribery—never mind. I'll give you a list."

"I'd like this agreement in writing," Shadow said. "And witnessed. I won't take the chance of you coming back on me at a later date."

Evan nodded. "Ok. But are you agreeing to it if it's put in writing?"

Formally, Shadow said, "If you're granting immunity for both Marvin and myself, I will take the job and do my best at it."

Evan said, "I'll grant immunity to the both of you as long as you uphold your end of the bargain and dispatch your duties to the best of your ability." Evan held out his hand to Shadow.

Shadow shook it and smiled. "Does this mean I get to go home today?"

"As soon as we get the written part done and I do the swearing in, sure. I'll go get Josie. She's very good at this stuff. Now, I'm going to trust you not to go anywhere until I get back," Evan said.

Shadow said, "I won't get very far with this leg."

"True." Evan stepped over to his desk and took something from a drawer. "I have a present for you."

Shadow looked at the glasses Evan held out to him. "Did Dr. Avery give them to you?"

"Yep. Try them on and see if they work for you. I need you to work during the day, at least partly."

Shadow reluctantly took them. He didn't like the idea of wearing glasses, but if they helped his eyes, he would try them. "I'm going to look ridiculous," he complained.

Evan chuckled. "Put them on."

Shadow did so and immediately felt relief from the glaring light. He smiled. "How stupid do I look?"

Thad came in the door and stopped. "You gave them to him?"

"Yeah," Evan said.

"Holy shit! He looks even scarier than normal," Thad said.

Shadow laughed. "They make me look scary?"

"Yeah. Come here," Evan said.

Shadow limped behind Evan until they came to a small mirror on one wall. The glasses did make him look even more menacing. The round shape of them was actually attractive and they gave him an added air of mystery because they hid his eyes so much. He smiled at his reflection. He chuckled at first, but it quickly grew into a laugh.

Evan and Thad joined him. Their mirth subsided and Shadow sat back down again as Marvin and Bree came into the office for their first visit of the day.

Marvin smiled at Shadow. "I see your glasses arrived. Good. How do they work?"

"Very well," he said.

"You're out of your cell," Bree remarked as she came to kiss him.

Shadow said, "I was let out for good behavior."

Evan said, "I'll be back. Shadow, why don't you fill Bree and Marvin in on your new job while I go get Josie?" He grinned and left. Thad took a seat over at Evan's desk to give the trio a little privacy.

Marvin asked, "What's he talking about?"

"Please just listen to me, Marvin. I'm doing this to protect all of us," Shadow said. "In exchange for immunity for you and me of any past crimes, I am accepting the position of deputy."

Marvin and Bree were shell-shocked. Fury blazed in Marvin's eyes.

"It's a trick!" he whispered. "Don't you see that?"

"No, Marvin. We're putting it in writing and it'll be notarized ... by you," Shadow said with a sly smile. "You've protected me all these years, let me protect you for a change. Please, Marvy?"

Bree looked between the brothers. She had no idea what to think about it all.

Shadow leaned towards Marvin. "Don't you see how this can work? You and I will have a fresh start and we won't have to worry about being arrested. I can't go to prison and I'll do almost anything to avoid it."

The possibilities ran through Marvin's mind and he did see how this arrangement benefitted them. He grinned. "Shadow, you've done a great thing here. You really have."

Shadow said, "We're going to have to play by the rules from now on. Well, mostly anyway."

Marvin said, "I understand that and that's not going to be a problem. No problem at all."

Shadow looked at Bree. "What do you think?"

She thought that maybe they could have a semi-normal life and it gave her hope for the future. She gave Shadow a kiss and said, "I think you'll make a very handsome deputy."

Shadow laughed and hugged her.

When Evan returned with Josie, she didn't know what to make of Shadow's appearance. It was unnerving and fascinating at the same time, much like she'd always found Marvin's demeanor. She was still getting used to the fact that Marvin had a twin.

"Hello, Josie," Shadow said. "It's nice to see you."

She gave him a small smile. "You, too."

Marvin said, "Sheriff, I am a licensed notary so I'll be able to notarize the agreement."

Evan asked, "Do you have proof that you are?"

Marvin kept copies of his credentials in his briefcase, which was outside in their buggy. "I'll go get it."

"You do that," Evan said.

While Marvin was retrieving his briefcase, Evan and Shadow dictated to Josie exactly what the document should say. Once it was done, Marvin read through it carefully and, finding it satisfactory, he notarized the paper. Thad and Bree witnessed it and the agreement was finalized.

Evan swore Shadow in and pinned his badge on Shadow's coat. As he looked down at it, Shadow felt a little bit lighter in his soul.

Evan said, "Once your bum leg is healed a little more, I have a special assignment for you that I think you'll really like."

"Which is?"

"It's tailor-made for you and I'll give you free rein in doing it your way," Evan said with a grin.

"Oh?"

"Your first duty will be to clean up the Burgundy House. I want all of the prostitution gone and the rowdiness cut down on as much as you can. When you walk in there, you have the full weight of this office behind you. Use it however you see fit," Evan said.

The more he thought about it, the more Shadow liked the idea. He enjoyed a challenge and the Burgundy House would be a big one. "Very well. I'll let you know when I'll start it."

"Good. In the meantime, I expect you to patrol town during the afternoons and get to know some of the townspeople. Your leg can stand riding, so doing that shouldn't be a problem. It's good for them to see law enforcement out and about and it's important to gain their trust. It's also a good deterrent to crime," Evan said.

Shadow wasn't used to being given orders and he wasn't crazy about the idea of patrolling, but if it meant staying out of jail, he'd do it. "All right."

"Good. You start at noon tomorrow, so get some shuteye tonight," Evan said. "Well, I guess that's about everything."

Shadow nodded and moved towards the door, motioning for Bree.

Marvin said, "I'd like a word with you, Evan."

"Fine."

They moved off a little from Josie and Thad.

"As a peace offering and a gesture of gratitude for what you've done here, I'm going to tell you the identity of Louise's baby," Marvin said.

Evan's gaze sharpened. "Who?"

Marvin leaned towards him and whispered in his ear. Evan gave him an incredulous look. Marvin's expression was grave as he said, "It's the truth. I have no reason to lie about it and no reason to withhold it. Thank you again."

Evan stared after Marvin as he followed Shadow and Bree outside.

# Chapter Sixteen

When Billy and company rode into Echo, they were greeted by many people. Lucky and Billy introduced Wild Wind, Otto, and Nina. They had all agreed to not mention that Billy and Nina were married until he told his family and Callie.

Billy's stomach was in turmoil about telling his parents that he'd gotten married while they'd been on the road. He knew that Nina was nervous, too, because she held onto him tightly. They parted ways with Lucky and Wild Wind because the Irishman and the other Indian were heading for the sheep farm while Billy and Nina were going to his folks house.

When they arrived at Arlene and Remus', Nina froze with fear and couldn't get off their horse.

"Honey, you have to get down now," Billy said.

Nina shook her head against Billy's back. "I cannot. They will hate me because of the way we were married and because I am not this other woman."

Billy rubbed her arms, which were still wrapped around his waist. "They're not gonna hate you. They'll be surprised about it all, but they won't hate you. My parents are very understanding people. I promise. Come on and get off now."

Nina reluctantly slid off the horse and stood by it while Billy dismounted. Billy hugged and kissed her. "It'll be ok."

She nodded, but wasn't completely convinced. Billy took her hand and led her towards the door. He didn't stop to knock. They went in the front door, but no one was in the parlor at the moment.

"Hello? Ma, Pa? I'm home!" he called out.

They heard a woman let out a happy sound from upstairs and then hurried footsteps sounded on the stairs. Arlene flew to Billy and embraced him tightly.

"We've missed you so much! Are you all right? How did everything go? You need a bath. You look good, though. It's so good to see you. Did you grow?"

"Ma, slow down," he said with a laugh. "I'm fine. Tired, but fine. Things didn't go exactly as planned. There's some bad news, but a lot of very good news, too. I don't think I grew."

Arlene kissed him and let him go. She noticed Nina then. "And who's your friend?" she asked, smiling at Nina.

"Is Pa around? It'll be easier just to tell you both," Billy said.

"I think he's out back. I'll go get him," Arlene said, giving Billy a curious look before going into the kitchen and out the back door.

When she returned with Remus, he grabbed Billy in a bear hug and slapped his back. Billy had missed his family and he was glad to be home.

"Well, come on and take your coats off and sit down," Arlene said.

They did and Billy and Nina sat on the love seat together while Arlene and Remus sat on the sofa.

"Ma, Pa, I need you to listen to me closely. I have a lot to tell you. First, I want to introduce you to Nina. Nina, this is my mother, Arlene, and this is my father, Remus," Billy said.

Nina gave them a shy smile and said, "It is a pleasure to meet you both." She had been rehearsing the greeting in her head all day and was happy that she got it out correctly.

Arlene said, "It's nice to meet you, too."

Remus nodded his agreement.

Holding Nina's hand, Billy said, "Nina is my wife. We're married."

His parents sat stone still and then looked at each other.

Remus cleared his throat and said, "I could have sworn you just said Nina is your wife. Did I hear that right?"

Billy nodded. "Yes, you did. It's a long story."

Nodding, Remus said, "All right. Go ahead."

In between questions, Billy and Nina told them their tale. Although his parents were surprised about the situation, they were supportive, which was a great relief to the couple.

Looking at Nina, Billy said, "We didn't expect to fall in love, but we did."

Arlene smiled and said, "We're very happy for you. You're going to have to talk to Callie."

Billy said, "I know. I'm going to do that now while Nina stays with you."

"Ok. She might be at your shop since it's early afternoon. She's been running it for you," Remus said.

"She has?" Billy asked. "Wow. That's really nice of her."

Arlene said, "She's a very nice young woman."

"I'm sure she is. Well, I'd better go get this over with," Billy said. He saw fear in Nina's eyes. "I'll be back soon, ok? It'll be fine."

Nina nodded and put a bright smile on her face. "I will get to know your parents better."

He kissed her and Arlene and left.

When Billy walked into his store, he saw how clean it was and smiled. Then he felt guilty for having to disappoint Callie. Gathering his courage, he looked around for her. *She must be in the back,* he thought.

Just as he was about to enter the back room, she came out of it.

"Oh! You startled me," she said with a smile.

Billy took in her black hair, pretty blue eyes, and very nice figure and thought she was a beautiful woman.

"Can I help you?" she asked.

He held out a hand to her. "Hi, Callie. I'm Billy."

Her eyes widened and she smiled. She shook his hand and said, "Billy! It's so nice to finally meet you!"

Grinning, he said, "Same here. Sorry about the way I look, but we just got back to town a little while ago."

"Think nothing of it. You'll want to get cleaned up, I'm sure," she said.

"Well, before I do that, I need to talk to you," he said. "I'm gonna close the shop so we can talk without being interrupted."

"Ok."

Billy flipped the sign to "closed". "Let's go to my apartment."

Callie followed him. Billy had turned out to be a very handsome man, she thought, but there was another man who appealed to her more. She hadn't gone in the apartment out of respect for his privacy. It was a cute little place. He motioned for her to have a seat on the sofa and he sat in the only chair in the room.

"Thank you so much for running the shop while I was gone. I'll make sure to pay you out of whatever you made," Billy said. "It's only fair."

Callie smiled. "I didn't do it for the money. I just wanted to help out."

Billy nodded. "I appreciate it, but you deserve to be paid."

"All right."

He was silent for a moment, which made Callie nervous.

"Callie, I feel so badly about this, but there's no way around it. I'm afraid your trip was wasted."

"What do you mean?"

Billy explained it all to her. Callie had been silent as he spoke, absorbing what he told her. It was quite a story and if she didn't know better, it could have been something out of book.

"So you're married now and in love with your wife?" she asked.

"That's right. I'm so sorry, Callie. I never intended for any of this to happen or for you to get hurt," Billy said. "I'm not that kind of guy."

Callie laughed. "I know that. Everyone says what a good man you are, how kind and funny. I don't think you purposely set out to hurt me. I have a confession to make and please don't be angry with me."

"I won't be," he assured her.

Playing with her skirt a little, she said, "I haven't done anything about it because I was waiting for you to get back, but I've developed feelings for another man. Like you, I didn't intend for it to happen, but I can't deny that they're there. I haven't said anything to him, although I suspect he feels the same way."

Billy grinned. "You like someone here in town? Who?"

"Ross Ryder," she said.

He grinned at the dreamy way she said Ross' name. "Ross? That's great. He's a good guy," Billy said.

"So you're not angry?"

"Not at all," he said. "I think things worked out the way they were supposed to. Maybe Ross is the man you're meant to be with. He'll treat you right. And I'm sure it doesn't hurt that he's not bad to look at."

Callie giggled at his teasing tone. "No, it doesn't. This is all a little crazy, but I'm so happy for you. It's always wonderful to see someone find love and I'm glad you and Nina did. I can't wait to meet her."

An idea came to Billy. "Why don't you come to my folks' house for dinner? I'll go and casually invite Ross and you can get the ball rolling."

She squealed and hurried over to hug him. Kissing his cheek, she said, "You're a wonderful man and I'm looking forward to becoming friends with you and Nina."

He laughed and said, "I think we did just become friends."

"I guess we did," Callie said. "I must go change so I really catch Ross' eye."

Billy liked the way her southern drawl became more pronounced in her excitement.

"Ok. That sounds good. I'll go invite him," Billy said.

Callie hugged him again and then hurried out of the apartment. Billy followed behind her and then continued on down the street.

Ross had just reorganized some meat in the case when Billy came into the store.

"Holy cow! Look what the cat just dragged in!" he said, coming around the case.

He shook hands with Billy and clapped him on the shoulder. "It's good to see you, buddy."

Billy smiled slightly and said, "It's good to be back, but I got a problem with you."

Ross' smile dimmed. "What do you mean?"

"You've been eyeing up my girl while I've been gone and I don't appreciate it," Billy said, barely keeping a straight face.

"What? No, I haven't. Well, I mean she's beautiful and nice and funny, but I never made any move on her, Billy. I swear," Ross said.

Billy couldn't hold back the laughter that bubbled up in his chest. "I'm just kidding you. You wanna hear a funny story?"

Ross was very confused. "Ok."

When Billy finished, he said, "So as you can see, Callie is fair game. She likes you, too."

Ross grinned ear-to-ear. "She said that?"

Billy nodded. "She sure did. Now, you need to come to my folks' for dinner. I invited Callie, too, so that'll give you a chance to talk to her and set something up with her."

Ross grabbed him in a crushing hug. "Thank you! I owe you."

"You sure do and I'll collect at some point," Billy said.

"Whatever you want," Ross said. "I can't believe you're married. That's great. I can't wait to meet her."

"You will, very soon. Make sure you clean up and dress nice for Callie," Billy said with a grin as he exited Ross' store.

# Chapter Seventeen

Nina stood in Billy's store, inspecting all of his paintings. They were beautiful and she could have spent hours looking at them, but they were going to bathe and change before going back to his parents' house. She'd had a good time with them. Remus had teased her about getting tangled up with Billy and Arlene had shown her about the cook stove and some other things around the kitchen.

Billy asked, "What do you think?"

She went to him and said, "I think I have married a very talented man. They're all so beautiful and none of them are the same."

Pride welled inside Billy. "Thanks. I'm glad you think so."

"I do."

"Come with me, wife. I'll show you our home," he said.

Entering the little apartment, Nina thought how strange it would be to live in a building instead of a tipi, but she would live anywhere if it meant being with Billy. She liked the little kitchen, although it needed cleaning. Of course with Billy being away for so long, things were bound to be dusty.

The parlor was a little plain, but she would take care of that. There was a tiny water closet and then the bedroom. She'd liked sleeping in a bed in the hotels where they'd stayed, so sleeping in their bed wouldn't be any different.

Billy anxiously waited for her to finish her inspection.

She put her hands on her hips and looked at him. "It needs a little color, but I like it very much." She smiled at him and he smiled back, visibly relaxing.

"I'm so glad. I was afraid you'd hate it. When we start having kids, we'll build a bigger place, but for now, it'll do," Billy said. "I'll go get the tub and get the stove going."

"You get the tub, I will start the fire in the stove. Your mother showed me how," she said.

He smiled. "Ok. You got it."

Nina felt very proud when she successfully built a fire in the cook stove. She found a couple of large pots, pumped water into them, and set them on the stove. It wasn't much different from hanging pots over an open fire.

Billy came in with the tub and sat it on the floor. Nina looked at it with a critical eye. "It will be strange bathing in that."

He said, "You'll get used to it. I'll help you get used to everything and other people will, too."

She nodded. "The water will take a little while to heat." She gave him a seductive look. "I have an idea how to pass the time."

Billy's adrenaline flowed faster. "Really? What's that?"

She began undressing as she walked back to their bedroom. Billy followed her, doing the same thing. Watching her shapely derriere and slim hips moving ahead of him, he knew he would never get enough of his green-eyed girl. In moments, he embraced her and made love with his wife in their home for the first time.

Afterwards, as their hearts settled into normal rhythms again, Nina said, "You have brought so much magic into my life." She took one of his hands in hers and kissed his palm. "You have magic in your hands. They create beautiful things. They bring things alive that make people feel things. When I look at them, I feel like I am right there seeing them. Yes, my husband is a magical man. I think that should be your Cheyenne name: Magic Man."

Billy was so moved that tears burned his eyes. "You just gave me a Cheyenne name. Thank you."

"You are welcome. Our water should be ready by now," she said.

Billy rose and scooped Nina up in his arms. "Then let's get our baths and get over to my parents' house. Ma hates it when people are late to supper."

Lucky had taken Otto home with him to get him used to the sheep farm and show him their tipi. Otto had seen tipis all his life, but he'd never seen sheep before. He looked around the tipi for perhaps five minutes before running back outside to play with the sheep.

Lucky had introduced his son and Wild Wind to Win and Erin and the four of them watched him run around petting the animals and playing with a couple of the early lambs.

Erin said, "He's adorable, Lucky. He has your smile."

"Thanks," Lucky said. "He's a smart lad, too. We've been teaching him English and he's caught on quick."

Win said, "I'm not surprised. You're no slouch intelligence wise, either."

Wild Wind grinned and Lucky said, "Not a word out of ye."

The other three laughed while Lucky scowled at them. Erin hugged him. He hadn't had a chance to tell them the full story about Avasa yet, not wanting to talk about her in front of Otto and upset him. He'd just told them that she hadn't been able to come with them. Erin knew Lucky well by then and she could see that under his playfulness he was hurting. She didn't say anything, she just offered some silent comfort, for which Lucky was grateful.

Win watched them a moment and then said, "I have some news that might interest you."

Lucky hugged Erin back and then let her go. "What's that?"

While Lucky stared at them in disbelief, the pair of doctors told him and Wild Wind about Shadow and how Evan had hired him to be a deputy.

When they finished, Lucky laughed and said, "Ye almost had me there. Ya spin a good yarn."

Win gave him a deadpan look and said, "We're telling you the truth. Marvin has a twin and Evan hired him."

"Has Evan gone nutters then?" Lucky asked.

Erin said, "That's what we thought at first, but once he and Thad explained it to us, we saw how crafty he was about it. Shadow has to uphold the law or Evan's going to put him in prison and that means even keeping Marvin in line. It also gives Evan a deputy at a very cheap price."

Lucky pondered that and saw the wisdom in it. "I can see how that could work."

"We're going over to Evan and Josie's for supper. You coming?" Win asked.

Lucky shook his head a little. "Not tonight. I'm tired and I want to get Otto settled in."

Wild Wind said, "I will come with you and meet all of Yelling Bear's other friends." He knew that Lucky wanted some privacy. Besides, he was very anxious to meet these people Lucky regarded as family. He liked Win and Erin and had a feeling that he would like the others, too.

"Great," Win said.

"I will go bathe and change. I will not be long," the brave said, running off to the tipi. They saw him go in and come back out with new clothing.

Erin asked, "Is he going to bathe in the stream? It's too cold for that."

Lucky smiled. "Indians bathe almost every day unless there's a lot of snow or ice. I have the fire burning in the tipi; he'll warm up by it for a few minutes and then be ready."

Win laughed. "I think we're in for some very interesting times."

"That ya are," Lucky said. "Otto! Come, lad. Time for supper."

Otto ran over to him. "What are we eating?"

"Mutton. You'll like it," Lucky said. He had Otto say goodbye to Erin and Win before taking him into the tipi.

Erin and Win smiled as they watched them walk away. "They look so cute together," Erin said.

"Yeah. It's a shame about Avasa. I can't even imagine," Win said, taking Erin's hand.

Erin moved closer and kissed him. "You don't ever have to worry about that."

"Mmm," Win said, kissing her back. "We could always stay home, you know."

She said, "No, we can't. I'm hungry."

"Ok," Win said in mock disappointment.

Wild Wind returned and put his dirty clothing in the tipi. Then he joined Win and Erin and the trio headed to the Tafts'.

There were so many people floating back and forth between the Tafts' and the Deckers' that it had turned into a homecoming party of sorts. Wild Wind was a hit with everyone and he teased Billy that Echo now had its first "real" Indian who wasn't afraid of blood.

Billy took it all in stride, smiling and telling Wild Wind that he was the only one with a genuine Cheyenne wife. Wild Wind was impressed with how accepting all of the white people were of him and he saw why Lucky was so fond of them. He enjoyed their food, even though some of it was strange to him.

Billy was also shocked by the news of Shadow and the fact that he now worked as a deputy for Evan. He wasn't sure how he felt about that, but he trusted Evan's judgement. Nina had been shy around everyone at first, but the women soon drew her out. She was glad that she knew enough English to get by and Josie and Erin knew some Cheyenne now and could help translate. Even though Billy had gone next door to his parents' house, Nina felt comfortable being left at the Tafts'. He'd told her he'd be back shortly and she wasn't worried.

Callie had been gracious about everything and she and Nina had hit it off.

"I'm so glad you married, Billy," Callie said to her.

"You are?"

Callie said, "Yes. I can see how much you love each other and I think it was meant to be. It's also a relief because I have feelings for another man."

Nina's eyes lit up. "Who?"

Callie said, "That big man over with Edna. His name is Ross and he's a friend of Billy's."

Nina casually looked in that direction and said, "He is handsome. He works with Billy."

"Yes. He's the nicest man and whenever he's around, my heart feels like it's going to beat right out of my chest," Callie said with a giggle.

Nina laughed and said, "I feel the same way about Billy. It is like my heart soars."

Someone knocked on Evan's door. Josie opened it and gasped. Shadow stood on the other side. It was uncanny how much he resembled Marvin.

Shadow was getting used to this reaction and, much like Marvin, he enjoyed it.

"Good evening, Josie. How are you?"

Recovering, Josie said, "Fine and yourself?"

"I'm well, thank you. Is your husband available?" he asked.

Josie tried to mask her fear of the man as she said, "Yes. Come in."

Shadow entered the house and conversation stopped. Quite a few lamps were lit and it was too much for his eyes. He put his glasses on.

Not everyone had met Shadow, so Evan stepped forward and said, "Everyone, meet Shadow, my new deputy."

Shadow held up a hand in greeting and there was ripple of subdued murmured greetings back at him.

Edna asked, "Evan, did you tell him about our game?"

"No," Evan said with a frown. "Will you behave?"

Shadow asked, "What game would that be?"

"Well, it's not a game exactly," Edna said. "It's more of an admittance fee."

Evan said, "Not now, woman. We have company."

Edna crooked a finger at Shadow and he walked over to her. She motioned for him to bend down so she could whisper in his ear. As she spoke, a grin stole over Shadow's face. He laughed as he straightened.

"Marvin was right about your aunt, Evan. She's going to be a lot of fun," Shadow said. "I'll remember that for the next time I come, madam."

"You better or you can just stand outside," Edna said. "Make sure you get something to eat."

"Thank you, but I'm actually on duty," Shadow said.

Edna said, "Well, all right, but you'll have to come to dinner sometime."

Josie stared at her, but Edna pretended not to notice. However, Shadow saw and pounced.

"I would love to and I'm sure Bree would, too," Shadow said. "Sheriff? A word? Have a pleasant evening, everyone."

Evan followed Shadow outside. "What's up?"

"I'm beginning my special assignment tonight and I just wanted to give you a heads up as promised," Shadow said.

Evan smiled. "Good. Remember, no senseless murder, unnecessary violence, and try not to cause too much destruction. Other than that, I'll leave it in your hands."

Shadow took off his glasses and put them in his coat pocket. "Very well. I'll give you my report in the morning."

"I look forward to it."

Shadow nodded as Thad came out of Evan's house. "Is something going on?" he asked.

Evan said, "Shadow's off to the Burgundy House."

Thad smiled. "That should be entertaining. Mind if I tag along?"

"If you like," Shadow said.

Evan laughed. "That's double trouble. Have fun gentlemen."

# Chapter Eighteen

Thad hung back a little as Shadow entered the Burgundy House. He was curious to see how Shadow would handle the situation. There was no way he could have foreseen what was about to transpire. Shadow assessed the situation as soon as he entered the business. The smoky atmosphere assaulted his nose and he was glad he was wearing his glasses to ward off the glaring light.

Saloon girls flirted with men or sat on their laps. Shadow's gaze followed the large staircase up to the long row of doors above the barroom. He knew perfectly well what happened in those rooms. The owner, Kevin Bartholomew, served drinks. Shadow unholstered one of his revolvers and shot the mirror behind the bar. The gun report combined with the noise of the shattering glass made everyone duck. The piano player stopped and hid underneath the piano bench.

"Good evening, everyone! I'm Deputy Earnest and you now have the unfortunate experience of making my acquaintance!" he shouted. "I want all the lovely ladies of the evening to clear out or I will haul you all to jail."

Kevin said, "You can't do that!"

"On the contrary, my good man," Shadow said. "This badge I'm wearing says I can and I will. Now, I would prefer to do things the hard way, but my boss won't like that. However, I've been given permission to do whatever is necessary to restore order to this den of iniquity, and since I'm here and he's not, I get to decide what that might be."

Used to constantly being on the alert when he was out, Shadow saw a man take out his gun and start to raise it. Shadow quickly reacted, shooting the man in the shoulder. "How unfortunate that he decided to test me," Shadow said. "Is there anyone else who feels the need to do so?" No one moved. "Good. Ladies, must I tell you again?"

There was a flurry of activity as the women ran upstairs or left the saloon.

"I will come back here every night if I have to in order to make sure things stay quiet. If I find any evidence of illegal activity, there will be dire consequences. Mr.—I'm sorry. I don't know the man I shot. What's his name?"

Kevin said, "Hank Vernon."

"Thank you, Mr. Bartholomew. Mr. Vernon found out the hard way that there are consequences when I'm not obeyed. Let that be a lesson to you all," Shadow said. He walked over to the bar. "I'd like a whiskey to drink while I wait, please."

Kevin looked at Thad. "Are you gonna let him get away with this?"

Thad said, "I'm a bounty hunter, not the law. Quit cryin' and give the man his whiskey. Give me one, too, while you're at it."

Kevin hesitated and Shadow growled. The bartender's face paled and he hurried to get the drinks. While he poured them with a shaking hand, Shadow pulled some money out of his wallet and laid it on the bar.

"This should be enough for a new mirror. I'm sorry for shooting it, but I confess that I wanted to make a dramatic entrance. How do you think I did?"

Kevin gave Shadow a sickly smile. "G-great. You did great."

Shadow smiled. "Thank you. Was there anything you thought I could have done better?"

It took great restraint for Thad not to smile or laugh.

"What?" Kevin asked.

"Are you hard of hearing?" Shadow responded.

"No."

"Then answer the question," Shadow said.

Kevin looked at Thad for help, but he received none. "Uh, no, I think that was a great entrance."

"Thank you," Shadow said. He downed his drink and then walked over to the piano. The piano player had sat down on the bench, but he moved again when Shadow shooed him away with a wave of his hand. Before sitting down, Shadow bellowed, "If you're not out of those rooms by the time this song ends, there will be consequences to pay! Do not make me come up those stairs!" In a quieter voice he said, "I sound like a parent at bedtime."

Thad laughed and Shadow grinned at him as he sat down at the piano. The song he played was a Beethoven number, and it shocked the patrons to hear classical music played on the piano instead of the rowdy songs they were used to. Thad was as surprised as everyone else.

Doors started opening upstairs and people hurried from the rooms and down the stairs. Giving Shadow fearful looks, they ran from the bar. When Shadow finished with the song, he stood up. "If there's anyone else up there, come down now and I won't shoot you!"

Thad snickered at his remark. No one else emerged from the rooms and Shadow stood back from the piano a little bit. He shot it in three places.

"Hey!" Kevin shouted. "What the hell are you doing?"

Shadow came back over to the bar and gave Kevin more money. "That piano needed to be put out of its misery. It was horribly out of tune, most likely because it's rotten inside. Get a new one. That'll be enough to replace it. Stafford's in Dickensville has some nice pianos from what I understand. Now remember, no prostitution, and try to keep the murders and so forth to a minimum. Good evening, Mr. Bartholomew."

Kevin looked at all of the money Shadow had given him and said, "Feel free to come back anytime and shoot up more stuff."

Shadow laughed. "You may come to regret that statement."

He and Thad walked out of the saloon. As soon as they were mounted, Thad cracked up. His laughter inspired Shadow's and it was a little while before they sobered.

"So, Thad, are you my babysitter?" Shadow asked.

"Nope. I just wanted to see what would happen," Thad said. "Thanks for the entertainment."

"Happy to oblige. It surprised me that you wanted to come with me. I *am* Marvin's brother, and you hate him. I would have thought that hate would have carried over to me,"

Thad had figured this topic would come up sooner or later. "I have a long history with Marvin. Most people around here do. You know what he did."

Shadow said, "Yes, I do. He loved Phoebe very much."

Thad's temper simmered. "I know he's your brother and you're loyal to him, but he has no idea what love is."

"On the contrary. Once you found out that Phoebe was seeing someone else, you ended your relationship. However, Marvin loved her so much that he was willing to share her for a long time. Yes, it gave him pleasure knowing that you were being cheated on, but the main reason he kept seeing her was because he loved her. He proposed to her five times and she turned him down. He begged her to give you up, but she wouldn't. He's mourned her as much as you have," Shadow said.

"I find that hard to believe. She was pregnant with my child," Thad said.

"True, and I'm very sorry for your loss. Losing Phoebe was bad enough, but losing a child at the same time must have been torture. Marvin feels terrible about that."

Thad snorted.

Shadow said, "Marvin loves children and it's deeply distressing to him that he can't have any. He feels sorry for anyone who's lost a child, you included."

"If you're trying to tell me that Marvin's a good guy, you can save your breath," Thad said.

"Oh, I'm not saying that. Marvin is what he's had to be in order to protect me," Shadow said. "He needed everyone to hate him so that people stayed away."

"Why did you need to be kept a secret once your parents were out of the way?" Thad asked.

"When Marvin found me, I was emaciated, had a speech impediment because of the emotional abuse I'd suffered, and I couldn't stand bright light. Add that to the fact that I'd never seen another living soul besides Father until Marvin came along and you can imagine what it would have been like for my existence to suddenly be known. I would have been put in an institution. We both know that such people are not always treated kindly," Shadow said. "He taught me how to do everything. Eat with utensils, what it was like to sleep in an actual bed, how to wear all types of clothing. How to bathe. Simple things that most people take for granted. As I began to understand just how different I was, I begged him not to tell anyone about me and he didn't. I didn't want to be ridiculed, beaten, or sent somewhere."

Thad felt a grudging respect for the way Marvin had taken care of Shadow. Marvin hadn't had to take responsibility for Shadow, but he'd done it. He'd also run a successful business at a young age when others wouldn't have been able to do that.

"So he sacrificed himself for you," Thad said. "Lookin' at it that way sort of makes sense. I'm not sayin' the way he went about everything was right, though. He's done a lot of rotten stuff that he didn't have to in order to keep you safe."

"Such as?"

"Sleeping with Evan's fiancée."

Shadow said, "That's true, but no one's perfect. However, it did serve the purpose of driving Evan away. It wouldn't have been good to be friendly with the sheriff."

"Nope. So Marvin was acting friendly with Evan to take his

measure. Good strategy," Thad said. "I've done the same thing in my line of work."

"Look, Thad," Shadow said. "I don't expect any of this to make you friendly towards Marvin. I'm just trying to make you understand a little bit."

"I get your point. I'll always hate him, so you're gonna have to accept that if you're gonna be around me."

Shadow said, "I already accept that people hate him and so does he."

"Good."

They reached town and turned in opposite directions—Shadow towards his home and Thad towards the Tafts'. He knew Evan would want to know what had happened and was most likely still up. When he got there and went inside, he saw that all of them were up.

Smiling, he said, "You're not gonna believe this."

Nina woke during her first night in her new home and didn't know where she was at first. Billy slept soundly beside her. Looking around the room, she smiled. *I am home with my husband, starting a new life.* She couldn't go to sleep again, so she rose and went out to the kitchen. Lighting the lantern there, she took it out into the shop to look at his artwork since she could take her time doing so.

As she moved from painting to painting, her appreciation for Billy's talent grew. His landscapes made it seem as though she could step right into them and walk along, seeing everything in them as if it were real. There were paintings of soaring eagles, buildings from around town, and still life works. She smiled as she looked at a painting of a furry, gray, tiger-striped kitten. It was so realistic that she wanted to pet it.

When she'd looked her fill, Nina went back to bed, snuggling up to Billy. Even in sleep, it was his instinct to put his arms around her. As he did, Nina closed her eyes, feeling safe and loved as she drifted off.

The next morning, Billy woke to the scent of coffee. Opening his eyes, he got his bearings. He'd been expecting to be surrounded by nature, not in his apartment. Realizing that his wife wasn't in bed with him, he got up and padded out to the kitchen. She stood at the stove in one of his shirts and he stopped to admire her shapely legs. She looked adorable in it and he thought that he would like to wake up to that sight every morning.

"Good morning," he said.

She smiled at him. "Good morning."

"That coffee smells good." His stomach growled. "We're gonna have to go to the store for some food."

"Yes. I am excited to see the store," she said, sitting two cups of coffee on the table.

Billy said, "We don't have any cream so we'll have to drink it black."

Nina nodded and sat down. Billy joined her.

"I looked at your paintings last night when I woke up and could not go back to sleep," she said.

"How come you couldn't sleep?"

She shrugged. "Sleeping in a strange place for the first time, maybe."

Billy sipped the hot brew and said, "Good coffee. What did you think of the paintings?"

"The same thing I already knew—I am married to a gifted man," she said.

His smile made her stomach do a pleasant little flip. It always did.

"Thanks. I'm glad you think so. It feels strange being home again," Billy said. "Good, but strange. I got used to being out on the trail."

"I know what you mean. I am not used to cooking on a stove, but I will get used to it," she assured him.

"You're a smart woman, Nina, so I'm sure you will," he said.

Someone knocked on the kitchen door, making both of them jump. Nina ran back to their bedroom since she wasn't dressed to receive company. Billy had put on a pair of pants and it didn't matter that he didn't have a shirt on. He opened the door to find Win standing on their back porch.

"Good morning," he said. "I know it's early, but I have a vet emergency to go take care of. Can you watch Sugar for me?"

Billy said, "Sure. No problem." He whistled and the burro walked into the kitchen.

Win hollered, "Hi, Nina!"

She yelled back, "Hi, Win!"

Win chuckled and said, "I'll be back for her when I can."

"Ok. Don't worry about it," Billy said.

Win left and Nina came out of the bedroom.

Billy rubbed Sugar's neck and said, "Sugar, this is my wife, Nina. Nina, this is my good friend, Sugar."

Nina grinned. "She is very cute." She held out a hand to Sugar so she could get her scent.

Sugar sniffed her and decided that she approved of Nina. She moved towards Nina and butted her to be petted. Nina giggled and scratched behind her ears, amused at the little grunts Sugar made.

Billy said, "Looks like you've been accepted into the club."

Sugar put her nose in the air and began sniffing.

"No. No coffee for you," he said. "Win will kill me."

Nina said, "She drinks coffee?"

"There's not too much she won't eat or drink. Every so often, Lucky gets her drunk, which really makes Win mad," Billy said.

Nina laughed. "I want to see that."

"I'm sure you will. Let's go shopping and then I better open the store. Back to the real world," Billy said.

Nina nodded, gave Sugar a final pat, and then went to get dressed.

Shopping in the Echo Canyon General Store with Nina was a very entertaining experience for Billy. She was fascinated with everything and asked him all kinds of questions. They bought a bunch of baking supplies and fresh food. They would go out to the sheep farm and get some goat's milk, too. Billy always got cow's milk from the Tafts' two cows since they always had plenty.

Billy enjoyed introducing his wife to Tansy and Reggie Temple, who owned the store.

"My goodness, aren't you a pretty little thing?" Tansy said to Nina.

"Thank you," Nina said. "Your store is very nice."

Tansy smiled. "How nice of you to say so. I can't believe you're married now, Billy."

Billy's eyes shone with love as he looked at Nina. "Me, neither. I'm a lucky man."

Nina blushed and lowered her eyes. Tansy thought they made a sweet couple. They paid for their merchandise and went back to their apartment.

After sitting their bags on the table, Nina opened cupboards and stood looking into them with a critical eye. Billy watched her, but made no offer to help. This was her domain and he wasn't going to interfere. Sugar had followed them to and from the store and now stood watching Nina, too.

Nina started putting their groceries away, moving things around until she was satisfied with their arrangement. She caught Billy watching her with a smile on his face.

"What?"

Billy said, "I just like watching you do wifely things."

Smiling, she said, "I am glad. What would you like for breakfast?"

"Do you want me to show you how to make eggs?" he asked tentatively.

"Yes. Then I can do it," she said.

Soon she saw that Billy was a fairly competent cook. He showed her how to crack the eggs into the pan and demonstrated how to flip them to finish them on the top. It looked easy enough. Then he showed her how to make toast and cooking the bacon wasn't hard. He put a plate of hot food on the table for her.

"You've made me breakfast so much, that I consider it an honor to make it for you for a change. Sit and eat before it gets cold," he said.

She smiled and kissed him. "Thank you." It was a strange thing to eat before him as well as not to have cooked the food. She thought it was very nice. "Mmm. You are a good cook."

"Thanks. I do all right," he said.

He finished making his food and sat down. Sugar moved closer, her ears pricked forward. Without being asked to, she sat down on her haunches, making them laugh.

"What is she doing?" Nina asked.

Billy said, "She thinks she's a dog. She's begging." He tore off a small piece of toast and gave it to Sugar.

The burro gently took it and chewed it happily, her ears twitching this way and that. They laughed at her and Nina fed her a piece of toast, too. Once breakfast was over and the dishes cleaned up, Billy and Nina went out to open the store.

"Nina, I have to go to the post office," Billy said. "I'll bet I have a ton of mail since I was gone so long. Are you all right staying here to mind the store while I go?"

She nodded. "Yes. I will be fine. Go." She would keep Sugar with her.

He smiled and kissed her cheek. "I won't be long."

As he ran down the street and crossed over to the post office, Billy waved at people who welcomed him home and responded to them. Some called out congratulations to him, too. Going in the post office, Billy went up to the counter.

"Hi, Ian. Good to see you," he said.

Ian held out a hand to him and they shook hands. "Good to see you, too. Congratulations on your marriage. That's not how you planned it, though."

Billy chuckled. "No, but I couldn't be happier."

Ian turned around and took a box from a shelf. "I saved all your mail for you. That should keep you busy."

Billy's eyes rounded as he saw how full the box was. "Dang! Look at all that. Yep. That'll take some time to get through. Well, I better get back. Nina's minding the store so I don't want to leave her for too long."

Ian's face took on a displeased expression as he looked beyond Billy. Billy turned around and started a little to find he now faced the man he knew had to be Marvin's twin. He hadn't met him the night before since he'd been over at his parents' house when Shadow had gone to talk to Evan.

Billy looked him over. Unlike Marvin, he wore casual attire of jeans, a black button down shirt, and a black sack coat overtop of it. He also wore a black cowboy hat and tinted glasses. He was Billy's height, but broader in the shoulders. His facial features were an exact replica of Marvin's. Billy hated him on sight.

Shadow saw the anger in Billy's dark eyes and smiled. "Mr. Two Moons, it's nice to make your acquaintance." He didn't bother holding a hand out to Billy because he knew that no handshake would ensue if he did.

Billy's eyes narrowed as they roamed over Shadow. He was familiar somehow and then it hit him—this was the man who'd dislocated his shoulder last June. Billy's right fist shot out, catching Shadow completely off guard. The blow landed squarely on his jaw and he staggered backwards a little. Billy followed up with a left to Shadow's stomach and he grunted from the force of the punch.

By then, Shadow's fighting instincts kicked in and he started fighting back, but mainly to block Billy's blows. He didn't want to hurt Billy for several reasons, but he wasn't going to just let himself be beaten up while Billy exacted his revenge. Billy could tell what Shadow was doing and it made him more furious. He hit harder and faster and got punches past Shadow's blocks.

Ian had run to get Evan and was glad to find the sheriff at the general store. Evan came on the run and hollered to Ian to keep people out of the post office. Entering he saw the battle taking place in the small space.

"Hey! Knock it off!" he yelled. He pointed at Shadow. "Stop!" he said as he got in between the two men.

Billy was still throwing punches and a couple caught Evan on the shoulder before he could ram Billy back against the wall.

"Billy! Stop! Quit it!" he shouted.

Dark fire burned in Billy's eyes. "He's the one I fought in the woods last year. I owe him!"

Evan looked at Shadow. "Is that true?"

Shadow wiped blood from his lip with the back of one hand and nodded. "Yes. It was me. I like the sheep and I used to go at night to see them since I can't during the day. Of course, I couldn't let anyone know I was there anyway, so when …" He trailed off into laughter for a moment. "When the burro attacked me, I ran so I wasn't found out. Mr. Quinn is very accurate with his bow and arrows. You'll be happy to know that I almost died from that arrow."

"I wish you would have!" Billy said between clenched teeth. "It would have served you right. What are you going to do about this?" he asked Evan. "I want to bring charges."

Shadow smiled a little as he looked at Evan. "I do believe we have an agreement."

Evan seethed. He wanted justice for Billy, but his hands were tied because of the document they'd drawn up.

"What's he talking about?" Billy asked.

Shadow said, "Mr. Two Moons, I would think twice about pressing charges against me because I have some that I could press against you and your business partners."

Billy asked, "What do you mean?"

"Oh, I think you know. I'm an excellent tracker. Does that give you a clue?" Shadow countered.

Billy knew that he was talking about them bringing the sheep through Creasy's Pass and running them through Marvin's land to cut their traveling time to the sheep farm in half. Shadow had him there.

"Fine," Billy said. "Neither of us presses charges. Agreed?"

Shadow extended his hand to Billy and smiled. "Agreed. I'll even let you assaulting an officer of the law slide as a gesture of goodwill."

Billy glared at Evan and said, "You're a witness to this agreement." He shook Shadow's hand with a crushing grip and then let it go. "Nice deputy you hired, Sheriff," he said with a smirk and left the post office.

Evan sighed. "How many things am I going to find you responsible for?"

"Nothing else," Shadow said. "I don't blame him for being angry. I would have most likely done the same thing. His fighting skills have greatly improved."

Evan didn't comment on that. "Go back to the office and finish that report. I want it done by the time I get back."

Shadow frowned. "I didn't realize that paperwork was going to be involved."

"I keep records of everything. Get used to it," Evan said and left the building.

Letting out a low growl of annoyance, Shadow also left, heading to the office to do as his boss had directed.

# Chapter Nineteen

"Is Evan daft?" Lucky asked Billy that night out at the farm.

Billy had taken Nina to show it to her and they sat outside around a fire where Lucky had made a pot of ham and bean soup. Win and Erin had joined them for the meal.

Billy finished the big mouthful of soup he'd taken and said, "I don't know, but I've never been mad at Evan before. I could kill him for hiring that…freak!"

Nina had never seen Billy this angry before, not even when they'd been forced to marry, and it was upsetting to her. He'd been unable to speak that morning when he'd gotten back from the post office. He'd walked in the store and had just paced, a black expression on his face. Nina hadn't said anything to him, figuring it was best to just leave him be. It had taken a while, but he'd eventually calmed down and told her what had happened.

Erin said, "I don't understand why he did it, either. Why would he do that?"

Win barely looked up from his soup bowl as he said, "Evan's got something up his sleeve. Trust me. Evan doesn't do anything without thinking it through and you all should know that. Besides, I'm sure Thad is in on it, too. You know that he and Evan work on this sort of stuff together."

Lucky said, "That's true, but what reason could he possibly have for hiring a monster like that?"

Erin said, "To be fair, Shadow is a product of what his father made him. He's only had Marvin to model himself after."

"So that excuses him for hurting me? Killing people?" Billy asked.

"I didn't say that," Erin rejoined.

Wild Wind, who had finished eating and now reclined back on his hands said, "You should not fight with each other over this. I do not know Evan or this Shadow, but in our culture when a captive is taken, we sway them over to our way of thinking by showing them kindness and respect until they become one of us. If I were Evan, this is what I would do. I would make Shadow like me and begin to be loyal to me so that he would choose me over his brother at a later date."

Erin looked at him. "You take captives?"

The brave nodded. "It is rare, but the Cheyenne sometimes did. Mostly they took orphaned children to raise in our culture."

Lucky said, "That's a possibility. I didn't think of that."

"It sounds like something Evan would do," Win said. "Let's not forget that Evan is really good at not giving away his motives until the time is right and by then, it's too late for his prey to escape. He's done it time and again since I've known him and Thad says he's cultivated that skill ever since his family was killed. He did help catch his family's murderers, after all, and he was only sixteen at the time."

Billy couldn't refute Win's statement. He sighed and let his anger at Evan subside. "You're right. There has to be a reason. We'll just have to trust Evan about it all, I guess." He smiled. "Boy, it felt great hitting him. I just wish he'd have fought back more. I tried to get him to, but he wouldn't and then Evan broke us up before I could make him."

Win smiled. "I'd have liked to have seen that."

Nina said, "There are two men coming."

They looked and a couple of them groaned upon seeing the brothers Earnest heading their way.

"By all that's holy, what do they want?" Lucky asked.

"I guess we're about to find out," Erin replied.

The brothers smiled as they saw their dismayed expressions.

"Good evening," Marvin said as they drew near.

"What do ya want?" Lucky demanded.

"Do you mind if I sit?" Marvin asked.

Win said, "We do, but you will anyway."

Shadow laughed. "They know you well, Marvin."

"So they do." Marvin sat and said, "I've come to discuss a business arrangement with you all."

Billy said, "We don't want to do any kind of business with you, so you're wasting your breath."

Shadow sat down close to Billy just to annoy him. "Well, actually, I think you'll want to hear this."

Billy wanted to gouge his eyes out with the spoon around which his hand was clamped. "The only thing I want to hear is the sound of the last breath you ever take."

The atmosphere around the fire became tense as Marvin and Shadow looked at each other. Marvin's mouth twitched and a snort of laughter escaped Shadow. The others looked on in disbelief as the twins rapidly dissolved into fits of mirth.

Marvin said, "I'm sorry, Shadow, but that was funny."

"No offense taken," Shadow said.

Lucky felt a shiver go down his spine. Their voices were so similar that it was like hearing someone talk to themselves and it gave him an eerie sensation inside.

"Well, now that the amusement is over, let's get down to business," Marvin said. "You have illegally moved livestock over my property and I felt it only right to let you know that I intend to press charges."

"What?" Billy yelled, looking at Shadow. "I thought we had an agreement!"

Shadow frowned a little. "We did. You and *I* do."

"Then what the hell is this?" Billy demanded.

Marvin said, "The problem is that Shadow isn't on the deed of the property because he doesn't exist. He holds no interest in our holdings or anything else. So he doesn't have the authority to enter into any such agreement. He didn't realize this, though, because he doesn't ever handle business matters, so he's not at fault. In the eyes of the law, I am the sole owner of our ranch. Therefore, you have no such agreement with me."

Lucky didn't want to upset Otto, who had come running over to him with one of the lambs, so he calmly asked, "What is it that ya want?"

Marvin said, "I'm willing, for a certain amount every year, to grant you a right-of-way easement through my property so that you can continue to bring your livestock to the farm."

Lucky fixed a suspicious stare on him. "And why would ya be willin' to do that?"

Marvin smiled at Otto. "He's a beautiful boy. Congratulations."

"Thanks. Now answer my question," Lucky said.

"Because it's beneficial to all of us," Marvin said. "I make some money and you have a quicker way to get your animals here."

"How much money do you want each year?" Billy asked.

"Well, actually, I don't want it in money," Marvin said. "I'd like it in livestock."

Erin asked, "Why would you want it in livestock?"

Win said, "Because he wants to put us out of business, that's why. If we give him livestock, he can breed it and make money from it the same way we do."

"And he knows he's gonna get quality stock because that's all we breed," Lucky said. "Very shrewd, Earnest."

Marvin smiled. "Although I appreciate the dubious compliment, I don't want to put you out of business. I know nothing about raising sheep, but you do. You have a lot of land, but eventually you're going to run out of it at the rate you're growing. You're going to need more land and more buildings to house your animals, I'm assuming. Am I correct?"

Lucky crossed his arms over his chest. "Aye. Ya are, but we can get more land."

"Oh? From where?" Marvin asked.

Lucky didn't like the predatory smile that curved Marvin's mouth. "Why would I tell ya that? I might be Irish, but I'm not dumb."

"I know that you're a very intelligent man, Mr. Quinn," Marvin said. "However, if you're planning on buying the Stratton's homestead, you're too late. I've already done so."

Lucky laughed hard at him. "And you're thinkin' about puttin' sheep on that land? Yer the one who's stupid."

"Oh no, not sheep. I do know that it's not appropriate for livestock. It would be good for growing hay, which is what I plan on doing," Marvin said. "You wouldn't have bought it for the sheep farm, either. Only because it's the only alternate way to go once you're through Creasy's Pass without having to use my land. However, now it's *all* my land. It's too bad you didn't have the funds to do it before I did."

Lucky was unperturbed, which seemed odd to Marvin. He'd just backed him into a corner and yet the Irishman only smiled at him. "That's nice for ya, but ya see, we don't need to buy any more land. We've got all we'll ever need. Now, back to the livestock. I don't understand where you're goin' with that."

Marvin said, "I would like to start my own herd, but not for meat. I want to get more into the wool production part of the business. So, you give me forty quality animals every year and you can keep coming through my land. I also won't press charges."

Lucky said, "I'll tell ya what. We'll confer about this and set up a meeting with lawyers if we can agree. Everything will be in writing so there's no misunderstandin' later on."

"Very well. Think carefully about it," Marvin said, rising. "Good evening, everyone."

Shadow also got up and smiled at them before leaving with Marvin.

Once they were gone, Win said, "Ok, Irish, where's all this land that we have?"

Lucky grinned and said, "Well, I was waitin' until the right time, but I guess that's now. See, I own another parcel of land besides this one. It's on the other side of Earnest's."

Billy asked, "You mean the old Mercer ranch? That's a big spread, Lucky. When did you buy that?"

"At the same time that old gent that sold me this land."

Win asked, "Who did you buy this land from?"

"Well, I believe ya know him as Darcy Fairchild," Lucky said.

"Fairchild? You ran into Fairchild in Colorado?" Win asked.

"Aye. If ya know him, ya know how much he hated Old Man Earnest, and he wasn't none too fond of this Earnest, neither. He was dyin' and he just wanted to get rid of the land, but he only wanted to sell it to someone who would make trouble for Earnest. I told him that I would do my best and since no one else had agreed, he sold this piece to me—the Mercer place, too. Now, since I hold the deed to the Mercer place, I can do anything with it I want to, including diverting the one and only stream that runs through the Earnest ranch. If we cut off their water, their ranch is worthless."

Billy let out a whoop and jumped to his feet. He ran over to Lucky and hugged him. "No wonder I love you! I can't wait to see his face! *Their* faces! Whooo!" He danced around a little. Otto laughed and started dancing with him.

Everyone else laughed, too.

Erin asked, "Is there any other land you own?"

Lucky shook his head. "There isn't. But that's all the land we need to raise good quality sheep and goats."

Billy picked up Otto and said in Cheyenne, "Your father is a very smart man, Otto. Did you know that?"

Otto smiled and said, "Yes. He is smart."

Lucky laughed and translated for Erin and Win. "We'll see about that," he said. "Now look, we can't act any different around them when we see them this week. Don't be smug, and don't tell Travis or Ross yet. Not until after we finalize a deal with Marvin. They don't ever press charges and we get an easement. In return we don't cut off their water supply. That's the deal we'll make."

Erin said, "That's brilliant."

Lucky's face grew a little warm. "All right, now. Go on with ya."

She crawled over to him and hugged him. "I missed you so much! It's so good to have you home and hear that Irish lilt again and see those smiling eyes!"

Lucky laughed and hugged her back. "Well, I missed ya, too, lass. It's good to be back home with all of ye."

Erin kissed his cheek and then went back to sit beside Win.

Smiling, Win said, "It's a good thing I'm not the jealous type."

She chuckled and hugged him, whispering something in his ear. Win's smile got bigger and he stood up. Grasping Erin's hand, he pulled her up. "Well, folks, it's time for us to turn in now. Have a nice night, everyone."

"Goodnight," Erin said.

Then the couple started running for their cabin, laughter trailing behind them.

Wild Wind and Nina looked a little perplexed. Billy and Lucky laughed.

"You'll get used to it," Lucky said. "We keep expectin' Erin to come up pregnant, but she hasn't yet."

Billy added, "It ain't for lack of trying."

"That's right," Lucky said. "Well, there's a little fella I better be gettin' off to bed, too."

Billy kissed Otto and set him down. "Goodnight, kid."

Otto smiled and said, "'Night."

Holding out a hand to Nina, Billy said, "I guess we'd better go home, too."

She let him pull her up and went to hug Otto goodnight and then bid farewell to Lucky and Wild Wind.

Nina wanted to cry. It had started out as such a good morning. Billy had woken very early by a dream he'd had about a painting. That sometimes happened to him. Now his creative juices wouldn't let him alone. He hadn't meant to wake Nina up, but he couldn't keep his hands off her and they'd made love. Nina liked knowing that he desired her so much because she felt the same way about him.

He'd told her to go back to sleep then and he'd gone upstairs to his studio to paint. She'd slept for a while and then got up and dressed. After that it all went downhill. Billy had made cooking eggs seem so easy, but it wasn't. She wasn't used to using a spatula and when she'd tried to flip the eggs over, the yolks had broken, the yellow liquid running all over the pan.

She'd tried several times, but with the same result. If she couldn't even cook eggs, how was she going to make more difficult dishes? Being a good wife was all she knew how to do and a big part of that was making meals. Becoming angry, she hurled the spatula into the sink and slid the pan to the back of the stove to cool down.

Billy came into the kitchen. He'd smelled the coffee and had come down for some. He smiled until he saw that she was upset. "What's wrong?"

She pointed at the pan. "That is wrong. I cannot cook them right."

Billy looked at the mangled eggs and barely stopped the smile that threatened. "Well, flipping eggs can be tricky. If that happens, you just make scrambled eggs, that's all."

"Scrambled?"

Billy picked up the pan and scraped the ruined eggs from it into a can that he would take to his parents' house and feed to his red-tick coonhound, Homer. "I'll show you."

She crossed her arms over her chest. "I should not have to be shown how to cook by my husband."

"Honey, you're not used to cooking the way we do. It's going to take some time, but you'll catch on quick. You're smart and a great cook. I know you can do this."

His confidence in her made her feel better. "I am glad you think so."

"I do. Ok. Ready for your lesson, Mrs. Two Moons?"

Nina loved it when he called her that. "Yes, husband."

Billy walked her through making scrambled eggs, which seemed easier than making them over-easy. She enjoyed watching his quick hand movements as he broke the eggs up with the spatula. From head to toe, Billy was handsome, but there was something about his hands that always drew her attention. He gestured gracefully whenever he talked and she couldn't keep her eyes off him whenever he was drawing. She hadn't seen him paint yet, but she was sure that it would be equally as fascinating.

They sat down to eat and Nina enjoyed the light, fluffy eggs.

"You are going to spoil me," she said in Cheyenne.

Billy said, "Some husbands in my culture do that with their wives. There is nothing wrong with it. I want to show you that I appreciate you."

"Thank you."

They heard someone come up onto the porch and there was a knock on their door.

"Come in!" Billy called.

The door opened a few inches and a white handkerchief was waved through the opening.

"I surrender," Evan said.

Billy and Nina laughed.

"Get in here, Sheriff," Billy said.

Evan came in, tucking his handkerchief away. "I wanted to make sure I was welcome after yesterday."

"Yeah, you're welcome," Billy said. "Sorry about that. Not about hitting Shadow, but being sarcastic with you."

Evan pulled the other kitchen chair out and turned it around, straddling it. "It's ok. I understand why you were mad. I didn't know he was the guy you fought with."

160

"It's not your fault. You're not a mind reader, so how would you have known?"

"Thanks. How did you know it was him?" Evan asked.

Billy said, "I recognized his shape and his hair. It must be because I'm an artist and I pay close attention to stuff like that."

"You've always had an excellent eye that way," Evan said and then smiled at Nina. "Is he treating you right?"

She nodded. "Yes. He made me breakfast yesterday and today. He is spoiling me."

"Good. You're newlyweds. He better spoil you," he replied with a wink.

Nina blushed and laughed. "He is a good husband. Is Josie busy today?"

"Nope. She doesn't have anywhere to clean today and she's caught up on her sewing jobs," Evan said.

"Do you think she would mind if I went to visit today?" Nina asked, shyly.

"No. She wouldn't mind a bit," Evan said.

"Ok. Thank you." She began clearing off the table. "I will wash these since you cooked," she said to Billy.

"Yes, ma'am," he said.

Evan smiled at the way Billy's eyes avidly followed Nina's movements. Who could blame him? Nina was a very beautiful girl. It was hard for Evan to believe that she'd already been married even though she must only be eighteen or nineteen. Of course some women in his culture were considered ancient if they weren't married by the time they were twenty-three, so he supposed it wasn't much different.

He shook himself out of his musings to say, "I know you don't like Shadow because of what happened between you two and because he's Marvin's brother. I know what I'm doing, though."

Billy rubbed his hands together. "Giving him enough rope to hang himself, right? You're just waiting for him to do something illegal and then wham! You'll put his ass in the clink, right?"

Evan said, "Well, not exactly."

"What do you mean? He's a criminal and you know it. Everyone knows it. I sure as heck know it. Marvin's the snake that made him or they were made together or whatever. I say cut their heads off and all the snakes will be dead!"

Evan and Nina laughed at him.

"While that's tempting, it won't do Echo any good in the long run," Evan said.

Billy groaned and put his head down on the table. "I'm not gonna like this, am I?"

"Just listen to me. The fact of the matter is that we need Marvin and Shadow, at least for the time being."

"Why do we need them?" Billy asked, raising his head again.

"It's the whole necessary evil thing. Marvin employs nine people who have families countin' on them to bring home money to pay for food and such. If I send Marvin to jail right now, those nine families are gonna be hard pressed to survive. You know that jobs are still scarce around here."

"I know," Billy said. "So why do you need Shadow?"

"I have a hunch about him that he's not quite like Marvin. They stick together, but if Shadow becomes friends with some other people besides Marvin, is he gonna be as loyal to him? He's a hell of a deputy, by the way. People are scared to death of him and that suits me just fine. He's the loose cannon and I'm the voice of reason, and I can control him. Which leads me to the favor I need from you."

Billy had a sinking sensation in his stomach as he looked into Evan's green eyes. "What favor?"

Evan pursed his lips a little and then said, "I need you to bury the hatchet with Shadow and warm up to him."

"What? No!" Billy's dark eyes brightened with anger. "I'm not gonna become his buddy! He's a murderer and God only knows what else he's done!"

"I know that, Billy," Evan replied. "Listen to me. I watched him with

Bree when she came in to visit him. There's good in the man." When Billy let out a sarcastic noise, Evan said, "No, there is! I know what he's done, but I also saw him cower in fear whenever I even tried to close the cell door on him. Imagine if you'd been locked up for the first sixteen years of your life. No light, barely any food, rags for clothing, Billy. Beatings, emotional abuse. He never knew a moment of kindness until Marvin found him. But if he's welcomed by other people and shown that he's been doing wrong to good people, I know we can turn him on Marvin, and once we do, we can control him."

Nina didn't like to interfere in men's business, but she could see the sense in what Evan was saying. She finished the dishes and sat down at the table. In Cheyenne she said, "I know that this is not a thing women usually discuss, husband, but you are a warrior and warriors use any weapon they can to defeat the enemy. As you know, part of defeating an enemy is not letting your anger cloud your judgment. Affecting your enemy's mind is also useful. If you can change Shadow by making him your friend, think of how much easier it will be to defeat Marvin later on."

Billy sighed. "What you say makes sense, but there is also the problem of these charges Marvin will bring against us. If he does, Evan will be forced to lock us up or Marvin will sue us and put us out of business."

"I do not understand all of this about the land because we have never 'owned' land. It is for everyone. What does it matter that you took some sheep across it?" She shrugged.

"I wish it were that simple, wife," Billy said and then fell silent.

Evan had no idea what they'd said to each other. It was a little annoying. "Will you do it? Will you help me with this?" he asked.

Billy nodded slowly. "Yeah. I'll do it."

Evan patted his shoulder. "Thanks. I knew I could count on you. I'm off to begin my part of it, too. You're not the only one who has to do this. I just keep tellin' myself it's for the good of the town. Think about Jimmy and Amy."

Billy frowned at the mention of the little boy and girl his parents had adopted after their mother had been murdered by their father. From that terrible night forward, Jimmy and Amy Patterson had come to stay with them and had never left. They'd become Billy's siblings and he didn't want them to grow up and be forced to leave their home because there weren't enough jobs. Worse yet, he didn't want Echo to die because the economy had worsened.

So far, their mail-order bride idea was working out. Even though he had married Nina, Callie was still staying in Echo because she and Ross had taken a shine to one another. He'd brought two women to Echo in one fell swoop. Thanks to Win, Echo now had a doctor. If Win was willing to marry a woman sight unseen, shouldn't he be willing to put aside his own selfish anger and do what was best for the greater good?

"You're right," he said with conviction. "Don't worry. I'm gonna make him like me and maybe gain his confidence. Slowly. I don't want to tip him off."

"Right. Ok. Well, I'll get out of your hair now so you can open the store," Evan said. "I really appreciate this. I owe you, so no matter if Marvin does try bringing trespassing charges against you, I won't arrest any of you. You'll just have to pay a fine."

"How did you know?" Billy asked.

Evan gave him a smile. "I'm not sheriff for nothing, Billy. This is my town. Besides, it was a dead giveaway the night you all kicked me out of the house when Lucky first told us about your plans, remember?"

Billy laughed. "You really are sneaky, you know that? Thanks. I appreciate it."

Evan smiled, kissed Nina's cheek and left. Nina wasn't used to men kissing her and she didn't know how Billy would feel about it.

"I am sorry," she said, looking at the floor.

Billy's brow furrowed. "Why?"

"I did not know that he was going to do that," she said.

"You mean kiss your cheek?"

She nodded.

Billy said, "Nina, it's ok. There's nothing wrong with that among friends. I don't mind."

Looking at him, she said, "I did not know what to think last night when Erin hugged Lucky like that."

"It doesn't mean anything. Now if you kissed anyone else the way you kiss me, then it would be a problem, but a friendly kiss is different," Billy said.

Nina's expression was startled. "I would never kiss any other man the way I do you."

Billy took her hand and said, "I know that. I never thought you would. I'll always be faithful to you, too. I promise. Besides, you're the only woman I love. No one else."

His eyes lowered to her mouth. All this talk about kissing made him want to do that very much. Leaning over he pressed a brief kiss to her lips and pulled back again. The hunger he felt for her was amazing considering the passion they'd shared not long ago. He saw the same feeling in her eyes, but he made himself stand up. He had a store to run and she had things to do, too.

"I'm gonna go open the store. Let me know when you get back, ok?" Billy said.

Nina smiled and nodded, but didn't move.

"What's the matter?"

"I need to go to the store."

"Oh. Ok. Are you nervous about going by yourself?" he asked.

Nina sighed. "No. I need money."

Billy chuckled. "Yeah, I guess that would be helpful."

He bent down and flipped back the rug in the center of the floor. He pulled up the board he hid his moneybox under and took it out of its hiding place. Then he put the board and rug back.

"That's where our money is, so when you need some, just get it out of here. Do you remember how to count it?" he asked.

"Yes," she said softly.

Billy could tell she was uncomfortable about taking the money.

"Nina, this is no different than me bringing game home for the family. It's my job to make money for us, just like it's my job to hunt so we can eat and to protect us. It's just a different way to do it, ok?"

"Are you sure?" she asked.

"Positive," he said, counting out some bills for her. "I don't know what you're buying, so take this so you have enough."

Nina took it and put it in her little pouch she used for such things. "It is a surprise," she told him with an impish smile.

"A surprise, huh? I like the sound of that," he said.

Her confidence had returned with his explanation. "You are not to come in the kitchen after …" She wasn't used to telling time by a clock, but Billy had taught her to read his watch. "Three o'clock. I will be busy."

Billy smiled. "Yes, ma'am. I'll make sure not to come in here and bug you after that time, ok?"

"Ok. Now, go get to work and make us more money," she teased him.

He saluted her. "Yes, ma'am!" Then he pressed a firm kiss to her lips and went into the shop.

Nina felt almost giddy as she walked through the shop, gave Billy a little wave, and left.

Billy watched her walk up the street as far as he could see her. He'd never wanted a woman the way he did Nina. He might not have planned to marry her, but he was no longer sorry that he had. She was sweet, funny, fierce, beautiful, and a great wife. He was eager for them to have a baby and he hoped Nina would conceive soon.

"I can't wait to have some little Two Moons running around," he murmured to himself. Then he got to work on an order for painting supplies. As he worked, he smiled, his thoughts repeatedly turning to his wife.

# Chapter Twenty

Josie and Edna were very happy that Nina came to visit them that morning.

"How are you settling in?" Edna asked.

Nina smiled. "Very good. Billy is a great husband, and his art is so beautiful. It is strange living in a house, but I am getting used to it."

Edna smiled. "Good. Billy is a good boy and I'm glad to see that he makes you happy."

"He does. He appreciates me," she said enunciating the word slowly. "He made breakfast yesterday and today. I am not used to a man cooking for me. My first husband never did anything like that. He was not a nice man. He was always drunk and mean."

Josie bounced Julia on her lap. "I'm so sorry, Nina. How awful for you."

Nina said, "He drank himself to death. I was happy to be rid of him. That sounds mean, but I cannot help how I feel."

Edna harrumphed. "I'd be glad to be rid of him, too."

Nina said, "I am glad you do not think less of me."

"Of course not," Josie said. "Who could blame you?"

Nina was quiet a moment and then asked, "Will you show me how to make some food for Billy? I have never cooked with a stove and I do not know what I am doing."

Josie's eyes lit up. She loved cooking. "I'd love to teach you and I can copy down some recipes for you."

"Thank you so much," Nina said.

Josie gave Julia to Edna and said, "Ok, Mrs. Two Moons, let's go to work."

Nina laughed and followed Josie to the kitchen.

Nina's cooking lesson with Josie and Edna was fun and informative. She caught on to using the stove fairly well and she felt better about her ability to cook for Billy now. Armed with recipes, she bid the Taft women goodbye and walked to the Temples' store. She hummed to herself a little as she picked out some spices she needed and some canned vegetables. On a whim, she picked up other items and took them up to the counter.

Tansy wasn't there right away, but Nina didn't mind. She just looked at some other things.

"Well, hello, sweetheart," a male voice said.

Nina looked up and saw a man leering at her. She didn't respond. Instead, she went back over to the counter to wait for Tansy. The man followed her, though.

"You're that sweet thing Billy married, aren't you?" he asked. "A white girl raised as an Indian. Perfect for an Indian raised as a white man, don't you think?"

Nina's chin rose. "Billy is a good man and I am proud to be his wife."

"That's very touching." He moved closer and reached towards her hair.

Nina flinched away from him. "Leave me alone and do not touch me."

"Aw, c'mon. I'm just being friendly," he said, smiling.

Looking into his brown eyes, Nina said, "You are being a … jerk! Do not touch me. My husband will make you sorry for bothering me."

Her insult angered him. "Look here, you filthy Indian slave—"

Nina started when strong hands grasped her upper arms and she was moved to the side. The man's eyes bugged out and he backed up. However, he wasn't fast enough and Nina saw Shadow close in on the man in a flash. He grabbed the man's coat and shook him hard.

"You will never disrespect this woman or any other again. If I find out that you have, I won't be so lenient. Now, get out of here and remember what I've said," Shadow said.

"Yeah. Sure." The man nodded his head vigorously.

Shadow gave him a rough push and released him. He stumbled and then fled out the door.

"Are you all right?" Shadow asked Nina.

Nina said, "Yes. Thank you."

He gave her a little smile and said, "Good. Have a good day and give my regards to your husband."

"I will," she said. He was wearing his tinted glasses and it was disconcerting not to be able to see his eyes.

He nodded went on his way. Tansy had come up to the counter while she'd been talking to Shadow, but she hadn't interrupted.

"Hi, Nina. I'm sorry I was so long in the back. I'm so sorry about that. I'm glad that Shadow was here to help you," Tansy said with a little shiver. "I don't like him any better than I do his brother, but I guess he's not going away, so … Anyway, was there anything else you needed?"

"No, thank you," Nina said. "It is not your fault. I knew that there would be some people who would not like me."

Tansy tsked as she rang up Nina's order. "Well, it's just not right." She gave Nina her total.

Nina concentrated on counting out the right amount of money and was proud that Tansy didn't have to correct her. She wanted to be able to do things on her own. Then she took her groceries and headed home.

"Well, there comes Mayhem," Evan said when Shadow entered the sheriff's office that afternoon. "What kind of trouble have you been causing?"

Shadow smiled and took off his hat. Bree had said he'd look good in one and she'd been right. She liked him in it so much that usually when he got home, she attacked him because she said he looked so virile. Since the first time they'd made love, she'd become bolder about her desire for him and it was incredibly exciting to see her inhibitions fading.

He smiled at Evan. "Nothing much yet. I helped Nina at the store when she was being harassed by a very nasty man. I made him see that such behavior won't be tolerated."

"Is she ok?" Evan asked. The thought of someone being mean to Nina made him angry.

"Yes," Shadow said as he sat down. "I made sure of that before leaving."

"Good. Now, before I forget, my aunt is summoning you and Bree to dinner tomorrow night. There's no sense refusing, either," Evan said.

Shadow leaned back in his chair a little as he considered this. "I can understand you pressing me into service, but why would want me as a guest in your home when you hate my brother?"

Evan said, "Because you're not your brother. I would never ask Marvin to dinner, but you're your own person."

"But I'm a murderer, among other things."

Evan shrugged. "I've killed a few people in my time."

"Yes, but that was for the right reasons," Shadow said.

"I'd call killing the man who was hurting Bree the right reason," Evan said.

Shadow straightened up a little. "You know about that?"

Evan smiled. "I'm good at putting two-and-two together even when it seems like they won't add up. Other people sometimes think I'm crazy for the way I think, but I guess I just see things from a different angle than most. That's how I found you, by thinking differently and speculating about some things."

Shadow smiled. "I'm impressed. You're craftier than people give you credit for."

"That's something you need to remember," Evan said. "I've always thought that Bree was the woman whose prints Billy and Lucky found. Those idiots, who were with the man you killed, left a clear trail back to the place near your secret entrance. Her appearance was right around the same time. Granted, Marvin didn't introduce her around until a month later, but I couldn't shake the feeling that she was the same woman."

"You're a very smart man," Shadow said. "Which is why Marvin needed to keep you and everyone else away so that I wasn't found. If Bree hadn't run in that direction that night, you would likely have never discovered me."

"That's possible. Would you rather have remained unknown? You've been out and about now for a couple of weeks. How do you feel about it?"

"I find it interesting and amusing. It's entertaining to watch people's reactions to me," Shadow replied.

"You enjoy intimidating people, don't you?" Evan asked.

Shadow smiled broadly. "Yes, I do. I guess it's because I was intimidated for so long that I like turning the tables on others."

"Even people who've never done anything to you?" Evan asked.

"It depends on the situation. Take the Burgundy House. I've had a very good time making sure that things are improving there and yet those people have never done anything to me personally," Shadow responded.

"True. What about around town?"

"Yes, I do, but only to a certain extent. It's amusing when I make them uncomfortable, but I don't do anything to cause it. They react to me that way because of their feelings about Marvin, not because of anything *I've* done to them."

Evan said, "I know and I'm sorry about that. You shouldn't be judged because of your brother, but you've done a lot of rotten stuff around Echo and if they knew—"

"They would come after the monster and burn me at the stake like a witch," Shadow said with a smile. "Why haven't you told anyone the real story about me?"

Evan said, "Because I think it's your own private business and no one else needs to know about it."

"So you're being loyal to me," Shadow said, perplexed. "Why would you when you know who and what I am?"

"It's called a sense of decency," Evan said. "Most people are taught it from the time they're little. You weren't. I'm not going to get all sappy on you, but I think there's a lot more to you than you've had a chance to discover. From the moment Marvin found you, you've spent your life making sure no one found you. What are you going to do now that you aren't preoccupied with causing trouble and staying hidden?"

Shadow pondered Evan's words. "Do you mean that I need to find a purpose? I have one. I'm now allowed to cause trouble for those who deserve it and I have a badge proving that I have such permission."

Evan laughed at Shadow's skewed view on his job. It was so funny that every time he tried to respond to Shadow's statement, he started laughing again. He was finally able to speak.

"Sorry about that, but the actual function of law enforcement is to protect the citizens of whatever town or city you live in. It's not to cause trouble for people," Evan said.

Shadow chuckled. "Well, if my trouble-making helps do that, so be it, but I guess we have a different outlook on it."

"I guess we do. Why did you help Nina today?"

"Because it was the right thing to do." Shadow stopped talking when he realized what he'd just said.

"Why did you help Bree and not kill her?"

Shadow growled and the sound made Evan uncomfortable. He showed no fear, however.

"You're trying to make me something I'm not," Shadow said.

Evan pressed his advantage just a little bit. "Shadow, you don't know *what* you are because you've never had the chance to find out. First you were controlled by your father and then Marvin told you what you were supposed to do. You've been guided by others for so long that you have no idea what it's like to be your own person. I think Bree was a step in the right direction there. You felt something for her, you connected with her and now look; you're in love and happy."

"You're trying to turn me against Marvin, aren't you?" Shadow asked, his temper beginning to simmer.

"No," Evan said. "I would never do that. He's your brother and you should love him. He's done a lot for you. I understand that. I'm just saying that maybe it's time for you to find out who Shadow Earnest really is instead of just accepting that he's what he's been told he is. Ok, I'm not gonna discuss that anymore. I've been in here all morning, so I'm going to go out and look around. You stay here in case anyone comes in."

Shadow's only response was a low grunt.

Evan put on his hat and coat and left Shadow to chew on all of the fodder for thought he'd given him.

# Chapter Twenty-One

Nina had everything ready by six that night. It had taken a little longer than she'd expected it to, but she didn't think she'd done too badly for it being her first time cooking in a kitchen. She was excited and nervous about serving Billy the meal. She went into the storeroom and called out into the shop from there.

"Billy, come to supper."

"Ok!" he responded.

Then she hurried back into their kitchen. Billy quickly closed the shop and entered their apartment. He was starving and whatever she was cooking smelled heavenly. He was very curious about what she'd made.

Nina stood by the stove in a soft yellow paisley dress, her hair done up in a French braid. Small pearl earrings dangled from her earlobes. She was beautiful no matter what, but there was something about seeing her in that dress with her hair in that style that made his heart start thumping in his chest. He noticed that there were two tall candles lit on the table along with a vase filled with early spring flowers.

He grinned. "You've been busy."

"Yes. I hope you like it."

In Cheyenne, he said, "By the way it smells, I am sure I will. You look very beautiful, wife."

"Thank you," she said. "Sit and I will get your food."

He sat down, watching her move around. Josie and Edna must have been teaching her and by the looks of it, she'd caught on quickly. In a few minutes, she sat a plate of roast beef, mashed potatoes, and succotash in front of him. His mouth watered as he looked at the food.

"That looks great, honey," he said.

"I hope it tastes good." Nina fixed her plate and sat down.

The roast was so tender that Billy barely had to use his knife to cut it. At first, he'd been going to put a big forkful of it in his mouth, but suddenly, he wanted to savor the first meal Nina had made for him. He modified the size of the bite and chewed slowly. The roast was savory and practically melted in his mouth.

"Nina, that roast has to be the best I've ever had and I mean that," he said.

"Are you sure?"

Billy nodded as he took another bite. "Mmm hmm."

Her relief was profound. "I am glad. I have been worried that it would be bad."

"No. Taste it. Come on and eat."

Nina did and found that she liked it. "It is good."

"Your potatoes are excellent, too. Everything is."

Nina watched him take smaller bites and eat slowly. "What is wrong?"

"Huh? What do you mean?" he asked in confusion.

"You are not eating like you usually do," she said, frowning.

He smiled. "It's so good that I wanted to slow down and enjoy it. It's the first time you've cooked like this for me and I wanted to remember it."

This made Nina so happy that tears gathered in the back of her eyes. To combat them, she smiled and said, "I am glad. I made dessert, too."

"You did? What did you make?" he asked.

With a coy look, she said, "You will see."

He chuckled and continued eating. In between bites, he told her about what had gone on at the shop and she filled him in on her day. She left out the incident at the store because she didn't want to upset him on such a nice night. Her first husband hadn't conversed much during meals and when he had it was only to request more or to criticize her cooking.

Billy was so different, though. He talked *with* her, not *at* her and made her feel worthy of his attention. He treated her as his equal, something that had never happened to her before. From the time she'd been taken as a captive, there had only been a handful of people who had treated her as anything but a captive. It bolstered her self-esteem that Billy had such high regard for her.

Billy liked seeing his wife so happy. Her animated way of speaking amused him as she told him about funny things Edna had said or how much she'd enjoyed playing with Julia and cooking with Josie. He was glad that she liked his friends and that she felt comfortable with them.

Dessert turned out to be shoofly cake, one of his favorite treats. Josie had given Nina the recipe and Billy thought it had turned out as well as any cake that either his mother or Josie had made for him. He ate two pieces in rapid succession, which made Nina feel good.

When he was replete, Billy said, "That was fantastic."

Nina asked, "Does that mean good?"

"It means far more than good," he said. "You are such a good cook. I knew you would learn cooking this way fast. You're a smart woman."

"Thank you."

For the second time that day, someone knocked on their kitchen door. A whole group crowded into the kitchen, led by Josie.

"Hi, guys! Oh! How did dinner turn out?" she asked.

Billy patted his stomach and said, "She cooks so good, I almost had to undo my pants."

Nina didn't understand that reference, but she laughed along with the others anyway.

Josie said, "We've come to get you two because we're going to Spike's and I want you to play guitar with me."

"Oh! Great! You'll like Spike's, Nina," Billy said.

"Ok," she said with an eager nod. He and Lucky had told her about the saloon and she was looking forward to going since she'd never been in one.

"I'll be right back. My guitar is upstairs," he said and ran from the kitchen.

Wild Wind had snatched a piece of roast from the serving plate. "This is very good, Nina."

"Thank you," she said.

Everyone wanted to try it and they all pronounced it excellent. Evan and Josie asked what seasonings she'd used since it tasted a little different than theirs, and they all started discussing cooking. They didn't notice when Billy came back. He watched Nina with their friends and smiled over how she scolded the men about eating all of the roast. He loved the way she laughed when Evan tickled her so she'd move away, allowing him to grab another piece of meat.

He closed the kitchen door and said, "Hey! Quit eating all our leftovers! That's my breakfast."

Evan said, "You eat roast for breakfast?"

Billy said, "Out on the trail, you eat whatever was left from the night before for breakfast. It was good enough then, so it's good enough now, too."

Nina said, "But I like your eggs for breakfast."

He rolled his eyes. "I really have spoiled you."

She laughed and said, "I told you. Now, quit complaining. I want to hear you and Josie play guitar."

Win laughed and said, "I guess she told you."

Billy grinned and said, "I guess she did. Better do as she says or she won't feed me tomorrow."

Erin helped Nina tidy up while Josie took care of the leftovers and then they got under way.

Watching Billy play guitar and hearing him sing with Josie was another magical experience for Nina. As she listened to the performers the rest of the saloon faded into the background of her consciousness. Josie and Billy's voices blended together seamlessly and their guitar playing was exceptional.

Evan happened to glance in Nina's direction and he saw how hard she was focused on Billy. He smiled because that's the way he was when he watched Josie perform. After all the heartache Billy had been through, he was happy that his young friend had found someone to love and whom loved him, too. It was clear that the young people were crazy about each other.

When the song was over, Nina clapped as enthusiastically as everyone else did. Billy smiled a little bashfully at the applause and then at her. She beamed back at him and signed to him that she loved him, which made him blush and laugh a little. Josie kidded him about it as they chose their next song and he shushed her.

They began another song and Nina felt a tap on her shoulder. She looked up into Lucky's smiling face.

"Mrs. Two Moons, may I have the pleasure of this dance?" he asked her.

"I do not know how," she said.

Lucky bent down so he could speak in a quieter voice. "That's all right. I'll show ya and then ye'll be able to dance with Billy after bit."

She nodded and stood up. Win saw what they were up to and pushed a couple of tables out of the way to give them room. Lucky was a very good dancer with natural rhythm and he was a fun, patient teacher. He made Nina laugh and she stopped being nervous after a little bit because Lucky entertained her so much.

Lucky enjoyed it as much as she did and she was a quick study. After dancing with Lucky for a couple of songs, Evan butted in and then Win took a turn with her. Billy had a good time watching his buddies teach

Nina a variety of dances. Seeing her laugh and smile made him happy and he liked that she was feeling comfortable in the new place.

When Lucky butted in the next time, he whispered something in her ear. She laughed and ran off to the bar. She went right behind it and took Spike by the wrist and tugged. At first Spike tried to resist, but Nina didn't let him. She already liked the slightly gruff older man and Lucky said that he liked to dance.

Everyone clapped when Spike came out to the dance floor with Nina. He taught her an older dance that most of the men there didn't know and she enjoyed learning it. Spike hadn't danced with a woman in a long time and it was a pleasure to do so with Nina. She laughed when she made mistakes and kept trying until she got it right. As the song finished, he bowed gallantly to her and kissed the back of her hand before going back behind the bar again.

Josie nudged Billy to go dance with his wife and he didn't need to be told twice. He took Nina in his arms and smiled at her. Her gorgeous emerald eyes smiled back at him and his heart grew a little fuller with love again. It seemed to do that every day—become filled even more with love for Nina. Dancing with her was a powerful experience and he'd never dreamt he'd ever be this happy.

As they moved, Nina could feel his love for her in his touch and see it in his eyes. It was still unreal to her that a man loved her the way Billy did. She couldn't thank the Great Spirit enough for her husband. Too soon the song was over and Billy went to give Josie a break so she could dance with Evan.

By the time they all left that night, it was late, but they'd had such a good time, that they didn't care. Evan and Josie said that Lucky should just leave Otto at their house since he and Julia were being watched by Thad and Edna there. Lucky thanked them and Billy suggested that he sleep on the sofa up in his studio. That way he could collect Otto in the morning and go on out to the farm.

Lucky took him up on the offer.

"Good," Wild Wind said. "I will not have to listen to you snore tonight."

"You're the one who snores," Lucky shot back. "It's a wonder ya don't suck in the tipi with the force of it."

Wild Wind laughed and said, "At least I do not sound like a bull moose when I blow my nose."

They went back and forth at each other until the group split up for the night.

Lucky regretted his choice to stay in Billy's studio that night. It gave him too much time alone to feel his heartbreak and sleeping was useless. Instead, he lit a lamp and looked at Billy's latest projects. Rarely did Billy finish one painting before going on to another. He'd get stuck on one and working on something different helped him get fresh ideas for the first one.

He was glad that he'd given Billy a nudge to get serious about his work. Billy got better every day, it seemed to Lucky. Picking up one of Billy's sketchpads, he began flipping through it. It was the one Billy had taken with him on their trip to Oklahoma. Lucky took it over to the sofa and sat down with it so he could take his time looking at it.

Even Billy's drawings were brilliant. He kept after Billy to frame some of his pencil drawings, but he hadn't been able to convince him to do it yet. Coming to a few drawings of Nina, Lucky chuckled.

"I knew ya were watchin' her."

He came to the drawings that Billy had done of him and Otto and he grinned at them. Billy had done several different poses: one in which father and son were looking right at Billy, one where they were both looking at something else, but his favorite was the one in which he and Otto were looking at each other with smiles on their faces. Turning the page, his stomach clenched painfully and his breath hitched in his chest when he saw that Billy had drawn a picture of Avasa and Otto.

Although Billy had only seen Avasa for a short amount of time, his brilliant artist's mind had captured her likeness amazingly well. Her beautiful face haunted Lucky all the time, but seeing it in Billy's sketch book brought it into painfully sharp focus and it cut him worse than any blade could.

Fighting the urge to crush the sketchpad, Lucky closed it and tossed it onto a chair close to the sofa. He couldn't understand how the woman he'd loved for so long had fallen in love with another man. He'd told her he'd be back for her and she'd known that he always kept his word. He'd been too long getting back, but he'd been building a life for them so that they'd have a good future together. Lucky was trying hard not to give into the anger and grief for his son's sake, but it was hard not to.

Dancing with Nina that night had been fun, but it had also made him even more aware of the loneliness in his life. Otto helped ease some of it, of course. Having his child with him was an enormous blessing and he was grateful for Otto's presence in his life. However, he'd always pictured the three of them happy together, living on the farm and working their business together.

Lucky knew that if he kept thinking about it, he'd go insane or destroy Billy's studio, so he found the bottle of whiskey Billy usually had stashed under the sofa and drank half of it as fast as he could. When he felt pleasantly drunk, he corked it and put it back under the sofa. Lying back, he sighed and started calculating how much money they would make that month. He fell asleep with tallies and dollar signs drifting through his mind.

# Chapter Twenty-Two

The next evening, Evan watched Josie move around their kitchen as they cooked together. He knew that she was not happy about having Shadow and Bree in their home and that she was only going along with it for his benefit. She'd only given him tight smiles and she'd been unusually quiet. Normally, they'd have been chatting and teasing each other, but that was absent.

"Josie, thank you for doing this. I know you don't see it now, but it really will be helpful. I promise," Evan said.

She gave him another tight smile. "I'm trying to trust your judgment on this, but I don't want him around Julia any more than I do Marvin. I know Shadow has been made by his father and Marvin. I understand that, but I do not trust him and I hate that you hired him."

"I know, honey, but I know what I'm doing," Evan said.

Josie felt guilty because this was the first time she'd ever doubted Evan about anything. Shadow was such an unpredictable, sinister character that she was terrified that her husband was making a huge mistake in giving Shadow one iota of his trust.

"I know," she said, trying to sound convincing.

Evan could tell that she didn't mean it, but he let it go. He didn't blame her for being scared. He knew he was taking a big gamble with Shadow, but something kept telling him that it would be worth it.

Outside, much the same sort of thing was going on, but it was Shadow who was suddenly nervous, not Bree.

"I'm not cut out to be a dinner guest," he whispered to Bree once they'd gotten out of their buggy. "I've never eaten anywhere else besides home. Evan has invited me to the diner a couple of times, but I'm terrified to go there. I don't want to hear the whispers while I'm trying to eat. I don't mind it when I'm out and about doing my job, but I like to eat in peace and enjoy my food."

Bree took his hands. "Shadow, they're just people. It's been a long time since I've done this, too, but you need to show them that you're not backwards or intimidated by them. I know they're good people, but they don't understand you. How could they? You have to let them get to know you a little and they'll start to see you for the intelligent, funny, kind, man you are."

"I am not kind and we both know it," Shadow said.

Bree wasn't going to back down from him. "Yes, you are. You've shown me nothing but kindness since the night you found me and you're kind to Marvin, too. You didn't think you had room for more kindness in you, but then I came along and proved you wrong. So stop doubting yourself and let's go eat. I'm hungry."

He gently squeezed her hands back and said, "I'll do my best to behave myself, but I'm not saying a blessing."

Bree laughed at his incongruous statement. "Why do you think I wanted you to?"

"I don't, but I was just making that clear right now," Shadow said, smiling. "Oh, I almost forgot." He took off his coat and handed it to Bree. His vest and shirt followed. "I don't want to disappoint Edna. This part I'll enjoy."

Bree giggled as she looked him over. "You're liable to make her have a heart attack by showing all of that delicious muscle."

He grinned. "Save some room and you can have me for dessert later."

Her laugh helped relax him and he thanked Fate for sending his little counterfeiter into his life.

Josie jumped when a knock sounded on their door.

"I'll get it," Evan said. "Honey, it'll be fine."

She blew out a breath and nodded. "I know."

He frowned a little and left the kitchen. When he opened the door to find Shadow standing on the porch bare from the waist up, he started laughing.

"I was informed by Miss Edna that this was the cost for being allowed to come to dinner," Shadow said, grinning.

"Get in here," Evan said.

Shadow motioned Bree ahead of him. She smiled at Evan and said, "I made sure he remembered his manners."

"Come on in, Bree," Evan said. "Good to see you."

"Thank you, Sheriff," she replied, entering their parlor.

Edna had just been rising from her chair to greet Bree when Shadow appeared in all his bare-chested glory. "Dear Lord! Warn a girl next time, Deputy Earnest!"

He held up his arms and turned around. "Do I meet with your approval?"

She crooked a finger at him. "I can't inspect you properly from all the way over there."

"Of course not. How silly of me," he said, walking to her.

She squeezed one of his biceps and nodded. "Yes, you'll do very nicely, I think."

"I'm glad to hear it. Do I get to return the favor?" he asked with a devilish smile.

Edna actually blushed. Evan saved her from answering by hauling Shadow away from her.

"Shadow, that's dangerous territory. Behave, old woman," Evan chastised her. "Put your clothes back on, Shadow. No one sits at the table unless they have clothes on."

Edna's blue eyes twinkled as she said, "Shadow is welcome to sit in here and eat with me."

"No, he is not!" Evan said.

Shadow chuckled as Bree handed him his shirt. He didn't miss the hunger in her dark eyes and he smiled at her.

Josie couldn't help being amused by Edna and she thought it was nice of Shadow to play along with her. Shadow finished dressing and they adjourned to the kitchen. Although he'd never been a dinner guest anywhere, Shadow had been groomed by Marvin in their youth about gentlemanly behavior and he'd had his brother give him a refresher course that afternoon.

He seated Bree and Edna, who was delighted with the attention. Taking the seat next to Bree, he caught sight of Julia and froze. He'd never seen a baby up close except in passing and it really hadn't given him a chance to examine one much.

The baby sat in her high chair between Evan, who sat at the head of the table, and Josie, who sat right around the corner from Evan. Her short, thick black hair was curly and there was a little white bow in it. Josie had dressed her in a pink and white dress that day and it was decorated with bows, too. She looked up at Josie and Shadow saw that her eyes were blue like her mother's.

Julia banged her little spoon on her tray and said, "Mumumum."

Josie smiled and said, "Yes, I'm your Ma. One of these days, you'll say it crystal clear because you're such a smart girl."

Julia smiled and let out a squeal of laughter. Everyone at the table except Shadow laughed. He smiled, but his ears hurt from the unexpected noise.

"How does something that small make such a loud noise?" he asked without thinking.

They laughed at him and it was disconcerting to Shadow. He'd asked a genuine question, but they thought he was teasing. Apparently he was funny without meaning to be. Not wanting to look like an idiot, he smiled and laughed a little.

Hearing the unfamiliar male laugh, Julia turned her eyes on Shadow and frowned a little. It was a cute expression and Shadow smiled at her. She frowned even more, though, and then started crying. Shadow didn't know what to do. He hadn't meant to upset Julia, but something he'd done had. It made him feel badly.

"Should I leave?" he asked.

Edna said, "Of course not. Babies cry at unfamiliar people sometimes. I have a hunch it's your glasses—she's never seen anyone wearing dark glasses before. Most of us haven't, but for babies it's harder to adapt sometimes."

"I see," Shadow said. "I have no knowledge of these things, of course. I would take them off, but then I couldn't see."

Josie remembered that bright lighting hurt his eyes. "I have a solution to that."

She got up and went over to one of the cupboards, withdrawing two candleholders and a couple of candles from it. After readying them, she lit the wicks and then turned the lanterns in the kitchen down.

"Is that better?" she asked.

Shadow took off his glasses and found that he could tolerate the lowered lighting. "Yes, thank you."

His voice drew Julia's attention again and this time when she looked at him, she smiled at him.

"She just wanted to see your eyes," Josie said.

Shadow's relief was great. "I'm glad that's all it was. I know I make people uncomfortable, and while I don't always mind that, I have no wish to frighten children and babies."

Evan chuckled. "Be honest, you like making people uncomfortable."

"Certain people. Well, most people, but not children and babies. Of course, children and babies have never seen me before, so I wouldn't have—" Shadow knew he was rambling so he shut his mouth a moment. "I'm terrified. Do you know that?"

No one responded.

"I can dislocate people's shoulders, snap their necks, and shoot them without any fear whatsoever, but sitting here, trying to have dinner with people other than Marvin and Bree, fills me with terror. I almost didn't come because the thought of it scared me so much."

Josie couldn't believe what she'd just heard. The man who frightened other people so much was actually afraid of something other than being locked in a cage again. Maybe Evan was right after all. Doing things you'd never done before was scary, like traveling all by yourself to a new life. She knew how nervous she'd been when she'd left home to come to Echo, but then she'd met Lucky and she hadn't been scared anymore. Maybe Shadow needed that same sort of thing.

Obviously he was as afraid of doing normal things as people were of dealing with him. Yes, he'd done terrible things, but there were reasons for that, Josie reasoned. He'd been taught that doing them was right. Could he learn a different way of life? Maybe with some more help, it was possible.

"Shadow, you have nothing to fear from us. I know you're not used to this type of setting, but it's not any different than what you do at home," Josie said. "You just have more people to talk to, that's all. I assume you talk while you eat, unlike Billy, who barely says anything at all because he's too busy shoving food into his mouth."

Shadow grinned. "Yes, I talk during meals."

Edna said, "That's good because I want you to tell me about some dark, sinister things you've done."

"Aunt Edna!" Evan objected.

"What?" she said. "I want to see if he's done something to someone I don't like. At least I'll have gotten revenge by proxy."

This appealed to Shadow's warped sense of humor and he laughed loudly. Julia liked his laugh and let out another squeal as if approving of the topic of conversation.

After that, things became easier for Shadow and he began relaxing around the Tafts. They talked about things related to Echo and the upcoming mayoral election. Bree enjoyed herself, too. Her association with Marvin had made her somewhat of a social outcast and having people act friendly towards her for a change was very nice.

Evan had been mulling something over during dinner and he finally decided to broach the subject. "Bree, I've never really had a chance to apologize for Thad's behavior the night we came looking for Shadow. He's not normally insulting towards women like that. Marvin had just shocked him by telling him that Phoebe was pregnant a little bit before that and he wasn't in a good frame of mind."

Bree smiled a little and said, "Thank you. I shouldn't have hit him, but I was so tired of being mistreated by men that I wasn't going to let anyone talk to me that way again."

Evan nodded. "I don't blame you. I wanted to smack him myself that night, but considering that he'd just learned that he was gonna be a father, I cut him a little slack."

Shadow chuckled. "He was right about you sleeping with Earnest, it was just the wrong one. Isn't that how he put it the night you captured me?"

"Yeah. That's how he said it. I couldn't believe you laughed at that. Of course, I couldn't believe he thought it was funny when you yelled, 'Surprise', either," Evan said. "Win and I thought he'd lost his mind."

Bree laughed. "Shadow and Marvin think things are funny that most other people don't, which is funny in itself. Like when someone insults them. I become offended, but they get a kick out of it and it usually makes me laugh in the end."

Edna said, "I remember that about Marvin. The more inappropriate something was, the funnier he found it. And while it wasn't really funny, it was, if that makes sense."

Shadow said, "It makes perfect sense to me. Like when Billy told me the other night that he wanted to hear me draw my last breath. He was completely serious. Most people would have gotten angry and been very offended, but Marvin and I thought it was hysterical."

Josie was confused. "Why would you find it funny that someone wanted to see you dead?"

Shadow chuckled. "I don't know. Maybe it's because I don't feel threatened at all by that sort of thing. I don't have an explanation."

Edna asked, "So if I told you I wanted to pluck your right eye out of your skull and pickle it, what would you say?"

Shadow did well at holding in his mirth until he heard Bree snicker. He was able to swallow the bite of roasted pork in his mouth before laughing. Josie watched him laugh and saw Edna grin. Suddenly, she found herself smiling and Evan chuckled.

"Marvin will love that," Shadow said. "I'll bet you never dreamt you'd be sitting eating dinner with Marvin's twin, did you?"

"Nope," Evan said. "But I'm guessing you never thought you'd be here, either."

"Touché," Shadow said.

When the meal concluded, Shadow and Bree thanked them for inviting them and took their leave. As they cleaned up, Josie punched Evan's arm hard.

"Hey! What was that for?" Evan asked.

"For being right," Josie said. "I actually like him a little more now and I felt so bad when he said he was scared."

Evan smiled and then said, "I was surprised by that, but I could see he was telling the truth. I'm sure there are gonna be a lot of things that'll be scary for him."

"You're right. It's a shame about his eyes. I can't imagine living in darkness for so long," Josie said.

"Me, either. So now do you think my plan is so crazy?"

Josie said, "Don't be smug, Sheriff, or you'll sleep alone tonight."

He just smiled and started washing dishes.

⌣‿⌣

Later that night, Shadow and Marvin sat out on the veranda the way they often did.

"I'm glad you had a good time tonight," Marvin said. "I was a little worried about you since you've never been a dinner guest before."

Shadow said, "I was scared to death, but I muddled through it and it got easier. Bree was a great help to me."

Marvin smiled. "Yes, she's able to work magic with you. I've seen a big change in you since she came along and I like seeing you so happy."

"Thank you. Marvy, what is our purpose now?"

"What do you mean, 'our purpose'?"

Shadow frowned. "Well, now that we're no longer concerned with keeping me a secret, what is our purpose? You still have all of the business to take care of, but what is *my* purpose in life? I have no reason to keep doing the things I was doing before in order to collect information to use against people to prevent them from finding out about me."

"Yes, I see what you mean," Marvin said. "I hadn't really thought about it. It's all second nature to me or perhaps first nature is more like it."

Shadow smiled. "I know. I still want to go causing havoc or spy on people, but what's the point now? I don't need to."

Marvin drummed his fingers on the arm of his rocking chair in contemplation. "No. I suppose not. Are we going to have to become normal?"

"What *is* normal? Nothing about me is normal."

Marvin sighed a little. "I suppose I'm semi-normal since I've led a mainly normal life."

"Now that you're not protecting me any longer, you're free to live a normal life," Shadow said. "You could actually find a wife now and have a family. There's always adoption."

That startled Marvin. Shadow was right; he could have a wife and family now, but what woman in her right mind would want him? Besides, there were very few women around Echo to begin with and all of them would be scared to death of him. Could he repair his image enough to entice a woman and could he find one who would be willing to adopt instead of having a child herself?

"You raise some very interesting points, Shadow. I'll have to think about it," Marvin said.

"There's something else we need to discuss," his brother said.

"Which is?"

"I assume I have a birth certificate."

"Yes, you do. I have it in my office in the safe."

Shadow said, "So it proves I exist. We'll have to do something about the death certificate, but I'm sure our lawyer would know what to do with it. Shouldn't I be on the deed to the ranch and have access to our accounts? What if I need to go to the bank or take care of some business because you can't for some reason? Right now, I can't do anything like that."

"Good God, you're absolutely right. I'm so sorry, Shadow. I'm just not used to you doing anything like that. I apologize for not giving that consideration. We'll start taking care of that immediately and whenever you're not working, I'll start showing you about the finances and such," Marvin said. "This is your home, too, and you should be on the deed and the accounts by all rights."

"Thank you. Will you go somewhere with me sometime this week?" Shadow asked.

Marvin smiled at him. "Of course. Where are we going?"

Shadow's smile was a little sheepish. "I want to ask Bree to marry me and I need to buy a ring."

Marvin grinned and reached over to grasp Shadow's shoulder and shake him a little. "That's wonderful, Shadow! I'm so happy for you! Soon you'll have little Shadows running around here. It will be a pleasure being an uncle."

Shadow frowned a little. "I've never dealt with children. It was a little, um, unnerving being around Julia tonight. I made her cry because my glasses scared her. They lowered the lighting so I could take them off, but I hated that I made her uncomfortable."

"That's not unusual and it can be hard telling what might disturb them. Don't take it personally. Look at Eva; there are times when she wants me and times when she doesn't," Marvin said.

Shadow smiled. "I can't believe Ronni stayed after all of the chaos.

You're good with Eva. You know, Ronni is a very pretty woman—"

"Let me stop you right there," Marvin said. "The woman drives me insane with her constant arguing. She's stubborn, opinionated, disrespectful, and—"

"And you want her."

Marvin put his forehead in his hand. "God help me, I do."

"She gets your blood going in several different ways," Shadow said with a laugh. "Which means she's perfect for you."

Marvin laughed. "I don't know about that."

"You should at least consider it. I like how she calls me Spider. I still laugh when I think about you telling her that I was dangerous spiders," Shadow said.

"I have to admit that was inspired."

"Yes, it was. Well, I'm going to bed since I have to be up in the morning. My body is still not accustomed to this new schedule. It'll take some time, I suppose," Shadow said.

"You're doing quite well."

"Thanks. Goodnight, Marvy."

"Goodnight, Shadow."

# Chapter Twenty-Three

"Well, now that we're all here, shall we begin?" Marvin asked as they sat in the formal dining room at the ranch.

"Let's do that," Lucky agreed.

Marvin nodded. "We're here to try to come to an agreement over the right-of-way and pressing possible trespassing charges against the owners of the sheep farm, of which there are four. You, Mr. Quinn, Mr. Two Moons, Dr. Wu, and Mr. Ryder."

Billy smiled at him. "Well, I've already admitted to Sheriff Taft that we committed that crime and he said that since it's a first offense that there would be a fine of $300.00 if you go forward with the charges."

Marvin arched an eyebrow at that. "Did he now? I'm afraid he doesn't get to set the punishment. It would go to the judge in Dickensville to be decided."

Win said, "Actually, according to the town bylaws, Dickensville doesn't have jurisdiction over Echo, so right now, Evan is judge and jury. He has every right to decide punishment."

Marvin looked over at Shadow, who shrugged. "I have no idea what the bylaws say," he said. "I haven't studied those yet. I'm sorry."

His brother then turned to his lawyer, Doug Brentwood. "Please find out if that's true."

"Of course," Doug said.

"Assuming you're correct," Marvin said, "I'll forgo the fine if we make the deal I outlined to you last week. In exchange for the right-of-way, I receive forty head of sheep from you each year. I think that's a fair exchange, don't you?"

Lucky said, "Actually, I don't. Ya see, I own the Mercer property, through which your creek runs before it gets to your ranch. I have plans for that land. I need to grow more grass to make more pastureland and I plan on diverting the stream so I can irrigate where I need to."

This news was shocking to Marvin. "Fairchild sold that land to you? When?"

Lucky enjoyed the surprised look on Marvin's face. "At the same time he sold me the other land. Here's the deed. It's all legal. I made sure of that."

He slid the documents over to Marvin, who carefully looked them over. They were genuine, Marvin saw. He had to hand it to Lucky. He was a shrewd businessman and he'd underestimated the Irishman.

"Bravo, Mr. Quinn. It would seem as though you have me right where you want me," Marvin said with a smile.

"Aye. We do. Now here's the new deal we're proposing. You don't press charges and we get the right-of-way. In return, we don't divert the stream and disrupt your water supply."

Marvin said, "Well, that would certainly work if I didn't have an alternate water supply. You didn't check your facts on that, Mr. Quinn."

Billy groaned. "That's right. You have a lake on the west side of the property."

"Yes, we do. Not only that, the water table here is quite deep and we have pumps out at the barn and the house, of course. It's how we're able to have flush toilets while others can't. So you can do anything to your stream you want, but it won't affect us since we don't really use it," Marvin said.

Win wanted to slap the smug look off Marvin's face.

"Which brings us back to my original offer. The easement for the livestock and I don't bother with the trespassing charges," Marvin said.

The sheep farmers had been prepared for this eventuality if Marvin had a way out of their agreement, which he did. Marvin didn't know animals and since he only wanted the sheep for their wool, he wouldn't need the younger animals, which were the best mutton producers. They could give him the older animals every year and that way they wouldn't be really losing anything.

Lucky frowned, acting as though he was very displeased with the arrangement. "Very well. I guess that's the best deal we're gonna make. Write it up and we'll sign it."

"Splendid," Marvin said. "Mr. Brentwood will draw it up and we'll send it over to Mr. Litwhiler to look over and make sure everything is in order.

John Litwhiler, the only lawyer who practiced in Echo nodded. "That's acceptable."

Doug said, "I'll get started on it right away and get it to you by the end of the week."

"Good," John said.

The men all stood and shook hands with one another. Before the four sheep farmers mounted up, they conferred by their horses.

Billy said, "I'm sorry about not thinking about their lake and all. That's my fault."

"Don't worry about it," Ross said. "We still got a good deal because we can get rid of our older sheep who would be tough mutton. We still keep our quality animals and get the right-of-way."

Lucky nodded. "That's right, Ross. So it all worked out just fine."

Win said, "Well, I'm heading for Erin's office to work on the vet office side."

Lucky said, "I'll come with ya and help. I've got time."

"Me, too," Billy said.

Ross said, "I would, but I have to get back to the shop. Callie's good enough to watch it for me, but I don't want to leave her too long."

Billy smiled. "How're things going with you two?"

"Great," Ross said. "We're taking things slow and getting to know each other, but it's looking good so far."

"Glad to hear it," Lucky said.

"If you get married, I get to be best man since I got her here," Billy said.

Ross laughed. "You got it."

May was a hectic time for everyone. The sheep farmers were kept busy since it was lambing time and also time to sheer the sheep. Wild Wind learned quickly how the process worked and he was a big help to them. He was also adept at butchering and helped Ross out at the shop whenever there was a bunch of meat to get ready.

Their business was rapidly starting to pick up and people were buying the goat milk and cheese as much as they were meat, which made them glad that Lucky had thought to diversify their products. Nina liked helping milk the goats and making the cheese. Lucky had also taught Otto how to milk the goats and he did fairly well for a three-year-old. He was growing and he rarely asked about Avasa anymore.

Lucky's heartache over Avasa had eased a small fraction thanks to things being so busy and the support of his friends. They were there to lend an ear when he needed one and they also tried to keep things light and fun for him.

Nina's grasp on the English language increased and she was now almost fluent. Between all of her new friends and Billy, she'd learned how to write better and had improved her math skills, which was all very beneficial to her. Usually on Fridays they went to Spike's where Josie and Billy played so others could dance. Nina loved the dancing and always made sure to dance with Spike. There were times when she helped tend bar a little if it got really busy.

Shadow and Bree had taken to joining them once his rounds for that

MAIL ORDER BRIDE: *Montana Adventure*

night were over. He still policed the Burgundy House, especially on the weekends, but it was a much quieter place now, which thrilled Evan. Shadow felt pride in his accomplishment and he was growing more comfortable socializing with people.

On the last Friday of May, the group of them went to Spike's like usual, with one exception. Shadow had convinced Marvin to come along. His twin had been resistant because he knew that he wouldn't be welcome. Shadow told him that he could just sit with him and Bree and have a good time together. Marvin finally had capitulated, figuring it couldn't hurt to try it one time.

When he walked in with Shadow and Bree, a hush settled over the place. Marvin was amused, enjoying the attention. He walked over to the bar and said, "Good evening, Spike. How are you?"

Spike was flabbergasted. "Fine. I thought I was seeing things. What'll it be?"

Marvin smiled. "Well, I didn't feel like sitting at home, so I thought I'd come hear Josie and Billy play. Whiskey, please."

Spike poured the drink. "I really don't know what to think about you bein' here. Don't cause any trouble or I'll kick your ass out of here."

Marvin smiled at his strong words. "I have no intention of causing trouble. Besides, the sheriff and his deputy are here, so that would rather stupid of me."

Spike nodded. "You want me to start a tab for you?"

"Yes. Thank you," Marvin said.

He took his drink and joined Shadow and Bree at the table they'd taken.

Marvin sat down. "This might be fun."

Bree smiled. "You're so bad."

"You know me well," Marvin replied. "Spike warned me to behave."

Shadow said, "Please do. I don't want to have to put my own brother in the clink."

Marvin said, "Don't worry; I'll be on my best behavior."

"That's not very comforting," Shadow said.

The three of them laughed.

Thad sat with Evan, Wild Wind, and Lucky at another table. "I can't believe he had the gall to show up here. I'd like to bash in his head with this beer mug."

"Thad," Evan said in a warning tone. "It's a public place and he's not doing anything wrong. I think we're going to have to get used to seeing him more places now since Shadow is out of hiding. It only makes sense that they would want to do things together."

"That's different. Marvin I hate. Shadow I like," Thad said.

Lucky said, "He does have a certain appeal."

Evan smiled. "My plan is working out very well."

"It sure is," Thad agreed.

Noticing that the other men's beer mugs were empty, Wild Wind said, "I will get us new drinks." He'd come to enjoy going to the bar.

"Ok," Evan said. "Thanks."

Wild Wind took their mugs over to the bar and Spike refilled them. He liked the Indian, who had a dry sense of humor.

"How's our other Indian tonight?" he asked.

"I am fine. It looks like you have a lot of business tonight. This is good," Wild Wind responded.

"Yep. That's what I like. Ok. You're all set," Spike said. "Do you want a tray?"

"No. I am fine." Wild Wind took two mugs in each hand and made his way towards his table.

A man sitting at a table along his route stuck his foot out just as the brave was passing. Wild Wind tried to avoid it, but there wasn't enough time. He tripped and beer slopped all over another guy at the neighboring table.

The troublemaker laughed. "Stupid Injun. You oughta look where you're goin' better."

Wild Wind glared at him. "You are an ignorant white man. I did nothing to you." To the man who was now soaked in beer, he said, "I am sorry for his stupidity."

The victim rose and said, "You probably did that on purpose anyway."

"No, I did not. It was an accident on my part. He tripped me."

The other man also got up and Wild Wind knew there was going to be trouble. As the first man swung a fist at him, the brave ducked and the blow ended up hitting the other guy. Suddenly pandemonium erupted and there were flying fists everywhere. Evan and Shadow immediately went into action, combating the fighters and working towards restoring order.

Marvin saw a man, whom he recognized as Tim Alderman, sneaking up behind Evan. He wielded a whiskey bottle and meant to strike the sheriff. Not usually one to fight, Marvin nevertheless wasn't about to let the man get an unfair advantage over Evan. He left Bree with Josie, Nina, and Billy, who was guarding them, and launched himself at the would-be attacker.

He grabbed the Tim around the waist and knocked him to the floor. The bottle of whiskey flew against the wall and smashed apart. Marvin followed up his attack by hitting Tim in the face twice, dazing him. The next thing Marvin knew, there was a blow to his back. It knocked the wind out of him and he fell sideways.

"I've wanted to do this for a long time," Corey Allen, one of Marvin's ranch hands said.

He started kicking Marvin viciously in the stomach and ribs. Marvin tried to get away from him, but the first two kicks had rendered him incapable of even crawling. In an attempt to protect himself, he curled up into a fetal position.

Shadow saw that his brother was in trouble and went after Corey. He aimed a kick at Corey's knee and the ranch hand went down with a scream as his kneecap shattered. Shadow wasn't done with him however. He was going to make him pay the ultimate price for hurting Marvin. He hauled Corey back up and prepared to break his neck.

He had his hands in position when Spike fired a warning shot into one of the walls.

"Next person to throw a punch is gonna go meet their maker!" he shouted.

The action had stopped, but Shadow was still intent on his mission. "You picked on the wrong person, Corey. Your time on Earth is up."

Just as he was about to complete the move, Bree shouted, "No, Shadow! Don't!"

Shadow stopped as she came closer. "He deserves it."

"I know, but if you kill him, you'll go to prison. Please don't leave me," Bree pleaded with him. "You don't have to do that. You've punished him enough. Please, Shadow. You don't have to be that man anymore."

Shadow saw fear and love in her eyes and he was torn between revenge and reason.

"Shadow, I need you with me, not in jail. You'll die in there and you'll never be able to see our baby," Bree said. "Please don't leave us."

Shadow jerked in surprise and looked at the hand Bree placed on her stomach. He made up his mind in that instant. He shoved Corey away from him. Corey hit a table and fell unconscious to the floor. In a second Shadow had Bree in his arms.

"You're pregnant?" he asked.

She smiled and laid a hand on his face. "Yes. We made a baby, Shadow."

He laughed and kissed her. He'd never intended to become a father, but now that he knew Bree was pregnant, joy surged through him at the unexpected news. Remembering Marvin, he released Bree and kneeled on the floor by him.

"Marvin. Are you all right?" he asked, shaking him a little.

Marvin couldn't answer because of the fiery pain in his abdomen. He shook his head and panted.

Looking around, Shadow spotted Erin. "Dr. Avery! Come here! Marvin needs help!"

Erin found the source of the voice and hurried over to Marvin. "Marvin, I need to look at you. Put your legs down, ok?"

Marvin tried, but the pain in his groin was unbearable. "Can't."

Erin brushed his hands away and began palpating his lower stomach area. Marvin let out a groan that bordered on a scream.

"What is it?" Shadow asked.

"His hernia ruptured. I need to get him to the office right now," Erin said.

Her response filled his heart with dread. He knew that such an injury could be fatal. He gently scooped Marvin up and headed out the door with him.

"Bree, you drive," he said. "I'll hold him still on the way."

"Ok." Bree got in the buggy and as soon as Shadow was situated with Marvin, she slapped the reins against the horse's rump and they soon moved along at a good clip.

"Hang in there, Marvy, ok? Don't even think about leaving me," Shadow said, looking into his brother's pain-riddled face.

Marvin nodded slightly as he concentrated on breathing. The pain in his groin worsened every time he took a breath. They were overtaken by Erin and Win, who galloped for the office so that they could prepare for Marvin's arrival. The doctors knew that every moment was crucial in treating Marvin's injury.

Evan rode up beside them. "How's he doing?" he called to Shadow.

"Not good. It's hard for him to breathe," Shadow responded.

Evan's expression became even grimmer. "They'll take good care of him. I'll meet you there." He spurred Smitty into a faster gait, leaving them behind.

As soon as they arrived at Erin's office, she started prepping for surgery. Win helped her.

"Have you ever done anything like this?" he asked.

"I've done a couple of appendectomies, but never a hernia repair. I sent Lucky to get Dr. Forrester over in Dickensville. He's done a lot of abdominal surgeries. I'm going to try to get Marvin stabilized until he gets here and can do a proper job. I might be able to buy Marvin some time. We're going to have to keep him heavily sedated," Erin said.

They finished turning the second exam room into a surgical room as Shadow came through the office door with Marvin.

"In here," Erin directed him.

Shadow eased Marvin down onto the table and backed up a little. He took Marvin's hand. "You have to fight, Marvin. I need you. You're going to be an uncle."

Marvin smiled through his pain and squeezed Shadow's hand back. "Happy for you," he whispered.

"So you have to be around for all of us," Shadow said, trying to keep tears at bay. "Do whatever they tell you so you get better."

Marvin nodded.

"Shadow, we need to begin. We'll be out with an update as soon as we can," Erin said kindly.

Shadow gave Marvin's hand another squeeze and left the room.

When Dr. Forrester arrived, Shadow showed him to the surgical room. The doctor entered and looked over Erin and Win's work.

"We have him stable, but there's a lot of damage," Erin said.

Dr. Forrester examined Erin's work and smiled at her. "You've done a great job in shoring him up until I could get here. We wasted no time, I assure you. Let's get to work, doctors."

Shadow held Bree's hand as they sat in the waiting room. Evan had sent Lucky, Billy, and Nina home, saying that he would stay with Shadow and Bree. He would give them an update when one was available. Evan couldn't help but feel bad for Marvin. Despite his past transgressions, Evan didn't like to hear of anyone suffering the way Marvin was.

He was also worried about Shadow. What if Marvin didn't make it? How would Shadow survive? He knew that Shadow had never experienced loss like that before. Would it drive Shadow over the edge? The way Shadow sat woodenly, staring at the opposite wall was disturbing, but Evan figured it was better than Shadow being agitated and demanding to know what was happening with Marvin. Evan stayed quiet so that he didn't snap Shadow out of his calm state of mind.

It had taken a while, but Billy and Nina had finally fallen asleep after the disastrous evening. They'd both been shaken and had lain holding one another, barely talking. Nina had dropped off first and Billy had followed a short time later. Nina had no idea what time it was when she woke up coughing. Her lungs were burning and as she became fully conscious, she realized that their apartment was full of smoke.

She shook Billy hard. "Billy! Wake up!"

He woke with a start and immediately began coughing. "What the heck? Oh no! The building's on fire."

They scrambled out of bed, running for the shop. When Billy felt the storeroom doorknob, it was hot. He knew they couldn't go that way. Running back into the kitchen, Billy threw the rug in front of the sink aside and yanked the loose board free. He pulled out their cash box and some important papers. Then they rushed to the kitchen door. Billy tried to yank it open, but it wouldn't budge. He tried everything to get it open, but something was stopping it.

"Stand back!" he ordered Nina.

He found the hammer he usually kept in one of the kitchen drawers and broke the glass in the door window. Fortunately, it was a large enough window for them to crawl through. He smoothed the glass from around the frame and helped Nina through it. He handed her the cashbox and documents and then pulled himself out of the window.

They ran around the neighboring building to the front street. Horror crashed down on them to see that their building was almost engulfed in flames. There was no hope of saving it, but they knew that the neighboring buildings were also in danger of burning.

"Go get help," Billy said. "I'm going to make sure everyone is out of the other buildings."

Nina nodded and took off.

# Chapter Twenty-Four

The battle to prevent more stores from going up in flames was an arduous task. Bucket lines constantly kept water coming so they could keep wetting the buildings down and also attempt to put out the fire. Evan had been alerted and was helping. Even though his brother was still in surgery, Shadow also came to assist. There was nothing he could do for Marvin, but he could be of use in combating the inferno. Bree would come get him if there were any developments with Marvin.

The Two Moons' building burned very quickly, the fire fueled by the various combustible painting chemicals, paper, and wooden frames. By eight o'clock that morning, the building was a burnt out shell of smoking wood. It was a complete loss. Fortunately, they'd been successful in keeping the fire from spreading.

Finally Billy and Nina sat down together on the other side of the now muddy street. As he stared at the ruins, Billy thought of all his lost works and didn't bother trying to stop the tears that fell from his eyes. Nina wrapped her arms around him and they cried together over the loss of their happy home and business.

Evan saw them and went over, embracing the both of them. Lucky and Wild Wind joined them, trying to comfort them as best they could. Billy grew angry.

"All of my paintings are gone. All of that income. Things were starting to sell and I had some portrait sittings lined up and now I have no paints, no canvasses, or anything!" Then he saw that he was upsetting Nina. He embraced her and said, "I'm so glad you're ok and that you woke up. I couldn't have stood losing you. We'll be all right."

She nodded against his chest. "Yes, we will. As long as I have you, that's all I need."

Remus came over to them and drew Evan away from them. "You need to investigate."

Evan asked, "Why?"

"This was deliberate. The kitchen door was padlocked shut," Remus said, fury evident in his craggy face. "They meant to kill those kids."

Evan's expression mirrored Remus'. "I know exactly who to go after. I'll take care of it."

Remus nodded and went back to Billy and Nina. "Come home with me, kids. We need to get you cleaned up and get something in your stomachs. You need to get some sleep."

Billy and Nina were bone tired from grief and working to help put out the fire. They rose stiffly and walked away from the street.

Their friends watched them go and Evan said, "They're gonna pay."

"Aye," Lucky said. "That they will."

Bree came running up the street, and found Shadow throwing water on some of the smoldering rubble of Billy's building.

"Shadow!"

He tossed his bucket aside and came over to her, searching her face for a clue as to his brother's fate.

She smiled and said, "He's got a long road ahead of him, but they're confident that he'll be all right."

Shadow grabbed her, a sob escaping him. He hadn't cried since he'd been a teenager and it was scary to be feeling such a strong emotion. Bree held him, crying and sharing his relief. Marvin had become very dear to her and it would have devastated her if they'd lost him.

Pulling back, Shadow asked, "Can we see him?"

"I'm not sure. Let's go see," she said.

He took her hand and said, "It's a good thing Marvin showed me how to take care of the most important business so that I can keep things going until he's up to it again."

Bree said, "I know you'll do a good job."

Shadow wasn't so sure, but he didn't say so. Everything was topsy-turvy and he hoped that he could hold everything together until it turned right side up again.

Once inside the clinic, they found Dr. Forrester in the office. Erin was in with Marvin.

"How is he?" Shadow asked.

Dr. Forrester couldn't see Shadow's eyes behind his glasses very well, but he could see the anxiety in his grave expression. "Well, he'll recover. It's going to take several months, but he'll be all right again. I can't believe how inept the surgeon who performed the original repair was. It was a long process, but we removed scar tissue and repaired the rupture. He'll have to be watched closely for infection. That'll be his worst enemy at this point. He'll have to stay here for a few days. He can't be moved right now."

"I understand. Thank you, doctor," Shadow said. "You'll be well compensated. Just send me the bill and I'll take care of it."

"Of course," Dr. Forrester said. "I'll be back the day after tomorrow to check on him, but he's in excellent hands with Dr. Avery. She's a top-notch doctor. If it wasn't for her and Dr. Wu, your brother wouldn't be alive right now. Well, it's been a long night and I've got a journey ahead of me. Have someone come for me if needed."

"Thank you again, Dr. Forrester. Can we see him?"

"He's not really with it, but I don't think it'll hurt for a few minutes," the doctor said.

Shadow and Bree followed him down the hallway to the door that led over to the side that was being built for Win's veterinarian practice.

"Where are we going?" Shadow asked.

"Well, there's not enough room over here for a bed and so forth, so Dr. Wu was gracious enough to let us set up a sick ward over here. It'll do until you can take him home." He opened the door and led them through it.

A short ways into the large room, a bed had been situated close to a window. There were a couple of tables near it that were littered with medical paraphernalia. Marvin was propped up against several pillows, his pallor rivaling the white linens on which he lay. His hair was wet with sweat and his under eyes were dark, but he was alive.

Erin was writing something in a chart and Win organized some other supplies. They looked up when the trio came in.

Erin smiled at them. "You can visit for a little bit, but he's going to need a lot of rest."

Shadow nodded and advanced on Erin. She backed up, her eyes going wide, and Win moved in their direction, but not fast enough. Shadow wrapped his arms around Erin and hugged her tightly. "Thank you, Dr. Avery. We will owe you for the rest of our lives. Anything you ever need, you have only to ask. Thank you."

Erin patted his back hesitantly. "You're welcome. That's what I'm here for."

Shadow released her and nodded. Then he held out a hand to Win and said, "The same goes for you. We are in your debt."

Win shook hands with Shadow. "You're welcome."

Shadow went over to Marvin and took his hand. "Don't worry about a thing, Marvy. I'm going to take care of you just like you've always taken care of me. Thank you for fighting so hard to stay with us. Your niece or nephew will be glad to have you around."

Marvin struggled to open his eyes and when he managed it, he gave Shadow a bleary smile and then gave Bree a wink.

She chuckled and said, "There's the Marvin we know and love. Now you be a good patient and rest. I'll have Ronni make you that beef stew you like so much."

"Ok," he managed to say and fell back to sleep.

"Hello? Where is everyone?" they heard Evan call out.

Erin said, "Back here in Win's side."

The sheriff stepped inside and saw the makeshift ward. "You guys got a nice set up going here. How's he doing?"

"He'll be fine, thanks to Erin and Win," Shadow said.

Evan said, "That's good."

Shadow speared Evan with a hard look. "Is it? Somehow I don't think you really feel that way."

Evan moved right over to Shadow. "Look, I've got my problems with Marvin, but he's still a human being and I know how much he means to you. So, yes, I'm glad that he'll be all right. Besides that, I owe him now."

Shadow frowned. "What do you mean?"

"Billy said that Marvin got hurt because he stopped a guy from bashing my brains in with a bottle. If Marvin hadn't intervened, I might not be here, so I owe him," Evan said.

Shadow smiled. "It seems like there's a lot of that going around today."

Evan said, "That's called being a good friend and watching each other's backs. That's how it works with most normal people. Now, go home, get cleaned up, and have a nap. Meet me at the office at two. We've got work to do. We're going after the men who set that fire." Evan clapped Shadow's shoulder, smiled at everyone else and left again.

When Billy had still lived with his parents, he'd had a room off the back of the house that Remus had built for him as a studio. Billy had ended up moving his bedroom out there since he was up all hours painting anyway. When he'd moved out, Jimmy had taken over the room, but Billy and Nina needed a place to live, so Remus and Arlene moved

Jimmy back upstairs to his old room so that the young couple could have the room.

The ten-year-old boy understood the gravity of the situation and didn't object. Billy had become his brother and he would do anything to help him. He felt bad about the fire and he and Amy were both grateful that he and Nina were safe.

Josie brought over some clothes for Billy and Nina to put on after they got cleaned up. She hugged them both, tears of grief and relief flowing down her face.

"I couldn't believe it when Evan told us," she said. "How could anyone do something so heinous?"

Billy raised an eyebrow. "What do you mean?"

Josie said, "I mean, how could someone deliberately set a fire with people inside a building? What kind of sick human being would do that?"

Billy and Nina looked at each other with stunned expressions and Josie realized her gaff. No one had told them yet that the fire was arson. She put a hand over her mouth. "I'm so sorry. I thought Remus or Evan had told you."

Nina shook her head. "They didn't tell us anything. What happened?"

Gently, Josie told them how someone had put a lock on the kitchen door and set fire to the shop, trapping them inside. Remus had come in on the tail end of her story and it was a good thing he did because Billy was going to go after the men he knew had to be the culprits.

"Billy, you can't do that. Evan is taking care of it," his father told him. "You need to take care of your wife and see to your business. That's your job right now. Don't go doin' anything stupid, son."

Billy had stifled his anger, but vowed to exact his revenge at a later time. For now, he concentrated on getting settled. "Ok, Pa. Ok. Nina, we should go to the store and get some more clothes."

Arlene said, "Why don't you eat and get some sleep?"

Nina said, "I can't sleep right now and I'm not hungry."

"Me, neither," Billy agreed. "We'll be back in a little while. Maybe by then we'll be ready for that."

Remus said, "Ok. Don't be long."

Billy nodded and he and Nina set out for town again.

# Chapter Twenty-Five

Along the way, Billy and Nina couldn't stay away from their store. They rode around back and Billy immediately regretted doing so. Because it had been the farthest wall away from the origin of the blaze, the kitchen wall was relatively unscathed. In black letters, someone had painted a very nasty message that called Nina a horrible name and said, "Leave town and take your Injun husband with you!"

Billy heard Nina gasp and squeeze him a little harder around the middle. Billy quickly moved their horse away from the area.

"Nina, don't you pay attention that. They're just ignorant asses and they're not worth your time or tears. Trust me. I learned that lesson," he said, giving her hands a squeeze.

He felt her nod against his back. "Ok."

"Good. We're gonna be all right. We'll rebuild. I can work at the house like I used to and get some paintings done again. We have some money and there'll be the money from the farm, too. We won't starve or anything," he said.

She nodded again. "Ok."

All the while they picked out some clothes and talked to Tansy, who expressed her horror and condolences to them, Billy fumed inside. Nina was weighed down by guilt and grief and barely responded to Tansy. They took their purchases home and put them away. Arlene made them sit down and eat a little bit.

Then they went into their new home and lay down. They held one another and rested, eventually succumbing to exhaustion.

They spent the next week sifting through the remains of the burnt out building for anything salvageable. There were two paintings that had survived and Billy found an easel that was still serviceable. Everything in their little apartment except some cooking equipment was lost to flames or smoke-and-water damage.

There was also the bank to deal with. It was a good thing that Billy had insured his shop, but it wouldn't cover the total rebuilding costs. Billy decided that he would have to down size and just rebuild the store for the time being. They could add on to the building when they had more funds.

Evan and Shadow had hauled the culprits into jail and Billy was hard-pressed to not go beat them up. Only his responsibility to Nina and their business kept him from doing so. One day when Shadow had run into Billy alone in the general store, he'd assured him that he'd exacted some revenge for him and Nina and that the arsonists had needed medical care. Billy had laughed and thanked him.

The town came together to help clear away the wreckage. Jerry used his Clydesdale stallion, Alonso, to help haul away debris and several of the ranchers also loaned their draft horse teams to the cause. By the time the week was up, there was only an empty lot where the building had once stood.

Nina tried not to look at it when she went into town for something because it depressed her and made her feel guilty. She mourned her first home with Billy in their little apartment where she'd first cooked a meal for him and they'd had so much fun. She missed the studio where she'd watched him create wonderful works of art and where they would sometimes make love.

Despite Billy's determination to rebuild and his assurances that everything would be fine, Nina felt more and more depressed. She hid her sorrow and guilt behind bright smiles as she worked hard to help get things off the ground again. However, she couldn't shake the feeling that none of it would've happened if she hadn't followed Wild Wind off the reservation. She should never have come with Billy to Echo.

A couple of weeks after the fire, Billy woke to find Nina already gone. She'd left him a note telling him that she'd gone out to the sheep farm to help milk the goats. He smiled as he pictured her with her hair in twin braids and wearing her Cheyenne dress. Then he thought about how the dress showed off her shapely legs and slim body and his mind pleasantly drifted over their lovemaking from the night before. Shaking off those thoughts, he went into his parents' house for breakfast.

He spent the day painting and drawing, only coming up for air to eat. Although still deeply upset over the loss of the store and all of his work, Billy was rising to the challenge of rebuilding, calling on his newfound fortitude to do it. He couldn't sit around crying and moaning about it. He had his wife and his family and friends and life went on. The guilty parties had been sent over to Dickensville and they would be going off to prison for arson and two counts of attempted murder.

When Nina wasn't home by supper, Billy rode out to the farm. He scratched on Lucky's tipi flap.

"Come on!"

Going inside, he found Lucky, Otto, and Wild Wind sitting around the fire. "Hi, guys. What's for supper?"

"Lamb stew," Lucky said.

"Mmm. Smells great," Billy said. "Is my wife in the barn?"

Lucky shook his head.

"Oh. She's up at Erin's then," Billy said. "I'll go get her."

"Billy, Nina's not here," Lucky said.

Billy said, "What do you mean? She left me note this morning that she was coming out to help with the milking. I just thought she spent the day out here."

Wild Wind said, "She hasn't been here at all today. We wouldn't joke about that." Over the past couple of months, his English had also improved.

"Where the heck is she then? She wasn't over at Evan's. I checked before I came out here," Billy said. "Oh, God! What if she got hurt on the way out here or something?"

Wild Wind stood up. "We'll help you retrace the way back to town and make sure she's not there somewhere."

Lucky took Otto to stay with Erin, and Win came along with them. They searched everywhere, even going to Spike's, but there was no trace of Nina anywhere. Arriving home again, Billy had a dark feeling settle over him and he hoped he wasn't right.

Entering their room, Billy pulled open Nina's drawers and found them empty except for her Cheyenne dress. He took it out of the drawer and a piece of paper fell to the floor. Picking it up, he read: *Thank you for showing me how to be a white woman like I should have always been. I'll always be grateful to you, but it's time I moved on. Nina.*

Billy sat down heavily on their bed, not believing what was on the paper. Hoping it was a mistake of some sort, he read it several times, but the words never changed. So that was it? Their marriage had been a lie and once she'd gotten what she needed from him, she was done? It couldn't be and yet... The pain of losing his store was nothing compared to that of losing Nina.

Lucky came in the door and saw Billy sitting on the bed. "Any sign of her, lad?"

Billy just held out the note to Lucky. As he read it, Lucky's eyebrows rose. He couldn't believe it any more than Billy could. He sat down on the bed with Billy.

"She used me," Billy said faintly. "All this time, she was just using me. She wanted to marry me right off, remember?"

"Aye, I do."

"She just wanted to get her hooks into me long enough to show her how to live in white society and then be rid of me. I thought she loved me, Lucky. I mean *really* loved me. It was in her eyes, her voice, and ..."

Lucky wasn't sure what to say. "Ah, damn, Billy."

"I'd like to be alone now, ok?"

"Sure, lad. I'll make sure no one disturbs ya," Lucky said and went inside the house.

Billy lay down on the bed, numb with disbelief and agony. He never closed his eyes that night, going over every minute since meeting Nina in his mind. By the time morning came, an iron-strong resolve to find his wife rose inside him.

Nina had made it to Dickensville by noon the day before. She'd sold her horse and bought a stagecoach ticket to Helena. She'd been disappointed that the stagecoach wouldn't leave until the next afternoon. Finding the cheapest hotel room she could, she'd locked herself in for the night and lay on the bed, watching the shadows move as the moonlight shifted directions. She longed for Billy, but she'd caused all of his misfortune, and she wasn't going to let anything else happen to him because of her.

He hadn't wanted her from the beginning and he'd been right not to. She was bad luck and he was better off without her. It was her punishment for being so happy to have him as her husband even though he'd been promised to another woman. It was Callie he should be with, not her. The Great Spirit had shown His anger with her meddling and she was now doing the right thing by removing herself from Billy's life so he could find the right woman to share it with.

In the morning, she didn't go out until close to time to board the stagecoach. She'd seen them, but had never ridden in one. Boarding it, she kept her eyes on the floor of the carriage because she couldn't care less about the passing scenery. Nina also didn't want to talk to the other passenger, a middle-aged woman, and made that clear by ignoring her.

She planned to work for a couple of weeks in Helena to make enough money to continue on her journey. She wanted to go east and away from Montana; it would be too tempting to go back to Echo if she were so close to Billy. She wouldn't do that to him. It was best to put more space between them. The rocking of the stagecoach and the monotonous sound of the wheels lulled her into sleep after a time.

———

Ever since the night two years ago when he'd completely given in to grief, anger, and heartache and destroyed his studio and had cut all of his hair off, Billy had worked hard on hardening his heart and mind against racism and discrimination. He'd developed a thicker skin against such things and he'd learned how to deal with disappointment without letting it keep him down.

When he'd started writing to Callie, he'd begun to have real hope that his romantic future was finally taking a turn for the better. Then Lucky had gotten that letter from Wild Wind and he'd had to leave before she arrived. He'd been disappointed, but had thought that it could be worked out when they'd gotten back to Echo.

Then Nina had entered his life and complicated it. He'd fought against his growing attraction to her, trying to honor his commitment to Callie. Then he'd kissed her and somewhere deep inside himself, he'd known that he would never marry the woman from Mississippi, but he'd still tried to stay true to the woman he'd never met.

When they'd been kidnapped by the zealot Peterson family and forced to marry each other, there had been a small part of him that had whispered that it was his destiny to be with Nina. After being with her that first night, he'd begun to experience what it was like to be truly happy in life, as though his life hadn't begun until meeting Nina.

Those feelings had been cemented on the trip back to Echo and the love he'd felt for her had been the most powerful, fantastic thing he'd ever had happen to him. It had only grown with time and Billy knew that Nina had felt the same thing for him. Evan had once asked him if he'd been mistaking sex for love and at the time, he hadn't thought he'd been, but looking back on it, Billy knew that the physical intimacy he'd shared with Shelby had only been one-dimensional.

With Nina, it involved every dimension there was: emotional, physical, spiritual, and mental. Every time they were with each other, it consumed them and Billy knew that Nina hadn't been calculating enough to put on such a convincing act. No, his wife loved him and unless he heard it directly from her sweet lips, he refused to believe otherwise.

With that in mind, he used his cunning to track down Nina's horse, confirming that she had been to Dickensville. He'd bought the horse back and, using a sketch he'd done of her, he'd gotten a positive identification from the ticket master at the depot that she'd gotten on the stagecoach bound for Helena. She was a beautiful young woman and she'd stuck in the man's mind. Billy had thanked the man and had gone after the stagecoach.

The third morning after Nina's departure, Billy closed in on the stagecoach, urging both horses into a faster canter to reach it quicker. Coming up alongside the stagecoach, Billy motioned for the driver to bring the team to a halt. The driver was resistant until Billy showed him the badge he wore on his vest.

When the stagecoach stopped, the driver asked, "What's the trouble, Deputy?"

"Well, I'm afraid you've got a horse thief on board here. A pretty blonde girl?" Billy said, imitating Evan's manner of speaking.

"A horse thief? That sweet thing is a horse thief?" the driver asked. "I can't believe it."

Billy wasn't going to tell the man that the horse in question was the other horse with him. "Yep. I'm just going to collect her and be on my way."

"Well, all right, then."

"Much obliged, sir." Billy backed up his horse and dismounted.

Opening the stagecoach door, he boarded and saw Nina lying on the seat asleep. Anger, relief, and joy flowed through his body. "Wake up, Nina," he said in Cheyenne. "Wake up!"

Nina heard him and thought she was dreaming. Her eyes popped open and she was only further convinced that she was dreaming. Billy was there, but he was dressed the way Evan and Thad did. Jeans, a buttoned down white shirt, and a black vest combined into an ensemble that many in law enforcement wore when there were no uniforms provided. Billy was even wearing black cowboy boots and a black hat. It looked like he'd cut his hair, too.

She sat up, still not convinced that she was awake even though she looked into his black, fury-lit eyes.

"Get up, Nina. I am taking you back to Echo," he said, still speaking in Cheyenne.

She shook her head. "No. I will not go with you."

Billy took her by the arm and said, "You do not have a choice. You stole a horse and I have been deputized and ordered to bring you back."

Her eyes widened in fear. "You are taking me to jail?"

"That is what happens to horse thieves, wife. Now move!"

He was too strong to resist so Nina went with him. When she saw her horse, she said, "That is my horse! How can you arrest me when you have my horse?"

Billy waved to the stagecoach driver to go on and said, "I recovered stolen merchandise, but that doesn't mean you still aren't guilty of the crime."

Since he'd switched back to English, she did, too. "You just used this as an excuse to be able to find me."

He smiled at her as he took off his hat and shook his hair loose. Replacing it, he said, "Pretty smart of me, I'd say."

"It's stupid to come after a woman who left you," she said.

"We'll see about that. Get on the horse, Nina," Billy ordered.

"No," she said.

"Nina, get on that horse or I'll put you on it myself and strap you to it," Billy said.

Looking at him, she saw that he was dead serious. Giving him a dirty look, she mounted and sat silently, refusing to look at him.

After mounting, Billy looked her over and saw that while she looked tired, she was fine. Her fatigue didn't diminish her beauty any; Billy's hunger for her was fierce even though they'd only been separated a few days. "How could you do this to me? How could you leave me like that?"

His softly spoken question made her feel much worse than if he'd shouted at her. She kept her eyes on the ground and stayed silent.

"I trusted you, protected you, and loved you. Wasn't that enough for you? You wanted to marry me right from the beginning and you got your wish," Billy said. "I was so angry at the time, but then I realized that I'd been developing feelings for you all along, even before those lunatics held that three-ring circus they called a wedding and we were forced to get married.

"It didn't take me long to see that we were meant to be together. You told me you loved me, Nina, and we made a life together, and I was so happy. You told me over and over how happy you were, whether it was in words, or the things you did, and I certainly felt it when we made love. Or did I imagine all of that? Was it all a lie? Look me in the eye and tell me the truth. If you can honestly tell me that you don't love me and want to be my wife, I'll turn you loose right now."

Nina tried to muster the hateful words and get the lies past her lips, but she couldn't. However, she couldn't go back to Echo with him, either.

"I'm waiting."

"Let me go. It's better if we're not together."

Billy moved closer to her. "Better? How so?"

"We'll both be free to live our lives. You can find someone better than me, who won't bring you bad luck the way I have," Nina said.

"Is that why you left? You think you're bad luck?" he asked.

Nina sat motionless.

Billy grabbed her shoulder and shook her. "Answer me! Is that why you left me? Is that why you tried to throw away everything we had together? Our love?"

"Yes!" she shouted, looking at him for the first time. "I have brought you nothing but bad luck since we met! I should have stayed on the reservation and then you would be married to Callie and happy. You would still have your store and all of your beautiful paintings!"

Billy's jaw clenched and he shook her again. "How could you be so blind? You've given me the greatest joy I've ever experienced! Those are all just material things and we can build them again, but I can't replace *you*! I don't want to. You're the only woman I'm ever going to love, Nina. Even if you don't come back with me, I'll never stop loving you and wanting you. Can't you see? As long as I have you, I can get through anything. Please don't throw away our future, Nina. Come home with me where you belong."

Meeting his eyes, she said, "It's my fault that we were forced to marry. I've always been bad luck. It's why I was captured when I was little, why I was made into a slave by the Kiowa, and why I ended up the wife of a man who never loved me and thought I should be a slave to him in all ways.

"When I ran away that night, I thought I was running to a better life. I met you and even though I knew you didn't want me, I tried to make you like me and see that I could be a good wife to you. You were so handsome and kind and funny. And you make beautiful things. Even when those men made us get married and you were angry, you showed me more kindness than my first husband ever did, and I was so happy and proud to be your wife.

"But I was selfish. I've always been told that I was bad luck, and it's true. I thought maybe the bad luck wouldn't follow me, but it did, and you lost everything because of me. Those people wouldn't have burned down the store and tried to kill us if I wasn't your wife," Nina said.

Billy said, "Nina, my whole life, I've been an outcast. My parents love me as much as they would love a child born to them and they tried to shield me as much as possible, but deep inside I've always known I was different than them and when I got older, I was made painfully aware of that by a lot of people.

"It doesn't matter where I would go, I'll always be discriminated against, but I've learned that it's not my fault that some people have small minds and small hearts. I used to think I was bad luck, because of the way I was treated, but thanks to my family and friends, I've learned that I'm not. I thought that my future was set in stone and that I would never find someone who accepted me for me and didn't just see my race.

"I began to see that I had to make my own luck and work hard to succeed and show people that I'm worthy of respect. That's what I've been doing the past couple of years and I knew it was time to start looking for a wife. No, you're not the woman I thought I'd end up with, but you know what? I know that I was never meant to be with Callie. The Great Spirit brought you and me together, Nina. Maybe we had to go through all of that bad stuff so we could be with each other.

"Think about it. If you hadn't been taken captive and I hadn't been raised here in Echo and met Lucky, who was part of your tribe, we wouldn't be together. Who would we be better with than each other? Two people from opposite races raised by the opposite cultures? What two people could understand each other more than you and I do? It's our destiny to be married and have babies and live a happy life together. Please come home with me, Nina."

Nina saw the wisdom in what he was saying. "You really don't think I'm bad luck?"

"No. You've only brought me good luck because of all the happiness you've given me." He stroked her hair. "I love you more than I thought I'd ever love anyone. How could there be any better luck than that?"

His words broke through her remaining resistance and she reached for him. Billy pulled her from her horse over onto his lap.

"I'm so sorry," she said as she started to sob. "I didn't want to hurt you. I loved you too much to keep bringing you bad luck; I would rather be miserable without you and know that you would have a better life than do that to you. I'm so ashamed that I hurt you so much when all you've done is love me. I've been so stupid."

Billy held her and stroked her back. "You're all the good luck I'll ever need. You did hurt me badly, Nina, but I understand why now. You did it out of love, but you can't ever leave me like that again. I couldn't take it. I couldn't believe that you didn't love me. That's why I came after you—I needed to hear it from you before I'd let go of you."

Nina put her arms around his neck and held him tightly. "I promise I'll never leave you again. I'll make you happy again. I'll never make you regret chasing me down. I'm so glad you did and I love you so much. You're my good luck, too. My Magic Man."

He laughed. "I love it when you call me that. I am yours and I always will be." Billy said in Cheyenne. "Let us go home, wife."

Nina nodded, wiped away her tears, and kissed him. Desire ignited within both of them and the kiss rapidly grew intense. Nina put an abrupt halt to it, looking around, glad that they weren't close to civilization at the moment no one could witness them.

She spotted some woods, looked meaningfully at them, and smiled at Billy. He returned her seductive smile and guided their horses to the forest where they tied them to a tree. There in the cover of the thick foliage the lovers held each other, making a new pact to stay together regardless of what fate threw at them. Nina promised to never let anyone get to her like that again. Billy was right; bigoted people's hateful opinions weren't worth throwing away a lifetime of bliss with him.

Billy vowed to do his utmost to make Nina feel cherished. He would help her gain the strength to brush aside hurtful remarks and to pity cruel people for their ignorance. Every day, he would show her that they could make their own good luck together and that no one could ever take that away from them.

# Epilogue

They took their time going home, treating the time away as their honeymoon. Although they didn't have much money by the time they arrived in Dickensville, they rented a cheap hotel room and they went to eat at a place that had good food at reasonable prices.

As they walked to a table, Billy heard someone calling his name. Looking around, he found the source of the voice and was surprised to see Shelby waving to him from across the room. She motioned to him. Billy took Nina's hand and walked over to her. Her children, Bruce and Renee, were with her.

"I thought that was you," she said smiling. "You look good."

Billy smiled. "You, too. Shelby, this is my wife, Nina. Nina, this is an old friend of mine, Shelby."

Nina had seen the appreciative way that Shelby had looked at Billy and she knew that this was the woman he'd told her about. She felt badly for Shelby for being stupid enough to throw away a man like him.

Smiling, she held out a hand and said, "It's nice to meet you. Billy's told me so much about you."

Shelby's eyes reflected her surprise. "You told her about me?"

"I sure did," Billy said. "There are no secrets between us. How have you been?"

"Ok," Shelby said, looking anything but. "Still working at the same place."

Billy nodded and said, "Boy, look at you two. You're getting big."

Bruce smiled. "Yep. How come you don't come around anymore?"

"Well, I've been busy with my art store and I co-own a sheep farm, so there's that to keep up with, too," Billy said. "And then this beautiful woman here keeps me busy." He put his arm around Nina, who leaned into him.

"You own a sheep farm and an art store?" Shelby said.

"Yeah. Luck has certainly shone on me, especially because of Nina," he said, gazing lovingly at his wife.

Nina laughed and said, "I'm very lucky, too. He's a wonderful husband and we're hoping to start a family soon."

"Well, it's been nice seeing you all again. We'd better eat and get going, honey," Billy said.

Both of them could see the jealousy in Shelby's eyes and the spiteful part of Billy enjoyed it immensely. They walked away and took a table on the other side of the dining room.

Sitting down, Billy said, "That felt good."

Nina giggled. "She was very foolish to not hang onto you, but it was my good fortune that she set you free," she said in Cheyenne.

Taking her hand, Billy said, "You are my good fortune, Nina Two Moons, and do not ever doubt it again."

"I will not, husband," she said.

By the time August started, Billy and Nina's new store was open. It was only one story, but they planned to add a second story later on, only this time, it would be an apartment for them to live in. They had built a studio on the back of the building and had special-ordered big windows that let in plenty of sunlight.

In addition to Billy's paintings, they sold the Indian moccasins and jewelry that Nina now made. The beautiful footwear and jewelry were becoming very popular, and they even took some to Dickensville every month. This helped draw people to Echo and when the visitors came, they usually ate at the diner and shopped at the Temples' store, too, bringing in even more income.

The sheep farm continued to do well and, per their agreement, the farmers gave Marvin their older sheep to be used for wool. This was actually a help to them since the older mutton didn't sell as well. It allowed them to get rid of the older sheep, preserving more of the grazing land for the younger animals.

Otto still had moments when he missed Avasa, but they were becoming less frequent as he adjusted to his new life. His loving father helped ease his pain and he now loved Lucky as much as he did Avasa. Between all of Lucky's friends, Otto had gained several aunts and uncles and Edna had become a surrogate grandmother, which thrilled her.

Although Lucky's heart still ached for Avasa, he told himself that each day he got through was one day closer to the time when he would be able to look back on the past without so much pain. Until then, he would love and raise his son to the best of his ability and glean as much joy as he could from life.

His friend Wild Wind also adapted to his new life among the citizens of Echo. Although there were those who weren't happy with his presence in the town, he ignored them and went about his business without giving them the satisfaction of getting under his skin. He proudly wore his Cheyenne clothing, not giving a damn if people didn't like it. He would always have the heart of a Cheyenne warrior and he wasn't going to change for anyone.

Billy followed Wild Wind's example and began doing the same. Any lingering fear he had of being an outcast in Echo was permanently erased from his psyche and he fully embraced his heritage. He also preferred his wife in her Cheyenne clothing and, although she sometimes wore regular clothing, most days that was her attire. She might be white by blood, but in her heart, she was Cheyenne. She was also now proud of her people despite the poor treatment she'd received from some of them. She'd learned who she was: the proud wife of the wonderful man the Great Spirit had given to her.

"Will you stop fussing at me, Ronni?" Marvin complained as the redhead tried to adjust the pillows behind his back.

He sat reclining on the sofa. He was healing well, but he still had a ways to go. He'd learned that "Ronni" was Veronica's nickname and had immediately begun using it.

"You didn't look comfortable," she said. "I was only trying to help."

Marvin became contrite. "I'm sorry. I don't mean to snap at you. I'm just restless and bored. I appreciate all you've done for me."

Ronni sat on an ottoman close to the sofa. "I know this has been so hard on you. You've been in so much pain and yet you don't complain very much."

Marvin smiled a little. "I've never been a whiner. What's the point of complaining? I just concentrate on getting through each day, and the pain is much better than it has been."

Ronni said, "I'm so glad, but I still worry about you."

Marvin snorted. "One wouldn't know from the way you constantly bicker with me."

"We're not bickering right now."

"I'm sure we will be soon," Marvin said.

She chuckled. "That's only because you're infuriating and rude."

"And you're churlish and argumentative," he retorted.

"You always start it, so you can't blame me," she said.

Marvin laughed a little. "I guess I do. You bring it out in me."

"Somehow I don't think it's ever far from the surface. I do worry about you. You've been so good to me and Eva and I don't understand why," Ronni said. "You insisted that we move in here and you made a nursery for her. Why did you do that?"

Marvin sighed. "I think it's because of Shadow. I know that being a single parent is hard and I can't bear to see children suffer. I know she wasn't suffering. You're an excellent mother, but—can't I just spoil her for no reason at all? Why must there be some big reason?"

Ronni laughed. "You're a coward, Marvin Earnest."

He was affronted. "Me? A coward? How dare you call me a coward? Ask anyone around here and they'll tell you I'm no such thing."

"Oh, I know how scared some people are of you, but they don't know you like I do. You're ruthless when it comes to business and you enjoy intimidating people, but when it comes to talking about your feelings, you're just like any other man. Scared to discuss them," Ronni said.

Marvin's temper got the best of him and he said, "So you want me to talk about my feelings. Very well, but remember you asked for it."

She crossed her arms over her chest and said, "Go on."

"You are the most stubborn, waspish, opinionated, infuriating, beautiful, alluring woman I've ever met and someday, mark my words, I'll have you," Marvin said, his eyes shooting sparks.

Ronni's mouth dropped open and her cheeks became suffused with color. She rose and moved away, staring at him. Then, without another word, she left the room. Marvin's laughter followed her out into the foyer, where she stopped, a hand over her mouth as she absorbed his shocking statements.

"Now who's the coward, Ronni?" he called after her, still laughing.

"Shut up, Marvin!" she shouted back.

This only served to make him laugh harder. Ronni giggled to herself like a schoolgirl as she went to begin supper. She admitted to herself that being with Marvin had crossed her mind quite a bit, but she hadn't known he'd also thought about it. As she prepared a chicken to roast, Ronni kept smiling to herself and wondered what the future held for her and Eva.

After Bree's revelation that she was pregnant, Shadow had wasted no time in proposing to her. He'd taken her to his favorite place—a glade in the woods where he always went to think or deal with some problem. Sitting there and listening to the sounds of the forest around him was soothing and helped him regain his equilibrium.

He had let his tender side shine through again as he'd gotten down on one knee, holding a ring box in his hand. "Sabrina Leigh Josephson, my little counterfeiter, you are the most kind, beautiful, loving woman I've ever known. I can't live without you and you'll never doubt how much I love you. You're my salvation and you've brought so much light into my world of darkness. Will you make me the happiest holy terror in the world by becoming my wife?"

With tears of joy in her eyes, Bree had caressed his cheek and said, "Yes, my holy terror, I'll marry you."

The ring he'd put on her finger was exquisite and she marveled at the way it shimmered in the sunlight. Then she found herself in his arms being kissed passionately. She responded to the man of darkness who gave her so much love and hope for a bright future.

Breaking the kiss, Shadow had placed his hand on her stomach and said, "I promise to love the both of you and provide and protect you. Neither of you will want for anything. I'll be a good father and our baby will know only love and happiness."

Hugging him, Bree said, "I have no doubts about that."

They'd stood in the sunny glade and made plans for their wedding, which they would hold just as soon as Marvin could stand for a little while since he was Shadow's best man. They'd decided to hold the wedding at the house, since it would be a small affair. There was no reason to go to the trouble of decorating a church and such. It didn't matter to them because they sought commitment and they didn't need a lot of fanfare. They only needed each other.

Watching Billy paint was always a joy for Nina. He was just putting the finishing touches on the painting of Lucky and Otto where the little boy was sitting on his father's lap. Although his sketches had all perished in the fire, he'd retained that image and had been able to create the painting from the picture in his keen mind.

"There. All done," he said. "What do you think?"

"It's beautiful. Lucky is going to be thrilled with it," she said, hugging him from behind.

He smiled. "I hope so. I just felt so strongly that the moment needed to be captured."

"And you did a wonderful job at it," she said.

Turning around, he embraced her. "It's all been quite an adventure, hasn't it?"

"Yes, it has. I'm glad it was with you. Knowing that I would end up with you, I would go through my whole life again just to get to you."

Billy hugged her tighter. "Same here. I used to feel like I didn't belong anywhere because I was caught between two worlds and didn't seem to fit in with either. But I know where I belong now: with you. You're my home, Nina, and I couldn't be happier about that."

Nina smiled. "Not even if we're going to have a little Two Moon soon?"

Billy stiffened and then tipped her chin up so he could look into her sparkling green eyes. "Do you mean what I think you mean?"

Her brilliant smile gave him his answer. "I am pretty sure I am pregnant since I have not had my cycle twice." She colored over discussing such a thing with him, but he'd never been bashful about those topics.

Billy did the calculation in his head. "That means a February or March baby, depending."

She nodded. "Yes. Are you happy?"

He picked her up carefully and swung her around in a little circle as he laughed. "How could I not be? Did you think I wouldn't be?"

She kissed him and said, "I just wanted to be sure."

Setting Nina on her feet again, Billy grinned and said, "I can't wait for our baby to come along. I love you so much."

He kissed her tenderly, trying to convey his happiness to her. Nina surrendered herself to him, reveling in the way his strong arms held her in a loving embrace. As they stood kissing in the sunlight that flooded the room, their love for each other grew again. It did so every day, filling their hearts so full that it seemed that they would burst from it.

And now they had created new life together. Holding Nina in his arms, Billy knew it was a sign from the Great Spirit showing His approval of their union and blessing them with more good fortune.

As the kiss ended, Nina smiled up at Billy and asked, "Are you ready for our next adventure?"

He laughed and said, "I'm so ready, it's not even funny. And I'll be ready for the next adventure and the one after that and whatever other adventures come our way."

"And we'll meet each other them together," she said firmly.

"That's right," he agreed. "Together forever."

Giving him another glowing smile, she said, "Forever."

### The End

Thank you for reading and supporting my book and I hope you enjoyed it.

Please will you do me a favor and review "Montana Adventure" so I'll know whether you liked it or not, it would be very much appreciated, thank you.

# Linda's Other Books

**Echo Canyon Brides Series**

Montana Rescue
(Echo Canyon brides Book 1)
Montana Bargain
(Echo Canyon brides Book 2)
Montana Adventure
(Echo Canyon brides Book 3)

**Montana Mail Order Brides Series**

Westward Winds
(Montana Mail Order brides
Book 1)
Westward Dance
(Montana Mail Order brides
Book 2)
Westward Bound
(Montana Mail Order brides
Book 3)

Westward Destiny
(Montana Mail Order brides
Book 4)
Westward Fortune
(Montana Mail Order brides
Book 5)
Westward Justice
(Montana Mail Order brides
Book 6)
Westward Dreams
(Montana Mail Order brides
Book 7)
Westward Holiday
(Montana Mail Order brides
Book 8)
Westward Sunrise
(Montana Mail Order brides
Book 9)
Westward Moon
(Montana Mail Order brides
Book 10)

Westward Christmas
(Montana Mail Order brides
Book 11)

Westward Visions
(Montana Mail Order brides
Book 12)

Westward Secrets
(Montana Mail Order brides
Book 13)

Westward Changes
(Montana Mail Order brides
Book 14)

Westward Heartbeat
(Montana Mail Order brides
Book 15)

Westward Joy
(Montana Mail Order brides
Book 16)

Westward Courage
(Montana Mail Order brides
Book 17)

Westward Spirit
(Montana Mail Order brides
Book 18)

Westward Fate
(Montana Mail Order brides
Book 19)

Westward Hope
(Montana Mail Order brides
Book 20)

Westward Wild
(Montana Mail Order brides
Book 21)

Westward Sight
(Montana Mail Order brides
Book 22)

# Connect With Linda

Visit my website at **www.lindabridey.com** to view my other books and to sign up to my mailing list so that you are notified about my new releases.

# About Linda Bridey

LINDA BRIDEY lives in New Mexico with her three dogs; a German shepherd, chocolate Labrador retriever, and a black Pug. She became fascinated with Montana and decided to combine that fascination with her fictional romance writing. Linda chose to write about mail-order-brides because of the bravery of these women who left everything and everyone to take a trek into the unknown. The Westward series books are her first publications.